T

The Light of the Capital

Three Modern Vietnamese Classics

Translated from the Vietnamese by

GREG LOCKHART AND MONIQUE LOCKHART

With an Introduction by

GREG LOCKHART

KUALA LUMPUR
OXFORD UNIVERSITY PRESS
OXFORD SINGAPORE NEW YORK
1996

Oxford University Press

Oxford New York
Athens Auckland Bangkok Bombay
Calcutta Cape Town Dar es Salaam Delhi
Florence Hong Kong Istanbul Karachi
Madras Madrid Melbourne Mexico City
Nairobi Paris Shah Alam Singapore
Taipei Tokyo Toronto

and associated companies in
Berlin Ibadan

Oxford is a trade mark of Oxford University Press

Published in the United States
by Oxford University Press, New York

First published 1996

British Library Cataloguing in Publication Data
Data available

Library of Congress Cataloging-in-Publication Data
The light of the capital: three modern Vietnamese classics/translated from the Vietnamese by Greg Lockhart and Monique Lockhart.
p. cm.
ISBN 967 65 3093 X (pbk.):
1. Hanoi (Vietnam)—Social life and customs—Fiction.
I. Lockhart, Greg. II. Lockhart, Monique, 1941– . III. Tâm Lang, 1901– Tôi kéo xe. English. IV. Vũ, Trong Phung, 1912–1939. Com thầy com cô. English. V. Nguyên Hông. Những ngày tho âu. English.
PL4378.9.L48 1995
895.9'223308—dc20
95–17326
CIP

Typeset by Indah Photosetting Centre Sdn. Bhd., Malaysia
Printed by KHL Printing Co. Pte. Ltd., Singapore
Published by the South-East Asian Publishing Unit,
a division of Penerbit Fajar Bakti Sdn. Bhd.,
under licence from Oxford University Press,
4 Jalan U1/15, Seksyen U1, 40000 Shah Alam,
Selangor Darul Ehsan, Malaysia

The image of a person pulling a rickshaw
with another sitting in it, the image of a person holding
two shafts and running with difficulty down a dusty road, has now
faded and withdrawn into the dark shadows of the past. The
young people of the present generation and those
following will not understand what the condition
of the 'horse people' was like.

Thuong Sy, 1974

I can invent stories that you will believe,
or I can tell you true stories that you will think
I have made up.

Vu Trong Phung, 1936

Preface

TODAY, Hanoi is developing rapidly. Yet it has developed rapidly before, and so contains the interplay of past and present, which has shaped this book.

The original idea was to try to recapture something of what had been lost in the 'time warp' to which Hanoi's foreign visitors have until very recently referred (Sheehan, 1992, p. 5). The intention was to search back beyond the epoch of war and revolution for texts to translate that might convey an authentic, inside sense of what life was like for ordinary people in the era that first made the city 'modern'.

This was the era that followed the French conquest of Vietnam between 1859 and 1884. Indeed, the modern city was largely built between about 1888 and 1910, a period when Henri d'Orléans described *Hanoi la Jolie* (Brocheux and Hémery, 1995, p. 177). There was another burst of activity in the investment boom of the 1920s. However, it soon became apparent that the literary record was, with much modern irony, richest in the decade that began with the Great Depression.

Hanoi writers of the 1930s have left not only an excellent record of a forgotten world that formed in the first four decades of this century, but also one that tells us much about literary modernism as a movement in Vietnam. It was, therefore, as a service to literature as well as history that this book was finally conceived.

It would have been possible to translate some novels or extracts of many. However, because of the direct access they give us to social issues and the concrete ways in which they epitomize the rise of the modern Vietnamese city, our attention was drawn to certain works of documentary social realism.

Two of the works presented in this book are works of urban reportage, a genre which first crystallized in the urban class—or underclass—formation on which modern Hanoi stands. Hence, Tam Lang's 'I Pulled a Rickshaw' (1932) and Vu Trong Phung's 'Household Servants' (1936) tended to select themselves, if only because they so strongly reflect the social alienation that was pervasive in old Hanoi. Especially when compared with the romance of others such as Thach Lam's charming 'Hanoi: 36 Streets' (1943), a further advantage of the realism of such works is that they also prefigure some of the social problems which have reappeared in the city today.

The third text is one of autobiography. Strictly speaking, Nguyen Hong's 'Days of Childhood' (1938) takes us out of Hanoi to the nearby provincial town of Nam Dinh. But as it reveals with realism the modern breakdown of the ancient institution of the family, it amplifies an issue of such fundamental importance in twentieth-century Vietnamese history and literature that it could have been set in Hanoi—where it was published. While the vitality of the writing made the first two works easy to include in a readable book about early modern Hanoi, it was the psychological depth and literary quality of the third that, in our view, helps to make it a valuable addition.

As usual, the last part of the work is also the one that appears first: the introductory essay. It was written with the idea of setting the stories in a modernist mould that some in Hanoi are thinking might well be dusted off and used again today.

We would like to thank the Australian Research Council for the support which has permitted us to produce this work, and a number of people who have read in whole or in part an early draft of the translations and offered valuable comments: Bruce Pollard, David Marr, Alexander Woodside, and Craig Reynolds.

Sydney
July 1995

GREG LOCKHART
MONIQUE LOCKHART

Contents

Introduction

First Person Narratives from the 1930s

Genres have histories, which is to say, times and places.

Kwame Anthony Appiah

'A New Way of Writing'

THE three stories that appear in English translation in this volume are classics of modern Vietnamese reportage (*phong su*) and autobiography (*tu truyen*). As such, they are long documentary narratives of social realism and self-awareness that have no strong precedent in Vietnamese literature. All were initially serialized in the Hanoi press in the 1930s, and soon after published in books. After various degrees of neglect in the revolutionary war years, all have been republished recently.

The first is Tam Lang's *Toi keo xe* [I Pulled a Rickshaw] (1932). Described by the critic, Vu Ngoc Phan, in 1942 as 'the first reportage in our country' (Vol. 2, p. 564), this work stimulated great interest in investigative journalism in the 1930s. It then dropped from view in Hanoi after the 1945 revolution both abolished the rickshaw trade and proved unsympathetic to such journalism. However, it was republished as a high-school reader in Saigon in at least 1969 and 1974, during the period when the country was divided between hostile northern and southern regimes from 1954 to

1975. Most recently, a complete edition was published in Hanoi in 1995.

Before its recent revival, the second work also rose in the 1930s and fell in the 1940s. Written by Vu Trong Phung, 'the king of reportage', this was *Com thay com co* [Household Servants] (1936), which was not much read after the Revolution. However, the literary establishment in Hanoi mentioned it (somewhat negatively) from time to time in wider discussions of Vu Trong Phung's major realist novels. Applying the Freudian notion of 'libido', for example, Nguyen Duc Dan made a typical remark in 1968: 'In "Household Servants" ... Vu Trong Phung once again maintains his argument about the domination of sexual desire in people and society' (pp. 107–8). However, the text was rehabilitated for its 'acute' social observation and 'filmic', 'documentary value' by Nguyen Dang Manh in Hanoi in editions of 1987 and 1989.

The third story is Nguyen Hong's *Nhung ngay tho au* [Days of Childhood] (1938). Unlike the other stories, which are works of 'reportage', it is usually described as the first fully-fledged modern 'autobiography'. However, it can also be classified as a 'memoir' or as 'reminiscences' (*hoi ky*), and there is no reason why it cannot be assimilated into this book as a 'self-reportage' (*phong su ve minh*). During the years of the great divide, it was republished in both Hanoi in 1957 and 1963, and in Saigon in 1969—at least partly because the depth and intimacy of its personalized attack on the ancient family system allowed it to appeal to 'modern' readers of either liberal or socialist leanings. It was reprinted in Hanoi in 1984.

Given its contents, therefore, this book comes (unwittingly) with a companion volume: Vuong Tri Nhan's *Phong su chon loc* [Selected Reportage] of January 1995. Even though both books were conceived without knowledge of the other—I only became aware of *Phong su chon loc* in March 1995—their parallel appearance in different languages is not a random coincidence. Both publish three works of 1930s reportage—Nhan's includes Tam Lang's 'I Pulled a Rickshaw', Trong Lang's *Hanoi lam than* [Miserable Hanoi] (1938), and Hoang Dao's *Truoc vanh mong ngua* [At the Witness Stand] (1938). Moreover, both may be interpreted as a response to the rapid, if still spotty, urban change that has followed the 'renovation' of public policy that was first announced in December 1986.

As the Vietnamese government turned away from the socialist internationalism of the war years, mid-1980s 'renovation' meant a large degree of integration with the world's capitalist economy. As this happened, the urban stagnation of the previous four decades ensured that the only local precedent which people had for thinking about urban growth was the experience of the colonial era. It was therefore reasonable to imagine, as the compilers of *Phong su chon loc* and this book did, that a revival of the reportage which flourished in the urban development of the 1930s would chime with mainstream concerns in Vietnam today. This was especially so when the social realism of that reportage suggests a great weakness in contemporary press constructions of social reality.

As the publishing profile of our first two stories suggests, the investigative journalism of the 1930s did not go on to flourish in the post-1945 period. It was, in fact, not until after 'renovation' in late 1986, that a string of realistic memoirs (*ky*) and works of reportage began to replace the press propaganda of the revolutionary war years. In 1987 and 1988, for example, detailed accounts of rural poverty and the maladministration of official 'bullies' (*cuong hao*) suddenly became typical of the new wave reportage in the major journal of the National Writers Association, *Van Nghe*

[Literature and Art]. Some of the journal's most cogent pieces were even republished in a popular anthology called *The Women Kneel* (Bao Van Nghe, 1988). However, it is well known that, along with the publication of some controversial fiction, the publication of this anthology—or at least the story from which it took its title, and another called 'What Night Was That Night?'—played a large part in the scandalous sacking of Nguyen Ngoc, the editor of *Literature and Art*, in December 1988 (Lockhart, 1992, pp. 7–8).

Since then, of course, there has been no revival of renovation reportage. What we find today is that, in the scramble for development dollars, corruption goes unchecked in the press, while social commentary tends to ply readers with moralistic advice. A recent article selected at random from *Cong an* [Public Security] is a good example of what I mean. Called 'The Result of Sick Love', it chronicles various crimes of passion and describes itself in an editorial blurb as 'good medicine' for the 'sentimental relations between men and women' that play a big role in upsetting social order (*Cong an*, 24 February 1995, p. 22).

Also, in keeping with the security approach, a recent war memoir by Nguyen Ba Tham in *Literature and Art* (25 March 1995, p. 7) has again unfurled the banner of the 'sublime sacrifice of the people'. This move comes at a time when conservatives in the literary world have a complex agenda that is partly designed to counter realistic and, thus, unheroic representations of the war—such as Bao Ninh has offered in fiction. But in the context of rapid, even, bewildering change for the old guard, it is also partly a substitute for what in fiction as well as reportage is an empty official line: one that includes a vapid concoction of very worn-out revolutionary romanticism with new elements of spiritualism, catastrophism, and international exchange (*Literature and Art*, 25 March 1995, pp. 2–3). Clearly, Nhan (1995, pp. 441 and 444) sees the social realism of 1930s reportage and its 'tendency towards democratisation' as a much-needed antidote for all this.

But what does he mean by the democracy of social realism? What he means is something that Hanoi editors had in mind in the 1930s: the publication of stories that people actually want to read because they represent a slice of observed social reality in which they can recognize their own lives. It is democracy in this sense that Nhan (1995, pp. 440–1) thinks people will find meaningful today, when they are 'obsessed' with such questions as 'How are we living?', 'What is happening around us?': 'People must find a way of living that is suitable to them personally. Our people don't only need advice, before all they want to see their own image. Newspapers must become a means of communicating, a mirror in which people can become self-aware.' And an interesting aspect of this contrast between the newspaper as a provider of 'advice' and as a 'mirror' in which people become 'self-aware' is the modern transformation it implies.

Ancient books could be described as 'mirrors'—or 'models' or 'examples' (*guong*)—too; but not ones in which people were supposed to see images of themselves. Since 'writing' (*loi van*) was often thought to be a manifestation of 'nature' (*thien nhien*), books were commonly assumed to be *Mirrors* or *Models of Nature* in which readers were supposed to see the reflection of a natural or moral order. The task of the serious reader was then to accept words of 'advice' so as to harmonize his or her behaviour with the received image of the moral order. It was not, through individual self-awareness, to promote reform and social change. It is from this radically modern perspective that Nhan is then assuming—rightly in my view—that a democratic transformation in the political, social, and literary consciousness during the colonial era produced 'a new way of writing', especially reportage, that has failed to flourish since the revolution in the 1940s. As they seek to revive a sense of Hanoi's early modern development, therefore, the companion volumes are assuming the popular interest that modern mirror images of society would create, if they came out in reportage again today.

New National–Social Categories: The Active 'I' and Class

A sure sign of the modern transformation was the 'astonishment' which Masson (1929) says onlookers expressed when the first rickshaws—two from Japan and six from Hong Kong—appeared in Hanoi in 1884, the year of the French conquest. More telling, however, is the surprise we still hear fifty years later when Tam Lang declares: 'I Pulled a Rickshaw'. For while the first gasps record the immediate shock of something awesomely new, that 'I' in Tam Lang's title is the sign of a more seriously developed, if still quite startling, relationship with it.

Tam Lang's relationship with a rickshaw is indeed emblematic of a whole world of change; one in which Hanoi grew rapidly into a modern administrative centre, as the French imperial project steadily integrated the plantation and mining sectors of the Vietnamese economy into world markets. In fact, by 1904, Hanoi had a modern French quarter with a cathedral, thousands of modern brick houses, some electric lights, a Post Office, an Opera House, and an electric tramway. As rickshaw factories in Haiphong as well as Hanoi produced a combined total of some 300 vehicles a year (Masson, 1929, Chaps. 4–6; Tran Huy Lieu, 1960, Chap. 3), the city was also well serviced by rickshaws and, of course, the people who pulled them: the urban rickshaw coolies.

This was, of course, one of the many new occupational groups that had begun to form in the new urban setting. By the early 1930s when Tam Lang counts about 1,200 rickshaws at work in Hanoi, therefore, we begin to see how, in a mirror image of urban change, the 'I' in his title suddenly finds itself standing on a new kind of social base: a class one that recognizes the subcategory of a rickshaw coolie class. But what makes this 'I' so startling is the new kind of relationship between people of different status it also suggests. No coolie would have declared 'I pulled a rickshaw'. He would have simply said, 'I am a rickshaw puller'. And so the really surprising thing about Tam Lang's 'I' is that it is associating someone who is higher than a rickshaw puller with a rickshaw and, by implication, making a *democratic–social* declaration of an affiliation with low-class people who pull rickshaws.

What we are dealing with in this new social arrangement is nothing less than the creation of new categories of self and collective identity that encompass and include everyone in the rise of the modern city. Yet, in so far as it suggests a new global formulation of human relations that is specifically social, Tam Lang's democratic declaration must also efface a more passive, autocratic past. It must represent an active assertion of self that, though not unheard of in pre-modern times, was not usually cultivated in literature before the destruction of the institution of the monarchy at the time of the French conquest.

Before the conquest of 1859–84, ideas of self were largely embedded in the vertical sense of moral hierarchy in family, village, and court around which it is generally agreed that the pre-modern state was structured. In this sense, a passive 'I' may be said to mark an autocratic system of government in which it was ideally thought that a good monarch nurtured his subjects as a father nurtures his children, and in which, therefore, the state operated like one great family (*dai gia dinh*).

In his *Dictionary* of 1651, Alexandre de Rhodes thus says the 'I' or *toi* was *humilitatis*, a humble form; or as Talberd put it almost 200 years later in his *Dictionary* of 1838, *inferiories*, 'inferior'. Talberd also includes the 'I' in various compound nouns which mean 'servant' (*toi to*), so that the idea of the 'I' as 'servant' brings us to a sense of family hierarchy in which the humble servant is ultimately the 'servant of the monarch'.

There are, of course, some qualifications to this sense. On the one hand, people within the family hierarchy usually used a range of pronominal forms that would not include the 'I', but that more instantly identified one's exact position in the hierarchy. On the other hand, when people of roughly equal age and status from different families and villages communicated with each other outside the hierarchies—as friends or negotiators in a market place, for example—it would have been necessary for them to use an egalitarian 'I'. In any case, with the strong sense of family hierarchy embedded in the usual pronominal forms of address, it was one thing to converse with equals in neutral territory, and quite another to do what Tam Lang had done when he wrote 'I Pulled a Rickshaw': stand up before a wide audience and act as though everyone in it was of equal age and equally humble status.

Clearly, this could only happen in the ruins of the ancient sense of hierarchy and communal order, which Tam Lang is not the only one of our authors to represent. Given the old political axiom that the king ruled his realm like the father ruled his family, nothing could be more symbolic of the destruction of the Vietnamese monarchy than, for example, the shocking portrait that Nguyen Hong paints of his father as a pathetic opium addict in 'Days of Childhood'. To the extent that his father's decline is central to Hong's own construction of himself, the idea of an autobiographical 'I' narrative is, indeed, itself, a by-product of the tremendous political shattering that followed the destruction of the monarchy.

With this shattering in mind, it is also relevant to argue that the rise of the 'I' narrative is structurally related to the theme of opium addiction itself. Recent research shows that the original French conquest of the north in the early 1880s was largely financed by revenues from opium farms in the south. Thereafter the colonial regime's finances were also heavily dependent on the drug. In nine years between 1899 and 1922, for instance, opium was the source of over 25 per cent of the entire budget of Indo-China (Descours-Gatin, 1992, pp. 165 and 223). As opium addiction therefore played a fundamental role in the destruction of the monarchical order, we can say that it had a strong bearing on the rise of modern 'I' narratives, such as 'Days of Childhood' and 'I Pulled a Rickshaw', where, appropriately, it has a strong thematic presence. Needless to say, opium addiction is a pervasive theme in early modern novels too.

Yet any act of destruction, fiscal or military, must be too negative in itself to explain the creation of our modern first person narratives. As they appear in the ruins of the monarchy, they are substantially the reflections of the new order that we have glimpsed in the rise of the rickshaw city. To give Tam Lang's active 'I' its positive potential, it is thus necessary to take another step. This is to define the new collective contexts within which the modern individual (*ca nhan*) may constitute its singular, sovereign identity.

For this purpose, we can do no better than begin with the new sense of class (*giai cap*) that crystallized between about 1900 and 1930 when Vietnam's population increased from an estimated 13 to 19 million people. Especially by the 1920s when population growth was encouraged by the post-First World War investment boom, the old Confucian Scholar, Peasant, Artisan, and Merchant categories of the population (*si*, *nong*, *cong*, and *thuong*) tended to be superseded by modern colonial bourgeois and working classes.

By 1930, some 39,000 French colonials had effectively displaced the old scholars from the highest policy-making apparatus and dominated the political, economic, and social life of the country. A further small number—no more than 0.5 per cent of the population—represented the indigenous, landowning bourgeoisie (*giai cap tu san*) which provided sons for the embryonic medical and legal professions and modern mandarinate. A larger petty bourgeoisie (*giai cap tieu tu san*) provided government clerks and small business people, while a significant number of Chinese and some Indians were included in the commercial classes. The appearance of a new Western-style class of 'intellectuals' (*tri thuc*) provided the schoolteachers, the journalists, and the writers, including ours, who would take such a strong interest in the new urban working classes (Marr, 1981, pp. 26–7).

While over 90 per cent of the population always remained peasants (*nong dan*), it has been estimated that, between 1906 and 1929, the number of modern tradesmen—mechanics, railway workers, telegraphists, masons, carpenters, cement workers, electricians, and many others—increased fourfold to 221,000. This number did not include the numerous workers in scattered handicraft industries, barbers, boatmen and women, ox-cart drivers, rickshaw coolies, and servants. Nor with the alienation of many peasants from their land in the formation of the colonial plantation sector did it include what Tran Van Giau (1958, pp. 169–70) described as the 'very many peasants who went to the cities and worked'. However, it is exactly this mass movement of people, exactly this formation of poorer as well as marginally richer working classes, which was fundamental to the construction of the modern city—and its reportage.

The displacement of individuals from families or villages and their movement into the city's lower working classes is, in various ways, a central theme in all our stories. Moreover, we have such richly detailed accounts of individual characters—Tu in 'I Pulled a Rickshaw', Dui in 'Household Servants', and Hong in 'Days of Childhood'—that they tend to personify the mass movements and modern class formation in which their personal tragedies are historically set.

In 'Household Servants', which gives us the most explicit sense of the mass movements, however, the paradoxical connection between the singularity of the modern individual and his or her mass affiliation is suggested in a different way in Chapter 6, which dramatizes the lot of a clumsy peasant lost in the urban 'labyrinth'. 'He' remains nameless and featureless and, with nothing more than attributions of exhaustion and hunger, 'he' plods from one street to another. But as 'he' finally falls in with a 'crowd' of people that, like him, are 'originally from the country', his anonymity makes him representative of the mass of restless people who swarm through the back alleys of the city. A new sense of collective identity is thus incipient in the crowd formed by uprooted, restless peasants.

One qualification to this atomized, individualized sense of the modern collective may be the tendency for the displaced people to re-establish the structures and kinship of village life once they have settled in the city. Yet kinship ties are still not a strong feature of our stories, which were written at a time when Hanoi had a large floating population—which increased from 75,000 in 1921 to 180,000 in 1937. Even for the rickshaw puller, Tu, who at least has a hovel and a wife and others around him, the sense of personal tragedy in the stories is actually associated with the disintegration of family ties. As a result, the subject of our stories tends to be a shifting mass of wretched individuals who have been shorn from the family and village and, thereby, constitute a new basis for individual as well as collective human relations, which has considerable potential for urban egalitarianism.

Hence the positive potential of the active 'I' in 'I Pulled a Rickshaw': it creates the modern (rickshaw coolie) class in its own image, while the class offers a new mass foundation for what is paradoxically the democratic sense of individual self-awareness. Detached from the ancient sense of hierarchy, Tam Lang's title is a self-reflexive construction of modern technological and social change.

There is, however, a point to add: Tam Lang's active 'I' cannot simply come into play with an idea of class. Because it assumes an egalitarian basis for human relations that is potentially equal and wide, the active 'I' easily spills out of class consciousness and, indeed, finds its limits in the new global formulation that we have seen makes Tam Lang's title so startling. In other words, Tam Lang's active 'I' is, finally, a self-reflexive construction of those culminating modern categories, 'nation' and 'society'.

As I have shown elsewhere (Lockhart, 1989, pp. 41–6; April 1994), neither of these categories exist in a modern popular sense in Vietnam much before 1900. By the 1910s, however, the idea of 'nation' (*dan toc*) is rooted in the fundamentally new political–social category of 'the people' (*nhan dan*)—as distinct from the old idea of 'people' (*dan*), as in 'the monarch's people'. As this shift clearly reflects the destruction of the monarchy, the idea of 'society' (*xa hoi*) comes into circulation to provide the complex, global sense of interrelationships that embody the national life. It gives us the global sense of the new family, organizational, occupational, and class categories within which the nation's people come democratically to identify their individual and collective human rights. Along with 'nation' and 'society', therefore, we find that various other new terms such as 'democracy' (*dan chu*), 'freedom' (*tu do*), and the 'individual' (*ca nhan*) *also crystallized in the disturbance* that followed the conquest.

A quite precise sense of the linkages underlying Tam Lang's title is not then difficult to develop, if we realize what the old monarch had to rule in his 'country' (*quoc*) before the conquest. These were his 'servants' (*toi to*) or 'subjects' (*be toi* or *dan*) or 'people' (*dan*). If we concentrate on the Vietnamese terms, what we notice is a series of semantic links in which the old 'I' and 'subject' were linked by *toi*, while ideas of the monarch's 'subject' and 'people' were linked by *dan*. At least loosely, old concepts of 'I' and 'people' were thus associated in a semantic field that was dominated by a sense of monarch and moral hierarchy. And so with the monarchy destroyed, we have the implication of a democratic revolution in which the rise of the active 'I' is associated with the rise of 'the people' and their 'nation', as well as 'class'. In sum, Tam Lang's active 'I' and rickshaw coolie class are not only linked to each other, but also to the nation and society as subcategories of 'the people'.

On this national–social basis, we may now turn to the institutional origins of reportage and social realism in reportage itself.

International Models, Social Realism, and the Democratization of the Press

One aspect of the national perspective which assumes defining importance in the rise of social documentary reportage in the 1930s must be the international context within which it is set. As a result, it will become clear that reportage was deeply influenced by that most democratic of international art forms, modern film. Of more primary importance, however, was the development of the modern press.

From its institution in Saigon in the 1860s, modern printing technology almost immediately had revolutionary effects. It is well known that it had led to the widespread use of *quoc ngu*, the romanized 'national language', as distinct from that of Chinese or Sino-Vietnamese characters. It had, by the 1920s, fostered southern initiatives in social realist fiction, which dealt democratically with low-class subjects. Moreover, it had fostered the publication of some early modern bourgeois 'I' narratives from the 1910s. I am thinking of such works as Pham Quynh's travelogues 'Ten Days in Hue' (1918) and 'Diary of a Journey to France' (1922). The women's writing that began to develop a new sense of feminine self-awareness in various journals from about 1918 also comes to mind (Huong Nguyen, 1995).

The distinguishing feature of 1930s reportage, however, is that unlike the early realist novel it was written in the first and not the third person. Also unlike the early bourgeois 'I' narrative, it offered a mirror image of the lowest urban classes. To understand how the first person low-class perspective of 1930s reportage came to constitute a major breakthrough in the development of Vietnamese social realism, therefore, it is necessary to begin with the transformation that began to occur in the northern press around 1927.

This was still the era of the post-First World War foreign investment boom when Tran Van Giau (1958, p. 166) says 'printing houses large and small were established in many big towns because the number of books, journals, and advertising increased a great deal'. Between 1923 and 1934, the number of journals in French and Vietnamese in all regions had in fact increased from 71 to 227 (Vuong Tri Nhan, 1995, pp. 435–6). We still await a detailed study of how the journals were financed and run, although it is clear that most were small-scale operations run by four or five people with a suitable bourgeois benefactor. Also, no study has attempted to show why it is that the Hanoi, rather than the Saigon, press produced most of the major reportage. However, while I will return to this issue, the activities of a certain Hanoi editor from around 1927 are worth pursuing because of the structural links they permit us to establish between international influences, the democratization of the press, and social change itself.

The editor was Hoang Tich Chu, and he is remembered for transforming the layout and content of Vietnamese journals after a trip to France to study journalism in the mid-1920s. To this time, journals did not actually publish much news. Rather, they published a range of fiction, poetry, translations, official reports, advertising, agricultural information, and educational essays—all in the same journal. But now, under the guidance of Hoang Tich Chu, the appearance of broadsheets with headlines, columns, and more local and international news than ever before meant that journals started to resemble modern newspapers (Nguyen Cong Hoan, 1971, pp. 141–3; Marr, 1981, pp. 164–5). And, as this happened, it is clear from a number of sources that the nature of published stories immediately went 'down'.

Hoang Tich Chu's newspapers themselves have not been available to me. But in Chapter 9 of 'Household Servants', for example, Vu Trong Phung mentions Hoang Tich Chu in his record of a discussion he had with his editor, Le Trang Kieu, on the extent to which it was possible to represent the 'seamy side of life'. As Nguyen Cong Hoan still remembered it in the 1970s, this had been an editorial preoccupation in the late 1920s when the columns of a number of newspapers like *Loa* [Megaphone] began to publish some quite rough prose—what he calls 'pornography' (1971, p. 141)—in place of the educational essays of old. A recent study of the press also says that another of Hoang Tich Chu's papers, which opened in 1929, was called *Dong Tay* [East–West], and that some said it was 'too Western' (Nguyen Thanh, 1984, p. 38). Consequently, there is no doubt that the transformation of the press coincided with the rise of a demand in the cities for a new kind of publication that was influenced by Western models and catered to popular taste.

It is also clear that this transformation was not a parochial one. It was part of the imperial process of urban class formation that brought its own international models for depicting the life of 'the people'. And there is no better way to demonstrate this point than to show how Tam Lang's idea to write a story about rickshaw coolies actually took shape.

In the opening section of 'I Pulled a Rickshaw', Tam Lang tells how Bui Xuan Hoc, his own modernizing editor on the *Ha thanh ngo bao* [Hanoi Midday News], had urged him to abandon some 'melancholy articles' and to get out into the world of 'investigative journalism'. The names of various globe-trotting French correspondents who were in New York, Shanghai, and the Soviet Union were mentioned as examples. Clearly, Vietnamese editors had become aware around 1930 that air travel had opened the new era of the international correspondent and provided opportunities for lively first-hand reports from interesting places.

More specifically, however, the 'melancholy articles' are a direct reference to the romanticism which had hitherto dominated the northern presses and, also, Tam Lang's literary education in the 1920s. (His first book published in 1930 had been a romantic novel called *Tears on the Perfume River.*) What Tam Lang is thus telling us in his references to the French correspondents is how the romanticism of the 1920s was going out of fashion under the influence of global change. In particular, the influence of the new on-the-spot reporting could not be resisted at a time when Hanoi editors were looking to modernize and democratize. And this was especially so when the kind of international models available were not only those of the high-flying correspondents.

Because he did not have the freedom to travel, the model which Tam Lang chose to 'imitate' was one that permitted him to do his investigative journalism 'close to home'. This was a reportage by the celebrated French lesbian, Maryse Choisy, called *Un mois chez les filles* (1929?). As a work about prostitutes, we know that to research it, Choisy had adopted a disguise which enabled her 'stoically to rub shoulders and patiently study [the girls] in order to understand and authoritatively tell of their pitiable distress' (1930, p. 11). And it is worth recalling that a similar method of writing from experience (if not a disguise) was very fashionable in the 1920s and 1930s. John Reid, Jack London, and John Steinbeck used it. Meanwhile, George Orwell was writing his seminal English documentary reportage *Down and Out in Paris and London* (1933), which interestingly contains a passage on rickshaw coolies, around the time that Choisy's book convinced Tam Lang that he should dress down as a coolie and investigate the rickshaw trade in Hanoi. By this time, Choisy had then moved on to another book in Paris, *Carnet d'une femme de chambre* (1933), which Vu Trong Phung mentions in 'Household Servants'.

Naturally, it was a condition of such internationalism that the models did not necessarily offer a perfect fit. Whatever the effectiveness of Choisy's disguise in France, for example, there has been considerable doubt about Tam Lang's in Vietnam: 'many knew that with his body, the author would not have been able to pull a rickshaw' (Vu Ngoc Phan, 1942, Vol. 2, p. 560). In fact, with what he calls his 'flabby' stomach, Tam Lang's disguise is so flimsy that we can only have adopted it—as a trace of Choisy's—for political reasons. Like the startling 'I' in his title, his venture into low-class reportage was so new he must have felt the need to justify it by highlighting its association with a prestigious foreign model—the one he explicitly decided to 'imitate'.

But the weak disguise does not detract from the work's creative impact. What is important about it is that as Choisy's example led Tam Lang to position himself as a socially centred eyewitness of the events he is describing, it realizes a shift in literary consciousness. Evidence that Tam Lang did pull a rickshaw a 'few times' will thus help us to link his adopted method with a particular construction of social reality.

A contemporary commentator who knew Tam Lang's work once explained:

> Tam Lang is a reportage writer, which means that he has involved himself in a profession where he must use observation before all else. Because of his profession he has made such efforts as to go right into a leper colony, or to sleep at night with the destitute, or to take the shafts of a rickshaw a few times to taste the hardship of the horse people. (Hoang Van Thiep, 1935, pp. 251–2.)

This is essentially Choisy's method. However, two fundamental reasons for using it have nothing directly to do with her, and these explain how Tam Lang's shift from 1920s romanticism to the realism of reportage is structurally interlocked with the democratic transformation of the northern press.

One reason is the profit motive: editors had to sell newspapers. To do this they had to write stories that interested people, and this often meant going down-and-out to find them—or publishing writers like Vu Trong Phung and Nguyen Hong who were already down-and-out. The other reason is that reportage writers commonly believed that by making people aware of social injustice, they could help to reform society. For both these reasons, editors in the 1930s had a common interest in encouraging people to read, and this led to various discussions about the need to abandon the old moralistic approach to literature and to write new kinds of stories that 'correspond with reality'.

For example, a 1933 editorial in the popular journal *Phong hoa* [Customs] said:

… if you want to teach morality, there are already whole books on moral principles; there's no need for stories and newspaper articles. A book or stories or a newspaper is the same, if you want to get people to enjoy reading them you must make people happy, or move them. And if you want them to be happy or moved, you need writings that correspond with reality. The situation of the times, things that the ears hear and the eyes see, are all living lessons, influencing people and making them ponder. (Viet Sinh, 1933, p. 1; translation by Woodside, 1976, p. 81.)

This is the shift in consciousness that I mentioned earlier transforms the idea of the book. The modern newspaper no longer forms a 'mirror' in which people see the reflection of a moral order to which their lives should conform. It is rather a 'mirror' of society in which people see images of *themselves*.

And notice how they got these: by reportage writers recording what the 'the ears hear and eyes see'. Some at the time even affirmed that this was 'only' what a reportage recorded (Trang Khanh and Viet Sinh, 1933). With such a purchase on social reality, we can then begin to understand how the pivotal role of the down-and-out or socially centred reporter creates an opportunity to project such a lifelike view of the world that a special name was constructed for it.

As it came into common usage around 1930, the term 'reportage' actually meant to 'blow up' or 'to enlarge' (*phong*) an 'event' or 'thing' (*su*). As we will soon see, this magnification of social reality has many facets. But to better understand what makes it work, we may note that reportage writing did not necessarily require an analysis of what the reporter heard and saw. It was enough to record it.

Rumour or gossip, such as the horror story about the witches' brew that opium addicts allegedly drank to combat withdrawal symptoms in Chapter 18 of 'I Pulled a Rickshaw', is a form of social communication that is often uncritically integrated into reportage. So too is the 'raw' information writers like Vu Trong Phung picked up at the cinema or read in novels. In fact, as long as it has a sufficiently strong grip on popular imagination to encourage people to read, the uncritical writing of gossip and other 'raw' information into reportage only tends to realize it as social reality. This is because it is a self-reflexive construction of the reporter's experience—or of the modern investigative method that comes more or less automatically with the democratization of the Hanoi press.

Meanwhile, to come back to a question I raised earlier: one may well imagine that the appearance of what I will now call this magnified social realism is in some way related to the dire consequences of the Great Depression. But, actually, there is no strong reason for thinking this. With reports of people 'dying beside the road' in Saigon and other places (Tran Van Giau, 1962, pp. 37–9), we cannot say with any confidence that the effects of the Great Depression were most acutely felt in Hanoi and, thus, in themselves, stimulated the sudden change in literary consciousness there in the early 1930s. What a Saigon–Hanoi distinction does suggest, however, is that the construction of magnified social realism was conditioned by a specifically northern sense of self-awareness that was realized in the democratization of the press and, perhaps, intensified by the effects of the Great Depression.

It is helpful to be aware that, compared with the north, a relatively free press had always existed in the south, that this corresponded with a relatively open social environment, and that this had given rise to some social realism in fiction by the 1920s (Cao Thi Nhu Quynh and Schafer, 1988; Hue Tam Ho Tai, 1992, pp. 120–1; Schafer, 1994, p. 108; Schafer and The Uyen, 1993). Turned around, this north–south difference strongly suggests that a deeply rooted sense of communal hierarchy in the north conditioned the emergence of first person reportage and autobiography—or the old sense of hierarchy intensifies the democratic impulse of the active 'I', which comes out in the self-reflexive 'blow-up' of magnified social realism. It could be argued that this is so in all our stories, but especially in the autobiography where Hong's projection of himself and the world is intensified in the deep introspection of his self-awareness.

In any case, it is the highly developed self-awareness of the autobiography that provides a good opportunity to tie up the main threads of the argument about how reportage realism was institutionalized in the Hanoi press.

When he explained in later life how he came to write 'Days of Childhood', Nguyen Hong told how the disintegration of his family had led to his great unhappiness as a child. He noted that what he wrote in his first documentary novel, *The Down-and-Out* (1936), was 'exactly what I saw before my eyes'. Finally, with certain works of world literature in mind, works which may be taken as models of democratic sensibility and social realism, Nguyen Hong said that he wanted to write a work which contained more of himself:

> I simply wanted to recount the bitterness of my life; give the public a 'me' without a mask, contrary to that which was habitually printed at the time. A number of characters from Maxim Gorky and Charles Dickens found a singular resonance in me and, without me knowing it, woke the memory of my own childhood. (Nguyen Hong, 1963, pp. 5–8.)

The foreign works Nguyen Hong had in mind were Maxim Gorky's autobiography, *My Childhood* (1913), and Charles Dickens's novel, *David Copperfield* (1850). I suspect that anyone who knows these works will sense the impact which their—especially Gorky's—vivid, sometimes satanic, sometimes saintly social realism had on Nguyen Hong's writing. Yet while the social details of Nguyen Hong's work bear no more resemblance to Gorky's or Dickens's than Tam Lang's or Vu Trong Phung's bear to Choisy's, the main point about the foreign models here is, still, their relevance in Vietnam. By defining the international context for a democratic national–social sense of self-awareness, these models are providing a ready-made focus and reinforcement for the structural changes in Vietnamese society and literature, which had begun with the French conquest. This, in sum, is how we get the magnified social realism of Hong's autobiography from that 'singular resonance in me'.

This is, moreover, how we get reportage realism from the singular and, by implication, democratic, resonances of modernity in all our writers. Yet these resonances had complex vibrations too. It is paradoxical enough that democracy was imposed by the conquest. But, then, in terms of its modernism, the conquest was hardly complete. As both a product and a precipitator of the modern transformation, reportage clearly represents the ongoing interplay of the old and the new, the local and the cosmopolitan. By demonstrating the main ways in which reportage realism constitutes each of our texts, we should then see how their modernism rests on an inherent sense of paradox.

The Ambiguity of Tam Lang's Social Contract

When 'I Pulled a Rickshaw' was first published, there were readers who actually responded with laughter and disbelief. Vu Ngoc Phan (1942, Vol. 2, p. 561) has said: 'I can still remember the time when they read it, many moralists were astonished and had the idea that the reporter had imagined the story for fun.' However, this reaction should not astonish us because the very idea of the moralist (*nha dao duc*) as a reader reflects the still untransformed communal hierarchy against which Tam Lang's text creates a new sense of social order.

In ancient times, moralists would have looked down vertically to the lowest strata of the population with what compassion they had. But, now, it is possible to show that what amused and confused them was the assumption of a new kind of horizontal, social relationship which is embedded in Tam Lang's text. Indeed, the new horizontal relationship is one between them, the moralists or the 'Dear Readers' to whom Tam Lang often addresses his remarks, and the rickshaw coolies or 'horse people'—a term which Nguyen Cong Hoan had already preserved for posterity in his 1931 short story, 'Horse People and Human Horses'. This new way of relating people with high and low status does not necessarily mean the vertical view has disappeared. However, a well-developed horizontal view does mean an ambiguous change in collective consciousness when it adds up, as it does in Tam Lang's text, to nothing less than a social contract.

In Chapter 19, where he clarifies the purpose of his earlier narrative, he asks and answers the following rhetorical question:

> 'Who is to blame for the class of people in our society that works like animals pulling other people?'
>
> ... I dare say you would answer honestly as follows: 'Society is to blame.'
>
> According to its strict meaning, 'society' is all of the people who come from the same origins and who all live together under the same system, and that includes you and me.
>
> Yes, you and me, all of us are equally at fault.

This gives quite a good definition of society and a participatory sense of social responsibility. But what is clearly fundamental to the construction of this passage—and to the entire story—is the pivotal role of the 'I' who dares to interrogate and to inform society about *itself*. In other words, it is around this first person turning-point that the 'you and me', the 'all of us', are 'equally' implicated in Tam Lang's narrative of society—his social contract.

Three points will help to clarify this. First, it is the reflexive nature of the 'I', or the function it has of creating society in its own image even as society creates it, that is crucial to the construction of Tam Lang's social narrative. It is, indeed, this reflexive function of the 'I' that allows the author to make *himself* an individual among *others* (rickshaw coolies as well as readers) and, thereby, relates the others with him and with each other, each as equal, sovereign particles in the social whole. More concisely, the operation of the reflexive 'I' is fundamental to the profoundly ambiguous sense of separation and connection that produces a democratic sense of social *inter*action between the 'you and me'.

Second, throughout the text, this sense of social *inter*action is fixed with new assumptions about social order and virtue. As distinct from old ideas of communal hierarchy that were accompanied by others of compassion and moral rectitude, the 'Dear Reader' finds that Tam Lang's text is justified by modern liberal ideals, such as 'social justice', membership of the 'human race', and the 'rights of man'. A horizontal sense of social responsibility thus crystallizes in an egalitarian conception of 'society', which did not much predate 1900, and which was still sufficiently new in 1932 for Tam Lang to feel the need to define it, as we have just seen he did.

In this horizontal context, the third point about the nature of the social contract brings us back to the modern investigative method: without the socially centred investigations of the reporter, he would not in fact have the necessary social detail to spin out the new social consciousness that catches the 'you and me' equally and independently in its web.

What lingered in the minds of many early readers of 'I Pulled a Rickshaw' was also what caused their initial surprise: its global account of 'all' the facets of the rickshaw trade (Vu Ngoc Phan, 1942, Vol. 2, p. 560). These range from the system of hiring out rickshaws to the method of pumping up the tyres and pulling them and from the social origins of the pullers to the tricks of their trade and to their way of life. As it tends to establish the rickshaw pullers' world as a specific one with a life of its own that is nevertheless of practical social interest to others, the detail also tends to implicate Tam Lang's 'Dear Readers' in a minute consideration of the lives of its low-class subjects.

What then clinches the implication of one urban class in the life of another may be drawn out from the detail of a short quotation. To illustrate the strong impression which Tam Lang's detailed descriptions had on him, Vu Ngoc Phan quoted in 1942 a long passage which describes various nuances of rickshaw pulling. The following is part of it:

> If you pull an old person, you have to call on people to keep out of the way as you run slowly; pulling a French man, you have to run strongly and not be afraid even at night when the street lamps are slow to come on; pulling rich young ladies and gentlemen, you must run with a sense of importance. In other words, it depends on the kind of passenger you have.

Alexander Woodside (1971, p. 58) has well described this passage as Tam Lang's 'urbanisation of the traditional reflexes of deference': the standardization of complex new and unpredictable stimuli of urban social behaviour in terms of conventions supplied by pre-modern culture. Indeed, the vertical view is still clear: the coolies still have to make various allowances for those who sit above them in the rickshaws. Yet what is also interesting about this passage is that, at the level of the text, something radically new is happening to the vertical view within the constantly changing patterns of concentrated urban life.

Now, those above—with whom we must identify most of the readers, including the moralists—suddenly find *themselves* being described, differentiated, and identified in terms of the modifications *they* cause in the coolies' pulling technique. Clearly, this could only occur in the projection of the view from the bottom up that, though already incipient in third-person realist fiction as it first developed in the south, did not have the same direct sense of unpredictable *inter*action as in a self-reflexive narrative of reportage realism—as it stems from the investigative method.

What we see in such a narrative has two important, inter-connected results. As indicated, the first one is that the vertical view is still intact, but we may now think of it as being horizontally crossed by the ambiguous and paradoxical sense it gives the reader of the *inter*action that occurs *between* people of *high-and-low status* in a concentrated urban setting: the 'all of us', the 'you and me'. The second result is that, while those above are being implicated in the lives of those below and vice versa, the narrative has not only reflected, but also promoted a change of perception and fulfilled the nature of a transforming text.

In relation to this, there is one other point to make: 'I Pulled a Rickshaw' is an early example of a long Vietnamese text that is structured according to a series of questions and answers. The importance of this modern interviewing technique is, of course, that it democratically assumes the social authority of any (even low-class) person being questioned, and thus provides spontaneous access to a range of social detail that was not necessarily available in a pre-modern text; all the facets of the rickshaw trade that so amazed the moralists who read Tam Lang's work, for example. Moreover, because it enters the social dialogue, an interviewing technique actually enmeshes the reportage text in the lives of the people who are providing the answers to the questions. As it reflects the speed of modern urban living and social change, this textual meshing in writing like Tam Lang's then means that the dialogue in it is brisker and more lifelike than ever before.

Critics have singled out examples of dialogue such as that where Tam Lang meets the rickshaw Supervisor in Chapter 2 as 'lively':

> 'Sir, I am from Thai Nguyen; my name is Ty.'
>
> 'Where's your identity card? Show it to me.'
>
> I took a piece of yellow paper from the pocket of my rough working shirt and gave it to him. It bore an official stamp and a set of fingerprints. It was folded into four, impregnated with sweat, and tattered on all four edges.
>
> 'Do you know anyone here?'
>
> 'Sir, I've just come from the highlands, and don't know anyone.'
>
> 'So who brought you here?'
>
> 'Sir, when I got off the bus, I asked a rickshaw coolie I met. He told me where to come.'
>
> 'Have you ever worked a rickshaw before?'
>
> 'Sir, I've never done it before.'

And to help explain the excitement that the spirited dialogue of this passage aroused in many contemporary readers, we come now to what Vu Ngoc Phan (1942, Vol. 2, pp. 562–3) observed was the influence of 'film'.

Like a 'close-up' on the modern screen, one of the effects of the above passage is to dilate the fine detail of a momentary exchange between two people and, thereby, create the sense of speed or rapid change. It is a passage which thus fits perfectly with the idea of 'reportage' or *phong su* as the magnification of social reality—in which we have a 'blow-up' or 'enlargement' (*phong*), an 'event' or 'thing' (*su*). Although I have seen no explicit statement of a precise connection, it does seem very likely that the cinema, which was well established in Hanoi by the mid-1920s, contributed to the construction of the term *phong su*.

But as the main elements of Tam Lang's social contract fall into place in *phong su*, this is a good place to turn to Vu Trong Phung's—not only because there is much speedy dialogue in 'Household Servants', but also because Vu Trong Phung's background happened to attune him to an important irony of modern development that significantly attracted him to film.

Vu Trong Phung, 'City Lights', and the Irony of Modern Development

One realizes almost immediately in 'Household Servants' that its author tends to upstage the servants in various ways. In Chapter 1, he stands out vividly in his newly acquired servant's clothes—his peach blossom shirt, shiny satin trousers, and dark glasses. In Chapter 2, he is the 'Big Brother' of an unemployed boy. In Chapter 5, he suggests he has an affair with the maid, Miss Dui, whose 'novel' he tells. In Chapter 7, he tries to cheer up some starving, abject people he is supposed to be investigating by singing folk-songs and popular poems. We get the feeling that Vu Trong Phung's reportage is bound up with his own play-acting, or almost because all this is told with such irony that, as Thach Lam (27 February 1938) commented in his review of the work, 'we cannot be sure if he is serious or not'.

One reason for this ambivalence is bound up with his humble origins in a poor village near Hanoi. Unlike Tam Lang, who came from a high-class background and for whom reportage writing was a democratic act of discovery and modernization, Vu Trong Phung was darkly sceptical about the possibility of reform. He knew his subjects and, ultimately, himself, too well. It could be, therefore, that his play-acting was a defence against deep pessimism and unease. However, there are at least two ways of showing that the ironic ambivalence of Vu Trong Phung is integrated with both the reality of social change and the filmic effects he uses to describe it in his writing.

The first way draws our attention to Chapter 9 of 'Household Servants', where we find more of the 'lively', 'filmic' dialogue we came across in Tam Lang's story. This is indeed a chapter where Vu Trong Phung actually mentions Charlie Chaplin films, which made him and his friends 'split their sides laughing'. Moreover, he calls Chapter 6 '*Anh sang cua kinh thanh*', which is his Vietnamese rendering of the title of Chaplin's world-famous film, 'City Lights' (1931)—and which we have turned back into English as 'The Light of the Capital', because such a translation seems more sensitive to the spotty nature of Vietnamese urban development compared with what Chaplin had in mind. But either way, there is no doubt that Chaplin influenced Vu Trong Phung's construction of social change.

There was, of course, the great excitement Chaplin caused when he visited Hanoi in April 1936, the month after Vu Trong Phung began serializing 'Household Servants' (Lockhart, 1994, Introduction). More fundamentally, however, the tragicomic pathos, poetry, and romance we find in that work has clearly been influenced by Chaplin's sensibility. Pham Van Khoa (1984, p. 108) has indeed shown how these elements of Chaplin's work generally impressed Vietnamese and in this context Vu Trong Phung's romance with Miss Dui may well be a variation on the one Charlie has with the flower girl in 'City Lights'. In any case, once Charlie's slapstick adventures finally lead him sadly down a poor, dark alley with the dazzle of electric lights all around, we are well prepared for the transposition of Chaplin's dark irony into Vu Trong Phung's Vietnam.

A central passage in Chapter 6 of 'Household Servants' tells of the electric lights that 'glowed with easy riches' and hung a 'halo over Hanoi'. The irony here, however, is one of modern development itself: attracted by the halo, peasants came from the countryside hoping to find a better life but found themselves 'curled up starving' beside foul drains in the city. Since there is no doubt that such false dreams were realized in Hanoi as well as in 'City Lights', we may conclude that the ironic ambivalence of Vu Trong Phung's reportage is as much bound up in film as in the reality of social change.

As a result of this double bind, the second example of Vu Trong Phung's ironic ambivalence will take us into the field of perception. It concerns the murky scene in the stinking, moonlit courtyard in the 'Tragicomedy' chapter of 'Household Servants': Chapter 7, where Vu Trong Phung has been trying to cheer up some miserable people by singing songs and play-acting. Suddenly, an ex-servant girl has an epileptic fit. She has had fits since being electrocuted while hanging out some clothes for her master on an electric power line. Being an ignorant peasant, she had known no better. The master dismissed her, and she found a job in another house. However, she had to flee after accidentally breaking a valuable vase. The scene in the courtyard thus ends with a policeman arriving to arrest the girl for breaking the vase, before she has hardly recovered from the fit.

This scene may embody some first-hand experience. But it is almost certainly a pastiche of servant horror stories—and perhaps flickering scenes from a modern detective film which Vu Trong Phung had seen. Anyway, the construction of the scene is filmic, if only because the idea of a 'tragicomedy' takes us back to Chaplin. Vu Ngoc Phan's (1942, Vol. 2, p. 575) description of the scene as 'extremely lively', as well as 'extremely tragic', may also be aligned with Nguyen Dang Manh's (1989, p. 7) recent description of how 'many passages' in Vu Trong Phung's reportage work—as though 'sections of film with documentary and artistic value are being projected in front of the face of the reader'. There is no doubt the constructed social reality of the reportage is again being called into existence by the agency of film, and this involves a major adjustment in social perception.

To describe this adjustment, it will be helpful to recall Walter Benjamin's 1936 essay, 'The Work of Art in the Age of Mechanical Reproduction'. But note first that this essay was exactly contemporaneous with 'Household Servants'—and a time when Vietnamese social reality was one of mass movements of people driven by economic and technological change. From this perspective, we may now appreciate the aptness of Benjamin's remarks about how the modern mass media work to reinforce the modernist consciousness of detachment from the past: the 'transitoriness and reproducibility' of modern 'magazines and newsreels', he says, brings out the 'sense of the universal equality of things'.

As film—like mass movements—thus involves what Benjamin called 'a tremendous shattering of tradition', filmic reportage like Vu Trong Phung's must represent, in the realm of perception, a democratic levelling of limitless scope. Remember that people all over the world could now watch the same film (in dark rooms that tended, paradoxically in terms of the mass nature of the audience, to create for each watcher a world of his or her own). The film audience thus epitomizes the modern democratic mass movement. But more than this, the film image itself also tends to epitomize social reality. As discussed, the construction of Vu Trong Phung's reportage is, to an important degree, bound up with the agency of film. We may say, therefore, that 'Household Servants' demonstrates one of the central arguments of Benjamin's essay: that the mechanically reproduced art form—film and reportage—involved in the realm of perception and thought 'the adjustment of reality to the masses, and of the modern masses to reality' (Benjamin, 1969, pp. 222–3).

Yet as Vu Trong Phung's writing is integrated into this limitless process, he also gives a strong sense of narrow limits in which it is difficult to imagine what might be described as the 'truth' of modern democracy. Towards the end of 'Household Servants', there is a scene in which—quite like Lesage's picaresque hero, Gil Blas de Santillane (Vu Ngoc Phan, 1942, Vol. 2, p. 575)—he turns the world upside down by getting the servants to denounce their masters. Once he has gone to the trouble of collecting their stories, however, he is concerned that they were all so 'bizarre', so 'crude and senseless' that, even though it would be impossible to 'invent' them, no reader would think they were real. He is not sure about whether he can publish 'the truthful passages' of his story at all.

In this situation he makes a strong statement, which includes the following ideas:

> Facing truth that is not normally considered worth writing down on paper, we find ourselves frightened and astounded by humanity.... Literature is one thing, life is another.... A rickshaw puller knows all the cruelty of human beings far better than a scholar. A room-boy knows more about the debauchery of humanity than a surgeon. A servant understands more clearly the behaviour of human beings than a realist writer.

There does not seem to be much hope of democratic 'truth' construction in literature at all. Ironically, however, the barriers of class, wealth, and education that seem to obstruct the 'truth' turn out to be more porous than this statement suggests.

In the age of mechanical reproduction, the reportage writer has in fact become a democratic representative of the rickshaw puller, the room-boy, the servant. In this capacity he might not know exactly what his subjects know, but, still, he or she is forced by the profit motive and his social consciousness to develop the best literary strategy he can for presenting their interests. For Tam Lang, who was a sincere liberal from the upper classes, this involved the development of an ambiguous reformist approach. But for Vu Trong Phung, who embodied and represented the deeply critical, often despairing, and incoherent view from the bottom up, the strategy was bound to be different, and, indeed, for him, there was that ready-made modern trope: irony.

On the fundamental question of how one gets around social barriers to democratic 'truth' construction, Vu Trong Phung concludes: 'I can invent stories that you will believe, or I can tell you true stories that you will think I have made up.' And in 'The Light of the Capital', such ironic ambivalence is reasonable.

Film clearly offered Vu Trong Phung and other reportage writers magnified mirror images of society. Although these were not exactly of Vietnamese society, we have seen they were easy enough to transpose and splice with reality. The political as well as the literary point of such adaptable mirror images was that, in their verisimilitude as well as their equal, wide presentation at the—universal—cinema, they tended democratically to break down old hierarchical barriers of wealth and status. It is possible to conclude, therefore, that Vu Trong Phung was drawn to films and filmic constructions of society because they permitted him to satisfy a democratic demand to tell stories that are both invented and real.

Without such an ironic play on truth construction, Nguyen Hong's story of downward social mobility offers a different approach to the social contract again.

Nguyen Hong and the Paradox of the Ancient Family in Modern Times

Beginning with a sentence that was very striking, if not shocking when it came out in 1938, the autobiography begins: 'My father was a prison warder, and my mother came from a family of traders.' Vu Ngoc Phan (1942, Vol. 3, p. 1144) indicated how radical this was when he emphasized that its tone was 'completely different' from that of the 'Family Register' (*gia pha*): 'My father came from a distinguished family, and thanks to his good deeds etc.' In the shift in sensibility thus marked, we have moved from an implication of what may be described as family- or ancestor-based morality to a detailed one of observed social reality that stresses occupation and class and, thereby, brings us into the world of reportage.

Yet unlike the social constructions of Tam Lang and Vu Trong Phung, Nguyen Hong's is not only bound up with the formation of new social or, in his case, anti-social classes—the orphans with whom he is eventually displaced in the modern city's streets. 'Days of Childhood' is primarily an attempt by the author to explain his own life and is accordingly bound up with the primordial institution of the old regime, the repository of what Nguyen Hong calls 'customs', 'rites', and 'old-fashioned prejudice': the family. Hence, Nguyen Hong's autobiography involved a virtually unprecedented undertaking to open up this bastion of the ancient Vietnamese order to the scrutiny of modern society.

A suitably complex response to such a radical venture was conveyed by Thach Lam (1938), whose introduction to the first instalment of the work said:

> Our people are good at hiding the truth, especially the sad truth of the family. Does this help? The days of childhood that Nguyen Hong has recounted below, I am not sure whether or not they should be told. I only feel in these painful old memories the extreme sensitivity of an innocent young soul who is lost in the rigid ways of a family that is about to break up.

Thach Lam is ambivalent about the propriety of Nguyen Hong's revelations. What holds his attention, however, is what happens in the 'break-up' of the family: the birth of an 'innocent young soul'. As the ramparts of the ancient family order crumble in a modern consciousness of its 'rigid ways', Thach Lam is unable to ignore the expression of individual sensitivities that give birth to a new social sense of self.

In some ways, this social self was already prefigured in various texts that were associated with the rise of feminine self-awareness in the enhanced publishing opportunities of the 1920s, and it will be helpful to set Nguyen Hong's autobiography against one of these. I am thinking of one of Tuong Pho's popular dream stories and personal confidences, her 'Lament of a Lady Friend' (1928), in which she presents the private feelings of a close friend—which are close enough to hers—and thus prepares us for the pivotal positioning of the 'I' in 1930s reportage, as well as the autobiographical self-awareness of Nguyen Hong. (It is not a coincidence that Tam Lang knew Tuong Pho well.) Moreover, her story clearly acknowledges certain features of the modern world. Great 'fighting' between countries, 'unemployment', and the poverty of 'machine civilization' are some of her sad laments. Yet as Tuong Pho's use of the first person pronoun *ta* rather than *toi* accentuates the feeling that she is thinking or speaking to herself, her understanding of the modern world does not form the basis of her self-construction. This is still a creation of the ancient cosmos.

It is, for instance, the ancient Confucian ideal of the 'Great Universal Harmony' (*dai dong the gioi*) against which she measures the depth of her despair. It is the evanescence of the 'great happiness' (*dai hanh phuc*) that heightens and intensifies the sense of deep, personal introspection pervading her lament. Except in so far as they are published, her thoughts are turned inwards and actually closed off from the modern world by a very strong, if not overpowering, sense of isolation within the vastness of 'the universe'. As she says, 'the universe is immense, but how narrow are people: each family only knows its own affairs; likewise each village, each country' (Tuong Pho, November 1928, pp. 428–32). What is so interesting about 'Days of Childhood', therefore, is that at the same time as it may be read as a lament which is set in these narrow pre-modern, pre-social categories (of especially family), these categories are still being perceived from a social point of view that shatters them.

After the shocking openness of Hong's first sentence, he essentially accounts for himself by saying that the family's disintegration and his misery 'resulted naturally' from central aspects of the old regime: 'the forced marriage of [his parents], the efforts to bear the situation, the resignation, and dark meaningless sacrifice'. The unhappiness of all this drives his parents into certain modern expedients: his father into an opium addiction, his mother into the arms of a lover, and both into lives of 'great hypocrisy'. Impoverishment, dislocation, and Hong's suffering follow. But notice the deep ambivalence of the construction.

On the one hand, the modern social problems of the parents arise from the ancient order of forced marriages. On the other hand, it is only in terms of modern urban social values, such as 'freedom' and 'rights' and 'education for women', that the ancient order can appear in a negative light. As the family has now been placed in a modern social context by the course of French colonialism, this modern consciousness is now at play in an ancient world where it had no structural foundations. Put another way, Nguyen Hong is paradoxically opening up a world that was still closed—and would become increasingly closed, because its failure to open and adapt to modernity was a condition of its disintegration. His ability to formulate his childhood so clearly in this paradox then explains the psychological insight and power of the autobiography, while the child's perception adds the poignant tone.

An early passage gives some idea of all this:

> It was on cold wintry afternoons, afternoons when the rain fell in a fine drizzle and seemed to be whispering an entreaty to the whirr of the wind, that the flames leapt brilliantly from the charcoal brazier at the foot of the wall, sparkling red and drawing our minds into a region of sadness that was especially desolate for my mother. This was even when she had me sitting on her lap, playing happily with my dolls; even when she could smell the aroma of various dishes commingling in the steam of the fragrant rice that wafted up in front of her face; even when she occasionally smiled warmly and always talked with graceful respect to my father.

The passage is loaded with ancient elements that could come from the *Book of Changes* [*Kinh dich*]: wind, water, and fire. These elements isolate Hong's mother and his thoughts in a desolate inner region. But at the same time as they turn Hong's psychological insights inwards to the smouldering sadness that lies at the heart of the work, these ancient elements do not set Hong up for the same withering sense of cosmic isolation as Tuong Pho.

He is also a bouncy boy. His relationship with his mother is central. There is a considerable amount of concrete, lifelike, social detail: the dolls he plays with, the various dishes, the communication between his mother and father. Brooding in the natural elements, the old introspection thus remains, 'even' in the face of all the social activity. But, of course, it is this 'even' that suggests the separation of the old universe and the new world of socially constructed behaviour. It is the sense of *society*—and the social contract— which is now heightening and intensifying the isolation of the inner region, not the withering 'immensity' of Tuong Pho's 'universe'.

Such an impression is created by many passages in the story, but it is quite dramatically revealed in one which reminds us of Vu Trong Phung's ironic play on 'The Light of the Capital'. This time, the irony of modern scientific development and social change is in the light of the cathedral at Nam Dinh in the chapter called 'Christmas Night'. Hong's father has already died and his mother is away trying to earn a living in Thanh Hoa. Standing in front of the cathedral, an orphan with 'no hat or shoes', Hong watches a five-pointed-star-arrangement of 'electric light bulbs' switch on:

> Mist swirled in the glowing beams of electric light, rising thickly and dispersing far off in the night. The sky looked like a dark blue velvet curtain that was about to be raised. Then, suddenly, parallel lines of bulbs which hung down from the bell tower to the stone steps of the church were also illuminated, forming a tree of dazzling rays.

The modern light bulb explodes against the backdrop of the night, immediately illuminating the new social order.

The cathedral doors opens to reveal a vault of candlelight interspersed with glowing beams of glass and crystal. French people chatted as they moved into the pews with covered cushions. Next came Vietnamese officials, 'people with power and wealth' so that the church warmed up with 'the shining colours of the congregation's clothes and the smell of make-up and strong perfume'. Then, the church wardens, who had been blocking the 'ragged, unkempt' crowd, dropped their arms and it surged in. Tired and roughly jostled in the tumult, Hong slips away, somewhat like Vu Trong Phung's peasants beneath the halo over Hanoi—for already revealed in microcosm by the tree of dazzling rays, the power and richness of modern society has not only obliterated the ancient darkness, but also become the backdrop for his modern life of dark despair.

This time from a social perspective, what has opened has also closed. For the rest of the story, the orphan Hong finds himself alone in the city's streets. At one point, after he has mastered a money-making street game called 'hit-the-coin', he dreams a modern kind of dream: that, like a profession, the game would enable him to enjoy a free and independent life. At other times, he expresses modern sociological opinions about education and human nature that stem from French enlightenment influences. For instance, Nguyen Hong says that 'each mischievous dishonest or wicked personality was the result of a family's degradation', a line that could come from Hugo. But the irony is that, like many who came to imagine in the aura of modern urban development that life could and should be better for everyone, Hong falls into a modern abyss. Miserable, poor, and unguided, all that awaits him is 'delinquency' in the streets.

The essence of the transformation that Thach Lam sensed in Nguyen Hong's work, and that all our stories represent in various ways, is that the old universe is no longer intact. It is being broken up so that, in the dissolution of the old regime and the emergence of a new one, the unifying sense is social. But this sense is not yet one of social integration; it is paradoxically one of social isolation and despair.

Conclusion

The final paradox of Hong's story is that it exists at all. As a product of the modern transformation, the view from the outside in—and the bottom up—is self-reflexive and democratic and, thereby, contradicts, the social alienation which leads to its projection. Modernity thus emerges in 'Days of Childhood', as it does in all the stories, as a contradictory process of alienation and national–social democracy. Literary modernism emerges as a suitably ambiguous and ironic strategy for the construction of social reality: Tam Lang's horizontal–vertical cross, Vu Trong Phung's democratic play on truth construction, and Nguyen Hong's interplay of worlds both ancient and modern.

Meanwhile, with the assistance of international models, the magnified social realism of 1930s' reportage was a function of the democratization of the press—and cinema—and their engagement of the active 'I' narrative in the mass movements of modern times. In this context, I have refrained from describing reportage as 'non-fiction', because this term does not sit very comfortably with the dilated sense of social realism as a 'blow-up'. As rumour, gossip, or foreign films are part of what the 'ears hear and the eyes see', there is, as Vu Trong Phung realized, a point at which fiction and non-fiction overlap in reportage—and all our writers were typical of many others in the 1930s who wrote both fiction and reportage.

From this perspective, it would be easy enough to demonstrate that, whatever the impact of fiction on reportage, reportage makes a seminal contribution to fiction as it begins to flourish in the Hanoi novel from around the mid 1930s. It has been said, for example, that Vu Trong Phung's major realist novels 'fictionalize' reportage (Vuong Tri Nhan, 1995, p. 451). An argument that could be developed, therefore, is that the realist fiction of the 1930s functions like social reportage that drops the 'I' and is written as a 'blow-up' in an active third person mode. Given the investigative method of reportage, the connection between it and the 1930s' detective novel also suggests the possibility of an interesting exploration. But this runs off into other discussions.

What concerns us here is that reportage was not fiction. Indeed, its method led most, including Vu Trong Phung, to think of it as creative documentary non-fiction that embodied a special sense of social mission. Writing in 1942, the critic Vu Ngoc Phan summed this up well when he argued that the advantage of reportage over classical memoirs and essays (*ky su*) was that it involved 'criticism' of society and, thus, an engagement in the 'big issues' of the day. As he thought of it, the new genre had created a 'lively and effective' work whose value lay in its ability to 'fix laws, correct punishments, and reform society' (1942, Vol. 2, p. 558).

The irony of this appreciation, however, is that it marked the passing, rather than the projection of the age of reportage. Only two years before in 1940, Ngo Tat To had published *Viec lang* [Village Affairs], one of the last major examples of the genre written in the 1930s' style. Although it was foreshadowed by some peasant novels, including one by Ngo Tat To himself, what is interesting about *Viec lang* is that, for a reportage, it is atypically set outside the city. It is thus a good example of the modern 'social' consciousness as it begins to splash over from the city into the countryside in the 1940s (Boudarel, 1991, p. 106). But as this happens, the limits of a modernizing urban consciousness are simultaneously revealed.

By the time of *Viec lang*, radical Vietnamese politics were indeed moving out of the city and into the collective, hierarchical traditions of the vast mass of the peasantry, where there was little foundation for the social interaction of the active 'I'. There was a considerable amount of first person reportage writing in Saigon in the 1960s. However, the genre had lost its transforming power from the 1940s, as the peasant revolution isolated Saigon and Hanoi crumbled for almost fifty years.

National independence was, of course, the democratic benefit of this decay. However, with the revival of urban development in the 1990s, we saw at the beginning of this discussion that questions are now being asked about whether it is possible to have democracy at all without 1930s' style reportage. Vuong Tri Nhan's concluding essay in *Phong su chon loc* emphasizes the 'tendency towards democratization' that is inherent in the modern 'mirror' image of society; the one in which 'people can become self-aware'. Referring readers back to the same 1942 passage in which we have just seen Vu Ngoc Phan emphasize the critical, socially engaged nature of our texts, Nhan then quotes another sentence from it: 'People who write genuine reportage are always people who defend reason and justice.' Does this comment hint at certain weaknesses in the present press regime? He does not say. However, in the very last paragraph of his discussion, he is quite explicit about why he thinks we should read 1930s' reportage again today.

With 1930s' reportage, 'society' had a Western-style conception of 'self-verification'. This made it ready to 'disclose inherent [social] defects' and, thereby, stimulate public discussion leading to 'reform and change'. And it is for this reason that he concludes people have already begun to re-read with 'great excitement' such stories from the 1930s as now reappear in his book and ours.

A Note on the Translation

The Vietnamese texts from which the translations were made are Tam Lang (1972) and Vu Trong Phung (1989), which are authoritative editions; and Nguyen Hong (1972), in conjunction with an original 1938 edition, that has some pages missing. In all cases reference has been made to the other texts listed in Section 1 of the References, except where they were unavailable to us. Those unavailable were Tam Lang (1932 and 1935) and Vu Trong Phung (1936).

While striving for accuracy in the translation, we have nevertheless thought it necessary to edit out the original Chapter 6 of 'Household Servants'. This was done with some reluctance, especially because this chapter contains some quite poetic details of the romance Vu Trong Phung claims he has with Miss Dui; ones that may have been influenced by Charlie's relationship with the flower girl in 'City Lights'. However, it seemed to us to pose so many problems of translation that we thought it better to omit it.

This means that the original Chapters 7–10 become Chapters 6–9 in our translation. Because in our view they unnecessarily weaken the text, four other passages in 'Household Servants' have also been edited out as follows: Vu Trong Phung (1989), p. 100, l. 31 to p. 102, l. 17; p. 106, l. 7 to l. 14; p. 120, l. 14 to p. 122, l. 29; p. 134, l. 15 to p. 135, l. 4.

'Days of Childhood' has also been edited in six places where it appears to us to be unnecessarily verbose or unclear: Nguyen Hong (1972), p. 67, l. 8 to p. 68, l. 3; p. 68, l. 17 to p. 69, l. 20; p. 86, l. 22 to p. 87, l. 22; p. 100, l. 3 to l. 22; p. 101, l. 12 to p. 103, l. 8; p. 104, l. 23 to p. 107, l. 11.

'I Pulled a Rickshaw' has not been edited at all.

References

1. Texts

Tam Lang, *Toi keo xe* [I Pulled a Rickshaw], serialized in *Ha thanh ngo bao* [Hanoi Midday News], 1932; first published in book form, Hanoi: Trung Bac, 1935.

____, *Toi keo xe*, with an Introduction by Thuong Sy and a Preface by Tam Lang, Saigon: Dat Moi, 1974.

____, *Toi keo xe*; long extracts appear in Phan Cu De (ed.), *Tong tap van hoc Viet Nam* [General Collection of Vietnamese Literature], Vol. 29A, Hanoi: Khoa hoc xa hoi, 1988, pp. 357–70.

____, *Toi keo xe*; the entire work has been republished in Vuong Tri Nhan, 1995.

Vu Trong Phung, *Com thay com co* [Household Servants], originally published in *Hanoi bao* [Hanoi News], No. 12, 25 March 1936; first published in a book with *Luc xi* [The Clinic], Hanoi: Minh Phuong, 1937.

____, *Com thay com co*; long extracts appear in *Truyen tap Vu Trong Phung* [Selected Works of Vu Trong Phung], with an Introduction by Nguyen Dang Manh, 3 vols., Hanoi: Van hoc, 1987, Vol. 2, pp. 61–90.

____, *Ky nghe lay tay—Com thay com co* [The Business of Marrying Frenchmen—Household Servants], with an Introduction by Nguyen Dang Manh, Hanoi: Hanoi, 1989.

Nguyen Hong, *Nhung ngay tho au* [Days of Childhood], serialized in *Ngay Nay* [Today], No. 133, 22 October 1938 to No. 140, 10 December 1938.

——, *Nhung ngay tho au*, Houston: Xuan Thu, 1976 reprint of Saigon 1967 edition.

——, *Jours d'enfance et autre récits*, translated by Lẹ Van Chat, Hanoi: Editions en Langues Etrangères, 1963.

——, *Truyen tap Nguyen Hong* [Collected Works of Nguyen Hong], 3 vols., Hanoi: Van hoc, 1983, 1984, and 1985. Vol. 2, pp. 193–265, contains *Nhung ngay tho au*.

2. *Selected Reportage from the 1930s*

Hoang Dao, *Truoc vanh mong ngua* [At the Witness Stand], serialized in *Ngay Nay* [Today]; first published in book form, Hanoi: Doi nay, 1938; republished in Vuong Tri Nhan, 1995.

Lang Tu, *No Van* [Slaves of Journalism], Saigon: Mai, 1938; Hanoi: Tan Viet, 1941. Republished in *Van xuoi lang man Viet Nam, 1930–1945* [Vietnamese Romantic Prose, 1930–1945], Hanoi: Khoa hoc xa hoi, 1990, Vol. 8, pp. 353–98.

Ngo Tat To, *Viec lang* [Village Affairs], serialized in *Hanoi Tan Van* [Hanoi Review], 1940; first published in book form, Hanoi: n.p., 1941; reprinted in a number of editions including *Ngo Tat To Tac Pham* [Ngo Tat To's Works], Hanoi: Van Hoc, 1977, Vol. 2, pp. 209–304.

Tam Lang, *Dem Song Huong* [Nights on the Perfume River], written 1932, published Hanoi: Nam ky, 1938.

Thuy An, 'Xa hoi an may' [The Society of Beggars], *Dan Ba Moi* [New Woman], Nos. 37, 38, and 40, August 1935.

Trang Khanh and Viet Sinh (Thach Lam), 'Ha noi ban dem' [Hanoi by Night], serialized in *Phong Hoa* [Customs], 1933.

Trong Lang, 'Trong lang chay' [Among the Thieves], *Ngay Nay* [Today], No. 3 February 1935 to No. 13, May 1935.

——, 'Dong bong' [Mediums], *Phong Hoa* [Customs], No. 163, 22 November 1935 to No. 173, 7 February 1936.

——, *Hanoi lam than* [Miserable Hanoi], Hanoi: n.p., 1938; republished in Vuong Tri Nhan, 1995.

——, 'Lam dan' [Being a Common Man], *Ngay Nay* [Today], No. 95, January 1938 to No. 120, July 1938.

——, *Lam Tien* [Making Money], serialized in *Ngay Nay* [Today], 1939; Hanoi: n.p., 1942.

——, 'Voi cac ong lang' [With the Medicine Men], *Hanoi Tan Van*

[Hanoi Review], No. 57, March 1941 to No. 73, July 1941.
Yen Dinh, 'Nhung due con hoang' [Illegitimate Children], *Ich Huu*, No. 108, March 1938.
Vu Trong Phung, *Cam Bay Nguoi* [How to Trap People], serialized in *Nhat Tan* [New Day], 1–2 August 1933 to 1 November 1933; Hanoi: n.p., 1934; Hanois: Mai Linh, 1951.
____, *Ky nghe lay tay* [The Business of Marrying Frenchmen], first serialized in *Nhat Tan* [New Day], from No. 69, 5 December 1934; Hanoi: Phuong Dong, 1936.
Vuong Tri Nhan (comp. and ed.), *Tam Lang, Trong Lang, Hoang Dao: Phong su chon loc* [Tam Lang, Trong Lang, Hoang Dao: Selected Reportage], Hanoi: Hoi nha van, 1995.

3. *Other References*

Anderson, Benedict, *Imagined Communities: Reflections on the Origin and Spread of Nationalism*, London: Verso, 1983.
Bao Van Nghe, *Nguoi dan ba quy: Tap truyen ky chon loc* [The Women Kneel: Selected Stories and Memoirs], Hanoi: Nong Nghiep, 1988.
Benjamin, Walter, 'The Work of Art in the Age of Mechanical Reproduction', originally published in German in 1936, republished in *Illuminations*, edited with an introduction by Hannah Arendt, and translated by Harry Zohn, New York: Schocken, 1969.
Berman, Marshall, *All That Is Solid Melts Into Air: The Experience of Modernity*, Harmondsworth: Penguin, 1988.
Boudarel, Georges, 'L'insertion du pouvoir central dans les cultes villageois au Vietnam: Esquisse des problèmes à partir des écrits de Ngo Tat To', in Alain Forest et al., *Cultes populaires et sociétés asiatiques*, Paris: L'Harmattan, 1991.
Brocheux, Pierre and Hémery, Daniel, *Indochine: la colonisation ambiguë 1858–1954*, Paris: éditions la découverte, 1995.
Cao Thi Nhu Quynh and Schafer, John C., 'Ho Bieu Chanh and the Early Development of the Vietnamese Novel', *Vietnam Forum* (Yale University), No. 12, 1988, pp. 100–11.
Choisy, Maryse, *Un mois chez les filles*, Paris: Montaigne, 1929?.
____, *L'Amour dans les prisons, reportage*, Paris: Montaigne, 1930.
____, *Carnet d'une femme de chambre*, Paris: Montaigne,1933.
Descours-Gatin, Chantal, *Quand L'Opium Finançait La Colonisation en Indochine: L'élaboration de la régie générale de l'opium* (1860–1914), Paris: L'Harmattan, 1992.

Goscha, Christopher E., *Vietnam or Indochina? Contesting Concepts of Space in Vietnamese Nationalism, 1887–1954*, NIAS Reports, No. 28, Copenhagen, 1995.

Hoang Ngoc Thanh, *Vietnam's Social and Political Development as Seen through the Modern Novel*, New York: Peter Lang, 1991.

Hoang Van Thiep, 'Hai nha van ta chan: Tam Lang va Nguyen Cong Hoan' [Two Realist Writers: Tam Lang and Nguyen Cong Hoan], *Dan Ba Moi* [New Woman], 2 September 1935.

Hue Tam Ho Tai, *Radicalism and the Origins of the Vietnamese Revolution*, Cambridge: Harvard University Press, 1992.

Huong Nguyen, 'Vietnamese Women Writers during the French Colonial Period', *Journal of Vietnamese Studies*, No. 8, May 1995, pp. 62–80.

Jamieson, Neil L., *Understanding Vietnam*, Berkeley: University of California Press, 1993.

Kwame Anthony Appiah, *In My Father's House: Africa in the Philosophy of Culture*, New York: Oxford University Press, 1992.

Lan Khai, *Vu Trong Phung (mo tai lieu cho van su Viet Nam)* [Vu Trong Phung (Presenting Material for the History of Vietnamese Letters)], Hanoi: Minh Phuong, 1941.

Lau Shau (Lao She), *Rickshaw Boy*, translated by Evan King, London: Michael Joseph Ltd., 1945.

Lockhart, Greg, *Nation in Arms: The Origins of the People's Army of Vietnam*, Sydney: Allen and Unwin, 1989.

——, Introduction to Nguyen Huy Thiep, *The General Retires and Other Stories*, Singapore: Oxford University Press, 1992.

——, 'Nguyen Huy Thiep's Writing: Post-Confucian, Post-Modern?', *Journal of Vietnamese Studies*, No. 6, January 1993, pp. 32–49; reprinted in Nguyen Xuan Thu (ed.), *Vietnamese Studies in a Multicultural World*, Melbourne: n.p., 1993, pp. 158–81.

——, 'Vietnam: Democracy and Democratisation', *Asian Studies Review*, Monash Asia Institute, Vol. 17, No. 1, July 1993, pp. 135–42.

——, 'Vietnamese Literature in History', Unpublished Seminar Paper, Faculty of Asian Studies, Australian National University, April 1994.

——, Introduction to 'Nhat Linh, *Going to France: Diary of a Journey Abroad (Using Humour to Cover the Truth)*', translated by Greg Lockhart and Monique Lockhart, *East Asian History*, No. 8, Canberra: Institute of Advanced Studies, Australian National University, December 1994.

Marr, David, *Vietnamese Tradition on Trial*, Berkeley: University of California Press, 1981.

Masson, André, *Hanoi pendant la périod héroïque (1873–1888)*, Paris: Libraire Orientalist Paul Geuthner, 1929.

Nguyen Cong Hoan, *Doi viet van cua toi* [My Life as a Writer], Hanoi: Van hoc, 1971.

____, 'Nguoi ngua va ngua nguoi' [Horse People and Human Horses], 1931, in *Truyen tap Nguyen Cong Hoan* [Collected Works of Nguyen Cong Hoan], Hanoi: Van hoc, 1983, pp. 106–14.

Nguyen Dang Manh, Introduction to Vu Trong Phung, 1989.

Nguyen Duc Dan, *May van de van hoc hien thuc phe phan Viet Nam* [Some Issues in Vietnamese Literature, Realism, and Criticism], Hanoi: Khoa hoc xa hoı, 1968.

Nguyen Hong, *Buoc duong viet van* [Along the Road to Writing], Hanoi: Van hoc, 1970.

Nguyen Khac Vien and Huu Ngoc, *Vietnamese Literature*, Hanoi: Foreign Languages Publishing House, 1978?.

Nguyen Thanh, *Bao chi cach mang Viet Nam* [Vietnamese Revolutionary Journalism], Hanoi: Khoa hoc xa hoi, 1984.

Pham Duy Ton, 'Buc minh' [Annoyed], *Dong Duong Tap Chi* [Indochina Review], 1914. For more information, see Schafer, 1994, p. 120.

Pham Van Khoa, *Sac-li Sa-plin* [Charlie Chaplin], Hanoi: Van hoa, 1984.

Phan Cu De et al., *Van hoc Viet Nam* [Vietnamese Literature], Vol. I, 1930–45, Hanoi: Dai hoc va giao duc chuyen nghiep, 1988.

Rhodes, Alexandre de, *Dictionarium Annamiticum Luisitanum et Latinum*, Romae, 1651.

Said, Edward W., *Culture and Imperialism*, London: Chatto and Windus, 1993.

Schafer, John C., 'Pham Duy Ton: Journalist, Short Story Writer, Collector of Humorous Stories', *Vietnam Forum* (Yale University), No. 14, 1994, pp. 103–24.

Schafer, John C. and The Uyen, 'The Novel Emerges in Cochinchina', *Journal of Asian Studies* (Princeton University), Vol. 52, No. 4, November 1993, pp. 854–84.

Sheehan, Neil, *Two Cities: Hanoi and Saigon*, first published London: Jonathan Cape, 1992; London: Picador, 1994.

Talberd, A. D. L., *Dictionarium Anamitico-Latinum*, Bengal?: J. C. Marshman, 1838.

Tam Lang, *Mot dem truoc* [That Night], Hanoi: Mai Linh, 1931.

Tam Lang et al., *Vu Trong Phung*, 1911–1939, *Tao Dan Tap Chi*, Special Number, December 1939.

Tap chi van hoc [Review of Literature], Hanoi, No. 2, 1990, has a series of articles celebrating the fiftieth anniversary of Vu Trong Phung's death in 1989.

Thach Lam, '*Com thay com co* va *Luc xi*' [Household Servants and The Clinic], *Ngay Nay* [Today], No. 99, 27 February 1938.

——, Introduction to *Nhung ngay tho au* [Days of Childhood], *Ngay Nay* [Today], No. 133, 22 October 1938, pp. 10–11.

——, *Ha noi 36 pho phuong* [Hanoi: 36 Streets], Hanoi: n.p., 1943.

Thuong Sy, 'Than the va su nghiep Tam Lang' [Tam Lang's Life and Work], Introduction to Tam Lang, 1974.

To Hoai, *Chuyen cu Ha noi* [Old Stories of Hanoi], Hanoi: NXB Van Hoc, 1994.

Tran Dinh Huou, *Nho giao va van hoc Viet Nam trung can dai* [Confucianism and Early Modern Vietnamese Literature], Hanoi: Van hoa thong tin, 1995.

Tran Huy Lieu, *Lich su thu do Ha noi* [A History of Hanoi], Hanoi: Su hoc, 1960.

Tran Van Giau, *Giai cap cong nhan Viet Nam: su hinh thanh va su phat trien* [The Vietnamese Working Class: Its Formation and Development], Hanoi: Su that, 1958.

——, *Giai cap cong nhan Viet Nam: tu dang cong san thanh lap den cach mang thanh cong, 1930–1945* [The Vietnamese Working Class: From the Time the Communist Party Was Established to the Success of the Revolution, 1930–1945], Hanoi: Su hoc, Vol. I, 1962.

Tuong Pho, 'Giot le thu' [Autumn Tears], *Nam Phong* [Southern Wind], No. 131, July 1928, pp. 13–18.

——, 'Mot giac mong: thu gui cho ban thuat truyen chiem bao' [A Dream: Letter to a Friend Recounting a Dream], *Nam Phong* [Southern Wind], No. 133, September 1928, pp. 228–44D.

——, 'Mot thuong-tam cua nguoi ban gai: tu tuong ve doi' [Lament of a Lady Friend: Thoughts on Life], *Nam Phong* [Southern Wind], No. 135, November 1928, pp. 426–35.

Viet Sinh (Thach Lam), 'Mot cai lam to' [A Big Mistake], *Phong hoa*, 17 February 1933, p. 1.

Vu Ngoc Phan, *Nha Van Hien Dai* [Modern Writers], 3 vols., Song Moi reprint of Saigon: Thang Long, 1959; first published Hanoi: Tan Dan, 1942.

Warren, James Francis, *Rickshaw Coolie: A People's History of Singapore (1880–1940)*, Singapore: Oxford University Press, 1986.

Woodside, Alexander, 'The Development of Social Organizations in

Vietnamese Cities in the Late Colonial Period', *Pacific Affairs*, Vol. XLIV, No. 1, Spring 1971, pp. 39–64.

____, *Community and Revolution in Modern Vietnam*, Boston: Houghton Mifflin, 1976.

Wright, G., *The Politics of Design in French Colonial Urbanism,* Chicago: University of Chicago Press, 1991, especially Chap. 4, 'Indochina. The Folly of Grandeur'.

I Pulled a Rickshaw

TAM LANG

TAM LANG is the pen-name of Vu Dinh Chi, who was born in Hanoi on 26 March 1900. Other pen-names he used were Thien Ly Kinh, Lang Tam, Chang Ba, Ba Phai, and Linh Phuong.

His father, Vu Dinh Chat, was from a well-known family of Confucian scholars in Ke Sat, Hai Duong Province. He resisted the French invaders in his early life, and supported the Tonkin Free School Movement. He then worked reluctantly as a colonial official because he needed to support his family. He died disappointed at the age of forty-five, leaving his wife, Vuong Thi Hao, to raise three sons and two daughters. The first son, Vu Dinh Tuong, became a doctor and playwright who died in 1942 during a typhus epidemic at the age of forty-three. Tam Lang was the second son.

At the age of five, he began to study Chinese characters, but before long entered a modern Franco-Vietnamese school. After passing his exams, he entered the Teachers' College in Hanoi. However, he did not complete his studies. Obsessed with the idea of building a new society, he turned instead to literature. He began working as a journalist in the 1920s, and became associated with a literary group led by Tuong Pho, the well-known lady writer of romantic laments and dream stories. She gave him the name Tam Lang, or 'Third Man', indicating that he was the third oldest in her group. Reflecting this association, he published a romantic novel, *Giot le song Huong* [Tears on the Perfume River] in 1930. However, his 1931 publication of *Mot dem truoc* [One Night], a collection of short stories, soon signalled a shift towards realism.

In the 1930s, Tam Lang worked as an editor on many newspapers and wrote a number of pioneering satirical and other columns which attacked social injustice: 'Films', 'To Speak or Not to Speak', and 'A Plate of Sweet Ginger'. In 1932, he wrote his classic reportage, *Toi keo xe* [I Pulled a Rickshaw]. Originally written for the *Ha thanh ngo bao* [Hanoi Midday News] in 1932, but not published in book form until 1935, it is presented for the first time in translation. In 1933, he married Nguyen Thi Mi, who came from a distinguished family. It is said that her culture and resourcefulness gave Tam Lang security and had a big influence on his work.

During the Franco-Viet Minh War, he first lived in the Viet Minh zone from 1946 to 1951. He then returned to French-occupied Hanoi at a time when many with upper-class backgrounds left the resistance, because the hard conditions were being coupled with increasingly oppressive Communist Party surveillance. In Hanoi, he revived an interest in theatre which he had begun to develop in 1945. After moving to Saigon in 1954, he was a foundation member of the Tu Do [Freedom] Newspaper Group. As well as his editorial work and journalism in a number of papers, he continued to write plays for the theatre and television. He died in Saigon on 17 January 1986.

1

A Coolie's Hat Is Placed On My Head

ONE day, Mr Bui Xuan Hoc, the editor of the *Hanoi Midday News*, slapped me on the shoulder and said: 'You have a talent for writing descriptive prose, and the era of investigative journalism is upon us. Others in your profession are going all over the world, investigating events and interviewing people: Albert Londres has gone to Shanghai, Maurice Dekobra is in America, Georges London has arrived at the Turkish–Russian frontier, Louis Charles Royer has gone to

Leningrad in the Soviet Union. But you, all you do is slave away in your office over a few melancholy articles. Why don't you throw down your pen and get out and see people? It would brighten you up. That would be better, wouldn't it?'

I thought about my friend's half-joking, half-serious comment and felt ashamed; felt ashamed, then sad; felt sad, then thought: 'My young cousin wants to go and work in Cambodia and still hasn't obtained the papers he requested some time ago; Shanghai and New York are further than Cambodia, so how will I be able to go to those places, and in order to do what?

'Interviewing and investigating, those two tasks require more than just a talent for descriptive writing. Not until we have put on our walking shoes and picked up a bag of knowledge and another one of money can we take up the staff of a wanderer and talk about such adventures.'

My conclusion: 'If I can't do it far away, then I should do it close to home.'

Thus imitating Maryse Choisy, the French journalist who disguised herself as a maid so that she could work in a brothel and write a book about it, I borrowed a set of working clothes from a labourer, put them on, and adventurously went looking for work in the rickshaw trade.

And so on one very hot summer afternoon, my friend, Mr Bui Xuan Hoc, put on my head the hat of a rickshaw coolie.

2

Facing Supervisor T

'Please, Sir, can I work a rickshaw?'

'Where are you from? What's your name?' the Supervisor asked rudely as though he was about to spit in the face of a stranger.

As he said this, the Supervisor opened his mouth wide and, revealing two rows of teeth that were covered in a mulch of food pulp resembling custard apple flesh, he took hold of his big leather belt—it was as big as a hunter's cartridge belt—and loosened it a notch.

'Sir, I am from Thai Nguyen; my name is Ty.'

'Where's your identity card? Show it to me.'

I took a piece of yellow paper from the pocket of my rough working shirt and gave it to him. It bore an official stamp and a set of fingerprints. It was folded into four, impregnated with sweat, and tattered on all four edges.

'Do you know anyone here?'

'Sir, I've just come from the highlands, and don't know anyone.'

'So who brought you here?'

'Sir, when I got off the bus, I asked a rickshaw coolie I met. He told me where to come.'

'Have you ever worked a rickshaw before?'

'Sir, I've never done it before.'

Supervisor T put the identity card into a pouch on his belt, turned and called to a person wearing a dirty, ragged shirt and greasy shorts, and told him to bring out a mattress and two covers. He then pulled a pencil out of his pocket and stood writing in a tiny notebook.

'Between now and 3 a.m., you must bring back exactly 60 sous to pay for the hire of the rickshaw; you must pull it on the right-hand side of the road; you must avoid cars and trams; you must bring the rickshaw back on time; understand?'

He threw me a set of old blue clothes with white hems and pointed to the first vehicle that was parked in a line of rickshaws along the side of the footpath.

'Rickshaw number 102, over there, the first one, do you hear? Go and get it.'

With my blue uniform over my shoulder, I followed my new workmates into a narrow courtyard enclosed by a wall, but with people coming and going through an open door. I bent down with my head against the wall, took off my trousers, and hopped into my work pants, one leg at a time.

Embarrassment eventually goes away, and in this situation it goes in the blink of an eye.

To join the white-hem brigade, all I had left to do was to roll my own clothes into a bundle, collect the rickshaw mattress with two strips of towel in one hand, put my other hand out to pick up a stained black conical hat, and then step outside the Supervisor's door.

After testing the shafts and checking the suspension and the hood of my rickshaw, I felt the pressure in both tyres and realized they needed more air. Picking up a pump that was lying near by, I unscrewed the cap on the valve on the wheel and attached the nozzle of the rubber lead from the pump. With one foot holding the wooden pump stand steady, I gripped the handle of the pump tightly with both hands, then, in order to fill the tube, I put my head down and pulled the handle up and pushed it down in long strokes, panting like a cow.

3

Holding the Shafts and Pulling

When I lifted my sleeve to wipe the sweat off my brow, it smelt like something out of a stable. As people often say, it was the smell of horse sweat. That smell came from the blue shirt I had just put on; the sweat of hundreds of people which had soaked into the cloth over many years and only been thrown occasionally into a bucket of water.

Holding two wooden handles that we call the shafts of the rickshaw, I stepped out in the rectangular frame with the afternoon sun on my back following the shadow it threw in front of me. My feet felt as though they were burning, even though to any passenger looking down at that time, the tarred road would have looked as cool as stone because it had just been sprayed by a public works water tanker.

First, I turned into the road along the river.

My feelings at that time? It wasn't me. Who could recognize me?

It was really very funny!

I felt like a naked man in the street pulling an ox-cart with a board mounted on it which bore my full name and, also, the names of the close members of my family. So acute was my embarrassment that, suddenly, it felt as though my ears had began to vibrate: sitting on the imaginary ox-cart, I was sure I could hear some people beating drums and clashing cymbals like those on the cart from the Quang Lac theatre when it goes around drumming up business.

On scorching summer afternoons, the road along the river is not usually crowded, but what a crowd I thought I saw there that day. It was as busy as the day of the celebrations of the fourteenth of July when cannons fire a 21-gun salute, as bustling as the Armistice festival when a rickshaw race is organized, and thousands of eyes stare at the professional horse person who is about to take the first prize of 2 piastres.

I had tried hard to maintain the courage I felt when, at home, I first took off my shoes and stepped out. But now I weakened and my courage collapsed inside me as I went along with a lowered head.

I was hot from head to foot, yet my body felt cold; as cold as a fellow with a fever who has to be dragged into hospital and stripped so that he can be dashed with water in a bathroom.

Now, in truth, there was no one at all in the street looking at me, but I still thought many people were staring, wide-eyed. No one wanted to know me at all, but I still thought they did. I still thought they knew my full name and, also, the place where I lived!

I was investigating! That's what I was telling myself.

But whatever you say, once your courage is gone, it doesn't come back; so I continued on my way with my face down and the sound of cymbals crashing in my ears.

4

Eight Advantages of a Conical Hat

Fed up, ashamed, shivering with cold, and feeling feverish, I lost my strength just as I lost my courage.

Remembering the most deserted area I could think of, I pulled the rickshaw into Hang Chuoi Street where I intended to lower the shafts on the sidewalk and have a rest until it was dark. I would then drag the rickshaw back and dump it at the Supervisor's.

'Whee-els!'

That call had no meaning for me at the time. Even though I could clearly see a Frenchwoman at the head of Hang Voi

Street waving her arms as she called, I pretended I hadn't heard a sound, and quietly pulled the rickshaw into a side-street where I also ignored a man who tried to help me by yelling into my ear: 'Hey, you, someone's calling you.'

At that same moment, from the road beside the Bank, two rickshaws came rushing out together. Seeing two members of my own trade competing to be horses, I honestly didn't have the courage to laugh.

Stopping by a stall an old woman ran in Hang Chuoi Street, I spent half a sou on a cup of fresh tea. As soon as it was down my throat, the water came straight out through the pores of my skin. I unbuttoned my shirt and, baring my chest, fanned myself with one of the flaps.

'Why don't you take off your hat and fan yourself? What's the use of leaving it on your head?'

Without letting me answer or waiting for me to ask his opinion, another rickshaw coolie, who was sitting at the tea stall with me at the time, started to prattle on about hats without drawing breath: 'A rickshaw coolie's hat is 3 sous, but has many more uses than a white umbrella costing 1 piastre and 20 sous. It's a hat of leaves, but it's ten times as good as one of those fine cloth umbrellas; no doubt about it. When it's sunny, you can put it on your head; when it's windy, you use it to shield the match that lights the tobacco in your water-pipe; when you're tired, you sit your backside down on it; when you're not near a tea stall and feel thirsty, you stick it under a water-pump. Then, when you're sitting in your rickshaw and sleeping, you cover your face with it to keep off the flies that are buzzing around; when you're hot, use it as a fan; when there's no time to go home and wash your shirt, wash it in the street, wring it out 'till it's dry, then wrap it around your hat and carry it on your head, drying it as you go; and, also, when you're hard up, your missus can use it as a basket when she goes to the market.'

It was four-thirty in the afternoon.

Ignoring the talkative fellow, I pulled the rickshaw to the other side of the street.

Placing the shafts of the rickshaw on the sidewalk, I put my hat on my belly, lay my back on the floor of the rickshaw, and dreamed.

The sound of cicadas came down from the trees.

The setting sun flickered through clumps of green leaves that danced in the wind, as though it was playfully sprinkling deep red and golden yellow coins all over my stained black hat—forming in red letters the word 'interview'.

5

——Pulling a Passenger from Don Thuy to Yen Phu——

Something gave the rickshaw such a strong bump from behind that I was thrown out of it. The street lamps had already been lit and, as I looked up from where I fell on the sidewalk, I could see their rays shining down along an absolutely deserted stretch of road.

Then someone appeared before me.

Before I had time to rub my eyes, that person had jumped into the rickshaw, planted his backside on the seat, stamped the heel of his shoe on the floor of the carriage, and yelled: 'Allez! Vite!' [Hurry up! Faster!]

I hurriedly slapped on my hat, picked up the shafts, and concentrated on pulling the rickshaw out into the street. Why did I accept this situation and proceed to pull another human being along the road? Actually, at that time, I did not know myself.

It now seemed as though my blood was running rapidly around my body. With my head forward and my elbows pointed up behind my back like a grasshopper, I stepped out and, with the first step, it seemed as though I could swallow miles of road in one gulp.

But the truth was very different.

By the third step, I already felt as though I had no flesh on my heels, that all I had left was bone which transmitted shooting pains up my legs. Being a fat person, I also felt that my stomach became flabbier and dangled like a pig's belly below the ribs.

'All-lez! Plus viite! All-lez!' [Hurr-ry! Faster! Hurr-ry up!]

Each time my passenger stamped the heel of his shoe on the floor of the rickshaw, it was as though the shock ran straight up the back of my neck and forced my head down. Usually, I walked with my legs evenly apart, but now it seemed as though they were bowed. My insides were painfully twisted from the navel up, my throat was like an overheated cast iron pipe.

With great difficulty I managed to get my passenger to the head of Dat Bridge. Breathing through my mouth, my nose, and, also, my ears with sweat streaming off me, I no longer felt like a human being, but like a steam engine.

From the Clock Tower, my pace started to fall into a rhythm, but I still panted through a wide-open mouth. The two rubber tyres continued to turn on the tarred road, but the carriage was still unsteady, as though it wanted to lift me off the ground or push me over on the sidewalk.

Nobody could say that I hadn't been able to handle the shafts. As far as I'm concerned, to be a rickshaw coolie you must bow to the command of two wooden shafts!

Usually, the row of electric street lamps seemed rather dim to me, but, that night, they all seemed like the glaring headlights of motor cars. They were twice as bright as usual, shining through my shirt and illuminating the hairs on my legs.

Along the road, there were many noisy, bustling sounds

which I heard and did not hear. Each time a car sped by throwing up the dust, I was sure there were passengers I knew inside it, pointing at me with contempt. There were also so many rickshaws around me, pulling people I knew! A strange feeling came over me. I put my head down and ran away.

'Out of the way!'

Perhaps because of my faint call, rather than his negligence, a person crossing the road failed to avoid me.

'Are you blind? What are you doing?'

Although it was the point of one of my shafts that poked him in the shoulder, he was still threatened by the French overseer sitting in my rickshaw.

Through the bridge underpass, past the bus stop, past the boiler house, past the old tobacco shop.

I was breathing flames, my chin was streaming with sweat like a broken piece of guttering from which water pours on rainy days.

'Assez!' [Enough!]

A heel stamped on the floor of the rickshaw once more.

I stopped in front of a house with a veranda on which an Annamese woman wearing white pants and a black blouse lay stretched out on an easy chair.

Pushing my blue shirt half way down my back, and using my hat as a fan, I squatted down on the sidewalk straight in front of the rickshaw. If at that time a servant had not come out and paid me 10 sous, I would have forgotten all about it.

'Could you please go back in and ask that man for some more money for me? I brought him from Don Thuy!'

The servant hadn't gone in when the long-nosed Frenchman came out fuming.

'What's the matter? What's the matter?' came the repeated question.

'He asked you to pay him some more.'

'Dix sous et encore pas content?' [Ten sous and you're still not happy?]

I stood up holding out the money the houseboy had just put in my hand: 'Monsieur, payez moi encore, monsieur, allez lointain.' [Mister, pay me more, you've come a long way.]

My passenger jumped out threateningly.

'Do you want a whipping? You dirty cow!'

As he unfastened the leather belt girdling his stomach, the brass buckle glittered.

At that moment I realized my passenger was, as people say, a curly haired blue-eyed overseer. Now that I'd heard him curse me, I wanted to see if he'd take the next step and try to beat me up, and so I had to maintain a stubborn attitude.

'Payez encore, moi pas connaitre.' [Pay me more, I won't take this.]

Sure enough, a blow came before I could avoid it, so I ran off crying loudly: 'Help, Police! Constable! Captain!'

A crowd of people rushed out into the empty street.

I clearly heard the voice of a woman: 'Ahh, it's the same old story, a rickshaw coolie being beaten up for wanting more money!'

Neither a Police Constable nor a Captain came!

Then the people in the street also ignored the fracas!

So did the woman in white pants who was still stretched out calmly on the easy chair as before.

I turned around and picked up the shafts of the rickshaw.

Another man from the white-hem brigade sitting with his arms around his legs beside another rickshaw under the street lamp said: 'It's nothing new coming from those overseers; you should have known!'

6

—*Remembering an Old Man Three Years Before*—

The breeze at Lake Truc Bach cooled me off.

Co Ngu Road was busy with cars that had shiny brass fittings, Torpedos and Limousines which their owners were taking out for a drive.

Bathing in the breeze, those people must have felt as light as a feather.

With the wind coming over the lake, the moon was reflected on the ripples on its surface, but I felt most uneasy.

The blow on the shoulder was not as painful as the one on my ribs, or the ache in the back of my neck or the soreness in my legs. And the ache in my bones was not as painful as the ache in my brain. But, at that time, both my brain and my bones ached.

It was as if my brain said to my bones: 'We're both in pain', then ordered my eyes to look at the road.

What do we see on the road?

We see a fellow as fat as a buffalo with four children—although without his wife to complete the family—all sitting together in a rickshaw that a coolie pulls along step by step.

Let's imagine that the coolie and the fat man changed positions. The latter wouldn't last more than three steps before pointing at the former, grinding his teeth, and saying: 'You cruel bastard!'

On summer nights we often hear ladies calling: 'Would you take me for a ride! How about 15 sous for an hour?'

Everywhere in the street, there are middle-aged women wearing heavy make-up. They sit sedately in colourful rickshaws, and the coolies have to run smoothly to give their lady-passengers a noble air. There are also big-shouldered fellows, as big as a Guardian Spirit, whom we see with their hair slicked back, lying full length in rickshaws that they hire by the hour. They draw on English cigarettes and roll their eyes in all directions like dragons.

'Fifteen sous for an hour? Would you take Madam for a ride?'

'Fifteen sous for an hour, makes 3 piastres a month. A bowl of sweat and blood, they value it at less than a nickel. Such cruel exploitation!'

As I sat thinking about the experiences I'd had after putting on the clothes of a rickshaw coolie, about the curses I'd heard and the beating I'd taken, I suddenly remembered an old man I met some three years ago.

Pulling a double-sized rickshaw—with a friend and me on board—the old man had run slowly.

My friend was annoyed and urged him on: 'Faster!'

The old man answered through his breath: 'You gentlemen will only understand, if you pull a rickshaw like me!'

My friend jumped down and would have slapped the insolent coolie, if I hadn't intervened in time.

That was three years ago.

Now, I'm sure that coolie is dead.

Working at this job, how can you live for long? You run all day. You don't have enough to eat. Your body is soaked in the rain and exposed in the sun.

People often say: 'Tropical fruit ripen early.'

I say: 'Rickshaw coolies die early.'

7

——*A Ten-sou Coin in the Cuff of a Coolie's Shorts*——

'I'm returning my rickshaw to the same street as you; have you got enough to pay for the hire of yours?' said a rickshaw coolie whose path converged with mine.

'After pulling the rickshaw all afternoon and evening, I've only taken 70 sous,' I replied. 'So after paying 60 for the hire, I've only got 10 left.'

'Good, it's almost two in the morning now. We can take our time to go back together. Follow me and I'll show you where to eat, and, after that, I'll show you a place to sleep.'

Putting the shafts up under my armpits, I stepped off with my new friend. As it was late and the street was deserted, I engaged my friend in some trivial conversation: 'Are 10 sous enough for a meal and a place to sleep?'

'Do you have a taste for wine?'

'I never drink at all.'

'Seven sous for rice, 2 for lodging, makes 9. Then ½ sou for a bowl of fresh tea, you are left with ½. But I've forgotten to include tobacco for your water-pipe.'

'No, I can't smoke a water-pipe.'

'So, there's nothing more to worry about!'

The clock struck two. We arrived at the place where we had to return the rickshaws.

Crossing a small courtyard, we arrived at the inside veranda where an American lamp shed a dim light. I recognized the man wearing the ragged shirt whom I saw the previous afternoon. Presumably, he was the Supervisor's assistant.

The Supervisor wasn't there, but on the canvas chair that he previously occupied I saw a woman sitting. This huge old woman, wearing no blouse, had her hair hanging down and was fanning herself vigorously. Under a bib that was smaller than a handkerchief, her breasts dangled like two coconuts as big as teapot holders.

Nearby, on a bare wooden bench, a number of half-naked fellows lay like sardines, sleeping heavily.

I could hear the sounds of people snoring, coughing, and talking in their sleep.

I took 60 sous out of my shirt pocket and handed them over.

'Rickshaw 102, wasn't it?' The bull-headed fellow with the face full of veins and the tattered shirt asked as he opened a notebook.

'That's right, so please return my identity card.'

'Is the rickshaw missing anything?'

'Everything's there.'

'You'll have to wait 'till I check it first.'

At that moment, another rickshaw coolie came in: 'Please, Sir, I beg your kindness, I'm 20 sous short today.'

'Shut up. If you haven't got enough for the hire, you'll have to pawn your shirt.'

'Could I make it up tomorrow?'

Without waiting for the coolie to finish talking, the old woman raised her shrill voice: 'We are not waiting 'till tomorrow! Where's his shirt? Catch him!'

'I've only got my shorts left, it wasn't a busy day today, please reconsider.'

At this moment, without warning, the Supervisor's assistant who wore the ragged shirt bent down and pulled a shifting spanner out from under a table, rushed at him, and struck his back three times.

'Oh, God!'

'You haven't paid the full amount, and you're being smart, aren't you?'

'How dare he open his mouth! Thrash him! Give him some more!'

The old woman quickly tied her hair up into a bundle and threw herself at the coolie. She grabbed his hair and pulled his head down and slapped him as she brought her knee up into his face and cursed.

On the wooden bench, the men, who were probably all coolies, continued to sleep soundly. One of them, who slept more lightly than the others, lifted his head and looked, then fell back to sleep.

'Search him,' snapped the old woman.

Throwing down the shifting spanner, the assistant in the ragged shirt searched the wretched coolie from head to foot.

Now, as the coolie shook like a trembling dog, the fellow carefully fingered the hem of his shorts: 'Ahh, he's hidden 10 sous here, the bastard!'

The assistant pulled out the 10-sou coin and then punched the coolie in the face: 'What's this? Damn your kind, you thief!'

The old woman pulled his head down and hit him again: 'From now on, quit your cheating!'

After receiving over ten blows, the wretched coolie put his hands on the small of his back and rolled over. Blood streamed from his nostrils, and a thick pool of it coagulated on the brick surface of the courtyard.

I shuddered and turned to the Supervisor's assistant and said: 'The poor man owes you only 20 sous!'

8

I Taste Beef Offal Soup for the First Time

Three o'clock in the morning.

With the friend I met on the road, I slipped into an eating booth that was dark and as constricted as a rat's hole. We sat down on a couple of low stools that were pushed up close to a table. The wooden tabletop was filthy with grease that had covered it for years, and on it was a container full of bamboo chopsticks with water dripping out of it, two tiny wine cups, and a pot with a broken spout, the fish sauce container.

I breathed in an air of fetid, choking smells. This stench

was called the 'chopping board smell', but this was only partly correct, because aside from the smell of stale fat, rotten fish, tainted meat, raw onions, and a hundred other kinds of food, there was, if you analysed it carefully, also the smell of excrement mingling with that of habitual sweat.

A small child brought out two shallow earthenware bowls, one covering the other with the bottom one containing 3 sous' worth of rice.

I turned the top bowl over, took a pair of chopsticks, divided the rice into two, and pushed one portion of it into the empty bowl.

In front of me, one bowl of beef offal soup stood with steam belching off it. Even though it was as hot as that, I predicted that it wouldn't be very tasty, because the soup looked like drain water with a few slices of offal floating around like drowned corpses with chopped onions. Next to this was a plate of cold tripe that didn't look any more appetizing.

With little money, you can't eat tasty food! Two sous for offal soup! Two sous for cold tripe!

Holding the rice bowl, I poured the soup into it, and I felt my stomach jump into my mouth. Perhaps the dish of large intestines was not carefully prepared, for after I'd finished one mouthful, I thought I had swallowed a whole field of bull shit.

Sitting opposite, my friend said as he sipped a cup of wine: 'You don't drink, so eat up.'

Holding the bowl of soup and slurping it down noisily, my friend smacked his tongue and said: 'The beef offal soup is delicious!'

I just sat there holding my chopsticks.

The soup, the tripe, the rice dish which was cooked with grain that had completely lost its colour and starch, and also the 'house fish sauce' that was mixed with brine to discourage consumption: even if I had tried to swallow, I would have thrown it all up.

Sitting, waiting for my friend, I looked at a food container just outside the house. Under a thin cover of steel netting was a pot of meat—sinewy meat whittled away from the bone—still waiting to be thrown into the pot to make the morning pork stew.

Three small freshwater carp, about the size of two crossed fingers that had been fried since I don't know when, were withered like grilled salted fish. They'd probably fallen into a frying-pan where they'd been cooked in fatty dregs, then landed on a plate which hadn't been able to tempt a customer for ages. A lump of pork brisket tied to a cord dangled like a string of coins. Some bean curd, fried for some days, had begun to change colour from yellow to dirt brown.

Coming in from the door, one saw a plank that was fixed to the wall; hanging from it was a long row of wine bottles, large and small. Inside the house was a big winnowing basket full of wet bowls pushed under a bench covered with a dirty sleeping mat. Fastened above it was a coarse curtain the colour of rice gruel and offal soup.

The food, the utensils, the curtain, the sleeping mat; it was as though everything was dried out by the light of two oil-lamps from which thick smoke rose as they burnt night after night.

I thought: 'In a setting like this, people can still lift their rice bowls and swallow the food with pleasure, but what food, what drinks are really good? All the discarded leftovers have come to the eating house: rotten eggs, spoiled meat, stale fish, diseased chickens, sick dogs! These leftovers don't include the meat that had already been boiled to extract the broth and then discarded, or the leftover potato dishes that had been thrown into a pot of rice water which had been removed by the kitchen hands in French restaurants and sold to eating-places like this.'

I felt nauseous.

Looking up, I saw my friend still slurping his soup, but this time, with a face as red as wine and feeling very pleased with himself!

Do we eat to live?

Do we live to eat?

9

In a Jar One Night

A rickshaw lamp swung beneath my friend's hand like a flickering firefly. Passing a dike a little over 2 metres high, we descended into a deep depression that was as dark as a grave.

No longer could we see the row of electric lights along the Don Thuy Road. Obscured by the long dike, they gave off a dull glow above our heads. What a sad scene.

I followed my friend's footsteps. There were no stars in the sky. A pulsating chorus of croaking frogs and toads and crickets resounded all around me.

That's the area of the southern slums!

The home of a group of poor, wretched people. A torn basket full of rubbish at the foot of a row of imposing villas!

There was no ray of light. Not one tyre mark. Here, the light of civilization is blocked by a wall of dirt; the wheel of progress is stopped by a long stretch of dike.

And yet something has managed to cross it!

This is the Opium Spirit with tortoiseshell red wings attached to its back. This is Miss Phu Dung, the spirit with the beautiful name that people know well how to call.

That night, I saw Miss Phu Dung lie there, in the compartment of a leaf-covered dwelling that was slanted on a twisted house post and in which ten people were packed as though in a jar.

I bent down and slipped through a doorway that was no higher than a metre. My friend pointed out Tu, who was lying beside an opium tray. Then, taking off his blue outer shirt, my friend said: 'This person wants to sleep here for a while.'

I nodded a greeting and handed over 2 sous I had just taken out of my pocket.

The person lying beside the opium tray lifted his head, raised his arm to take the money without uttering a word.

He was about forty, pale, and with sunken cheeks. His eyes were also deeply sunk into his head. His arms were as thin as reeds. His pants were rolled up above his knees, showing two legs that were no stouter than his arms.

Without being invited, I sat down on the bed beside our friend who was lying there smoking opium.

After exhaling a long trail of smoke, he sat up, drew his knees up, undid the flask on the opium pipe, bared his chest, rolled his sleeves up to his shoulders, and scraped the residue out of the flask.

In one corner, a number of others, all men, some wearing shirts, others bare-chested, were sitting on a piece of sleeping mat with their heads converging around a smoky lamp on a tray. They made noisy cries as they gathered around playing a kind of card game called 'Bat': 'Pull', 'Turn it over', 'Bat', 'Damn your mother', 'Damn your father'.

Rickshaw coolies robbing rickshaw coolies; crippled chickens scratching around the grinding stone to peck at empty husks!

A woman holding a child lay on a hammock that was hidden in the darkness. She popped her head out from time to time, opened her mouth and asked: 'Did the "wooden fish" win, or who?'

My friend who brought me here, joined the group playing cards. I was left with Tu, and, having the opportunity, I coaxed him with a question: 'Each day, how many pipes do you smoke?'

After putting the top back on the flask, he looked up at me: 'Did you say this is the first time you've been here?'

'Yes. The other man has just brought me here today.'

'You look as though you're from Hanoi.'

'No, I just came down from the highlands a few days ago.'

With the opium pipe standing at the foot of the bed, Tu took a long draw on it. Without giving him the time to judge me, I asked again: 'Each day, how many pipes do you smoke?'

Lying down slowly, Tu invited me to join him.

Inserting the point of the opium pick into the ball of residue and holding it up to the lamp, Tu said as he prepared the opium: 'Twenty sous a day, as I have only one session at night. Mixed opium can be smoked many times and the residue lasts.'

'So, in that case, how many pipes?'

'Three pipes, sometimes four, but no more, because the residue gets too strong and damaging, and I haven't got the strength to draw on it.'

'At 20 sous, you must spend 6 or 7 piastres a month.'

'No, not that much. I cook the residue again, so that I save a bit each month.'

'Smoking like that, surely you can't work at night?'

'No, I only hire a rickshaw and pull it at night. During the day, it's extremely hot and very hard work.'

'So if you work at night, when are you able to find the time to smoke opium?'

'At 2 a.m. I return the rickshaw. I get back here a little before you just arrived. I smoke 'till morning. After eating, I sleep until five in the afternoon, get up, eat again, and go to work.'

'Money for hiring the rickshaw, for opium, and also for food; how can you make enough to afford it working only for seven or eight hours?'

I asked him his story, and he smoked as he responded. By now, his cold attitude had completely disappeared. Hearing me ask the last question, he just laughed and did not answer.

Seeing I didn't ask any more questions, Tu turned his eyes towards me. Perhaps I had revealed a little of my true identity beside the opium-lamp, because, now, I clearly heard him ask: 'If I'm not mistaken, I see you don't have to work at this occupation. For how many days have you been pulling a rickshaw?'

I remained calm without fearing that he would unmask me, and answered with a sincere expression on my face: 'True. With a body like mine, who could say I've had a hard time. Up in Thai Nguyen, I used to have a house. During my childhood, my parents spoiled me, and I didn't study. When I grew up, I led a debauched life, drank and smoked opium, lost all my wealth, and, then, my parents got angry and disowned me. I came to Hanoi, where I intended to take up a trade. But without an education and with no specific skills, I couldn't get anything. I was hungry and had to crawl on my knees. People said I should go and get a job as a rickshaw coolie. I thought that for someone as half-baked as me, there wasn't any other occupation.'

The group playing cards had broken up. It was almost morning.

On a few flimsy bamboo beds, over ten coolies, who had just been fighting to fleece each other at cards, now lay rolling around exhausted, offering a sweaty banquet to the mosquitoes that swarmed above them.

Lying beside the miserable opium tray and preparing the opium for Tu to smoke, I had become his close friend.

Through the sounds of children crying, the heavy snoring

of the half-dead gamblers, we continued to exchange confidences.

I didn't sleep throughout the whole night.

As he realized I wanted to know about his ten years as a rickshaw coolie, Tu was happy to tell me his story.

'Twelve years ago. . . .'

10

Tu's Twenty-eighth Year

'Twelve years ago, I was like you are now; I'd left home, walked for three days from Thai Binh to get here, and hoped to find a job in order to survive.

'I say I'd left home. Actually, at the time, my home was seized by some people, and I lost everything!

'My father, a scholar who taught Chinese characters, lived at Tan De. Because he committed the offence of making a false seal, he was arrested by the government and sent to Son La where he died. I was the only child and lived at home with my mother. My mother loved my father very much and, despite her old age, cried for him every night. After that, she went blind. At that time, I took every single thing in the house and sold it to pay for treatment to try to save my mother's sight.

'I spent all the money, and my mother stayed blind.

'That year really was an extremely miserable one for me, although I still had a roof over my head. Coming from a scholar's family, I didn't even know how to truss a chicken, so I didn't know what I could do to look after my mother. At that time, my father's students all went in different directions. Desperate, I finally went to the province capital and brought a rickshaw home to work it.

'Pulling a rickshaw in the provinces in those days was not like it is now. You still wore a long dark tunic, tucked into a waistband; you had a turban wrapped around your head and wore a proper lacquered hat. People also allowed me to pay gradually for the rickshaw I worked and, finally, to own it. At that time, in the country, people who were able to run a rickshaw were no different from people who rowed a ferry-boat. Whatever the difficulties of running a ferry-boat, they were the same when pulling a rickshaw. Although it was a very hard way to make a living, nobody despised you, especially me: everyone knew I was a student who had fallen on hard times.

'After pulling the rickshaw for two years and looking after my mother, I had paid off the instalments on the rickshaw and was able to own it completely. Seeing my old mother provided with food and comfort, I didn't mind the hard work.

'But, my friend, fate stepped in again. One day, the customs police came to search for illicit alcohol. I don't know how it happened but they found a basket full of rice dregs behind the back garden. I was arrested and taken away, and my thatched house with three compartments was confiscated together with my rickshaw.

'After I was taken away, I wasn't able to find out clearly what my mother's situation was.

'I was imprisoned for three months in the province jail, and when I was released, someone else was living in the house and my mother had been dead for some time.

'I enquired of an old woman who had a tea stall right next to the jetty. She told me the story: a notable in the village was entrusted to sell my house, and a Mr Ly Cuu bought it. Seeing me get mixed up in an offence that put me in prison, my mother died just five or six days after I was taken away. Feeling pity, the village bought the coffin made of wood from a kapok tree to bury her, while the relatives all disappeared, complaining bitterly about the situation.

'I asked where my mother was buried and visited her grave. Then, wiping my tears, I picked up my bundle and left immediately, without a house, without knowing anyone I could rely on for food, looking for somewhere to live.

'From Tan De, I headed south. I spent one night trying to sleep here and there on the roadside, and early the next morning I headed for Phu Ly. I slept one night in a boarding-house there and, having no money for food, I had to beg the housekeeper to let me pawn my tunic before I was allowed to leave.

'Thinking of that story, I'm still ashamed by it. Wretched, with only three bowls of very low-grade rice and a few leaves of green vegetables that weren't worth 5 sous, the owner insulted my ancestors and also seized my long black tunic for which he could still have got 50 sous even if he sold it cheaply.

'I was full of self-pity and wanted to cry but had no tears left.

'I was twenty-eight!'

Seeing that Tu did not say any more, I stopped preparing the opium and looked at him. From the holes in which his eyes were set deeply in his skull, my friend shed without emotion a few tears that seemed to be mixed with blood.

I also fell silent and rolled the ball of opium residue around in the cold flame of the oil-lamp.

Tu sat up, wiped his nose with a brown hand towel, sipped some water, then lay down again waiting to smoke the ball of opium I was rolling to put into the flask.

11
The Horse Follows Its Own Path

'So, you left Phu Ly with nothing except your identity card?'

'My old identity card—the day I arrived in Hanoi, I had to hand it over to the rickshaw Supervisor. And it was fortunate that I still had it; if I hadn't, I'd have starved to death.'

'Did you work a rickshaw from the beginning?'

'There was nothing else to do! But I was able to get a rickshaw with rubber tyres, and was able to exchange my rough brown clothes for a decent set of blue ones. This was better than before.

'Also, at that time, the rickshaw rent was still quite low: 20 or 25 sous for the 4 a.m. to 1 p.m. shift; 40 or 45 for the 1 p.m. to 3 a.m. shift.

'With plenty of customers, it was easy to make a living, but the work was very hard and more exhausting than in Thai Binh. If you could bear running all day, you had money for food and were able to put aside a few sous; so if you didn't find any customers or were too idle to work, there were days when you could use that money to pay for the hire of the rickshaw; and if you didn't have it, the Supervisor would take your shirt or shorts and return them when you had enough money to make it up.'

'Are Supervisors related to the rickshaw owners, or do they just work for the owners?'

'They are neither related to nor work for the owners; they are bull-headed scoundrels who stand in for the owners and rarely get paid by them. They live on the backs of the coolies.

'Like now, all day and night, the Supervisors squeeze the coolies for 1 piastre and 10 sous: 50 sous for the day, 60 for the night. So for each rickshaw, they only pay the owner 70 sous' rent, keeping 40 to put in their pockets. The rickshaw owners know that, the coolies know that, but the Supervisors are still needed, because the owners are never able to hunt down the coolies who short-change them, and the owners do not trust the coolies enough to give the rickshaws directly to them.

'There used to be owners who rented out their own rickshaws, but the coolies got away with a lot of rent or abandoned their rickshaws on the side of the road and didn't return them; the owners lost a lot of time going to find them, and, also, without a ruffian for a Supervisor, the coolies weren't afraid of them. After that, seeing they were losing a lot, the owners had to use Supervisors to stand in for them.'

'If a coolie gets away with the rent, does the Supervisor have to reimburse the owner?'

'Yes, but they rarely suffer a loss. When the time comes to return the rickshaws, they open their notebooks, see which ones are a little slow to return, jump on their bicycles, and ride around the streets looking for them. When they find a coolie who is still hanging around, they grab him, give him a good thrashing, and search him in the middle of the street. It's an unlucky coolie who is short of a few sous; he just gets more punches in the face, the chest, the ribs, the kidneys; then, jumping on his bike, the Supervisor accompanies the coolie right back to the house.

'We have an expression: "As cruel as a Rickshaw Supervisor!"

'But they are not only cruel, they are also cunning. They are the overseers who prosper on the sweat and tears that are wrung out of coolies. They are able to purchase rice fields and houses. Some even establish estates, keep eight or nine wives, and have bigger funerals for their parents than are held for a province chief.

'They really are evil. They rob the pickings of the poor, they live on the backs of the destitute. Scoundrels like that are allowed to live comfortably, while we toil away in the heat of the sun and the cold of the night.'

Leaving Tu to curse, I put my hand up to my forehead, and lay dreaming to myself.

Outside, beside the river, mulberry trees had appeared in all their green.

The story, that had gone on all night in the low thatched dwelling, flickered out with the flame of the opium-lamp.

12

The First Lesson from an Opium Tin

'Since you have been able to survive for twelve years pulling a rickshaw, I think I can put up with it. Today, I'm still very tired and don't need to work, so I'd like to rest here with you. After paying for the bus and some cakes on the way down from Thai Nguyen, I have 2 piastres left. I want to smoke a few pipes to regain my strength; here's the money, tell someone to go and buy some opium.'

I gave Tu a 1-piastre note.

Taking the money, he threw a brown sweat rag over his shoulder, and, feebly lifting his shrivelled body off the bed, took a small tin box from the opium tray. In a rasping voice, he then said: 'How about you stay here and replace the wick on the lamp? To get good stuff, I'll have to go myself.'

'Loose or packaged?'

'Loose, but you get a good smoke out of it; there's plenty for four pipes.'

'Incidentally, could you buy some more oil?'

'Ah yes, I nearly forgot, could you give me the flask at the foot of the bed?'

Half an hour later, Tu returned with a flask of oil, a tin box of opium, and a packet of twenty powdered sweets.

'A good pipe followed by these sweets is wonderful! Please see if the teapot is still hot.'

I picked up the teapot, took the steel top—which was the top of a Nestlé milk tin—off it and emptied from it a few drops of deep red tea water.

'Is it finished? Let me boil some more water. We'll pour it in, the tea leaves are still good!'

Tu carried a battered brazier and a few sticks of bamboo and put them straight on the bed. The bamboo was young and didn't fire easily, and the flames rose slowly in the thick smoke.

I poured the oil into the lamp's rusty steel well and lit it. Assembling the flask, Tu tested the opium pick on his lips, and praised his set of implements, despite their shoddy appearance.

With our pants rolled up to our thighs, Tu and I now lay on either side of the tray with our bodies tilted towards it.

The opium stick spluttered in the flame like a roasted plum; from the tin box of opium, Tu's story spluttered like roasted rice: 'Working a rickshaw, you toil all day, eat hastily, and the only leisure you get is when you lie beside the opium tray.'

Tu then wrinkled his cheeks and laughed: 'For rickshaw pullers, pulling a pipe gives so much pleasure and pulling people causes so much pain!'

He seemed very satisfied with this remark. After I had finished preparing the opium, I invited him to smoke first and pretended to make a stupid complaint: 'I only pulled the rickshaw for one shift yesterday and I'm aching all over. My bones are rattling around as though my joints are loose, especially in the legs. They're still very sore.'

'At first, it's painful for everyone. But if you know how to pull, and know how to massage your muscles, it helps a lot.'

'So how do you do it? Tell me what to do.'

'Don't worry, staying here with me, you'll be skilled before long.'

'But my body's very painful now. What do I have to do to get relief?'

'You go on and prepare that pipe! I know a way, don't worry.'

After smoking about ten pipes in a row, Tu stood up and went out behind the house.

When he returned, he held a pot containing something that looked like cooking dregs covered in water. Putting the pot on the brazier, he took a bamboo taper and lit a fire beneath it. Steam rose from the liquid and gave off a pungent stinking odour that smelt like urine mixed with medicinal herbs.

Pouring the foul dregs into a dirty rag, Tu gave it to me, told me to make a wad of it, and to rub it on the painful parts of my body, including my legs.

I did that and asked him about the concoction as I rubbed.

'In half an hour you'll be better. Anyone can make this medicine. Whittle a little rice husk and pound it, pour some urine into it, and heat it up. Each muscle, each joint, each welt you've taken in a beating, rub them and you'll be cured!'

'Is that all?'

'If you can drink the juice from bamboo leaves, it's better. Pluck a few leaves from young bamboo and dry them. After they've begun to wilt, wash them, cook them in a pot, and drink a few bowls of the juice.'

Twisting and bending my creaking body, I lay down again.

I went on preparing the opium for Tu to smoke, and asked him about the method of pulling a rickshaw.

'Pulling a rickshaw is a trade. Anyone can pick up the wooden handles and pull, but one must know how to pull and to run to conserve one's strength. I'm sure you ran a whole journey, and were panting when you dropped the shafts. That means you don't know how to pull. People who know how to pull properly don't breathe heavily like that.

'Working a trade where you run all day year after year, your body would gradually shrivel up if you didn't know how to run and panted each time like a cow, weakening your lungs, and developing coughing and asthma. With no nutritious food to eat, living in a hole, being exposed to the wind, soaked in the rain and dew, and dried in the sun: all that would wear down a stone, let alone a human being. But that's our fate and you can't resist it! You have to know the best way to survive.'

So saying, Tu stood up without showing any emotion, took the teapot, and drank straight out of it.

He sat down again and, noiselessly taking a sweet and putting it in his mouth, he said as he crunched it: 'When you pick up the shafts, you take a look at the way the passenger is sitting and work out the balance before you start running. If the passenger is sitting back in the seat, you must take a long shaft; if sitting forward, you take a middle position; if leaning to one side (with the cushions supporting his elbow), you take a short shaft. Before setting out, you must set yourself between the shafts. Once you've taken the shafts, don't change the position when you turn a corner or you'll be unsteady and the rickshaw will bounce and tilt to one side. Don't run on a full stomach, and make sure your belt is tight; if it's not, you'll have no support for your midriff, and if you eat too well, you'll throw up. When you are running, keep your lips closed and only breathe through the nose, not the mouth. Controlling your breath like that will conserve your strength, while panting through an open mouth will immediately make you feel tired. Keep that up until you really need some air, then open your mouth and let out strongly one big breath before closing it again and continuing to breathe through your nose.

'Now, when the rickshaw has stopped and the passenger stepped down, release your breath, but don't sit down straight away. You must take a few steps to allow your legs to loosen up before you sit down and have a rest. Fan yourself to dry the sweat, before you have a drink of water.'

Tu taught me that first lesson in many bits and pieces.

Each pipe was a full stop at the end of a string of words, each sweet a comma!

But how indifferent he was! Throughout fifty or sixty sentences, he didn't use a single question or exclamation mark.

The first lesson Tu gave me came out of an opium tin.

And now that I'd had the first one, I was able to learn many more difficult ones—from other tins of opium.

13

My Teacher Opens His Heart

That day, we were very intoxicated.

People say opium is cooked with blackbird bones, and it is possibly true, because it was as if my landlord sang like a blackbird when he told me everything he had inside him.

A trade that requires you to run head first down the street after a few sous each day soon teaches you your left from your right and alerts you to pitfalls that ordinary people can't see. To be clear about this, there are various tricks of the rickshaw trade, just as there are of any other.

The bartender adds water to alcohol; the contractor adds sand to cement; the restaurant owner soaks raw rice in limewater to fill many bowls; the Chettyars lend money at 30 per cent, but force the borrowers to sign receipts at 10 per cent, following government regulations. What do we call such dealings?

Trade secrets!

The bartenders' business, the contractors', the restaurant owners', the Chettyars', each one has its secrets, and so, no less, does the rickshaw pullers'.

I had just learned many of them from a veteran of more than ten years.

Unlike journalists, magicians, and apothecaries, Tu was truly a fellow who did not know how to keep his trade secrets. He did not hide a thing. Today, he had revealed all the clever tricks he knew, released them from a little tin of opium that had been prepared with blackbird bones.

'Working in the rickshaw trade, you have to know what's on the passenger's mind,' said Tu, adopting a serious tone and the dignified air of a teacher who is instructing a pupil.

Now, at this point, Dear Readers, allow me to interrupt and interpret Tu's ideas in a more sophisticated way: 'Rickshaw coolies must know the psychology of their passengers.'

Tu went on: 'Once you know what kind of passenger you are pulling, you know whether or not you can ask for a few extra sous without being kicked or slapped.

'Going into an expensive Chinese restaurant, there are times when people order dishes for over a hundred sous and don't touch them, but they bargain hard for a sou or two when they use a rickshaw. In 1 piastre, there are 100 sous, and while 100 sous can be thrown without any fuss into the drawer of a fat Chinese restaurant owner, 1 sou thrown into the torn hat of a rickshaw coolie is such a big thing. Ninety-nine out of a hundred passengers are like that. They think that the extra sou they give the coolie is bigger than the rickshaw wheel.

'If you think about it, it's not really strange, because no one needs to keep face with a rickshaw coolie. The places you need to keep face are in big stores, expensive restaurants, and theatres.

'If a passenger regards 1 sou as a big sum, then the person pulling a rickshaw must play down its value. Doing this does not mean that you undervalue 1 sou because it cannot buy much, but because it makes it smaller in the eyes of the person who thinks it is big!

'If you want to close the eyes of the passenger, you must first know what sort of person he is.

'You see, even though you're running, you must always use your head. Let me give you an example. One day about five in the afternoon, I'd just taken the rickshaw out and immediately picked up a rich young man. He was well dressed. I only knew he had money, and didn't know what he was dressed for.

'The trip was from Hang Dau to Hom Market, and he bargained for 8 sous. I asked for 10; he was resolved not to pay that much. But because it would have been bad luck to refuse the first passenger of the day, I agreed to pull him.

'The rickshaw ran to the top of Hang Dao Street. Six or seven steps ahead of me was another rickshaw. It carried a young woman. I couldn't see how she was dressed, but from the back, she looked fashionable enough.

'The street was packed, so the crowd of rickshaws ahead were not travelling very fast. Taking advantage of the opportunity, I slackened my pace to fall in with the traffic, thinking: why bother trying to get through the crowd.

'From that moment, I felt the springs shaking on my rickshaw. I guessed straight away that the young man was impatient to overtake the rickshaw ahead, but because the street was narrow and crowded, it wasn't possible for him to hurry me, and, if he had ordered me, I'm sure he would have been embarrassed.

'Knowing his weakness, I shouted for people to get out of the way, and tried to get through the crowd. As soon I managed to overtake the rickshaw in front, I slackened my pace.

'The rickshaw left Hang Dao Street and entered the road along the edge of Hang Guom Lake. The road was wide and I meant to run so that the second rickshaw could stay beside us, but I also kept my rickshaw just ahead.

'The springs on my rickshaw then settled down, and didn't shake as before. Knowing my passenger was satisfied, I maintained that pace.

'Passing the Post Office, the other rickshaw stopped at the Brodard patisserie. I ran at a slower pace as I came to the old Crossroads Depot, then I ran as fast as I could, overtaking a tram going in the same direction.

'When we reached Hom Market, the young man pointed to the place where he wanted to stop and paid me a full 10 sous.'

I interrupted: 'He might just be a generous man. You never know.'

'Not at all. A fellow who bargains so hard for a few sous before he gets into the rickshaw, how can he be generous!'

'But during that trip, whether you ran fast or slow, your passenger neither attracted the attention of that girl nor wooed her, did he?'

'There's no need to woo the girls. To dress up and go out looking at girls, and to attract their attention with your slicked-back hair, your smart clothes, your shiny shoes, and the perfume you wear, that should be satisfying enough.

'But it depends on the person; not everyone is the same. If you pull an old person, you have to call on people to keep out of the way as you run slowly; pulling a Frenchman, you have to run strongly and not be afraid even at night when the street lamps are slow to come on; pulling rich young ladies and gentlemen, you must run with a sense of importance. In other words, it depends on the kind of passenger you have. If your passenger is a gossip, you have to chat as you run; if you have one who looks down on you as an inferior, you have to keep your mouth shut; a passenger who is not a mandarin still has to be treated like one; a woman you know has a bad reputation and who is dressed up when she gets in the rickshaw also has to be treated like a great lady! Even when you see a black African or a Chinese whom you don't know anything about, you still call them Sir, as you would a shopowner, and invite them to step into your rickshaw, so that you can take them wherever they want to go.

'There's nothing to lose with a flattering word. What they do is their business as long as they get into the rickshaw, and don't mind if you beg for a bit more once you lower the shafts.'

'Where did my teacher intend to take me next?' I asked myself, as I lay there absorbing all the information.

As he scraped the residue with a knife, my teacher dissected many people, and I was one of them.

What could be more laughable than that?

As you are well aware, Dear Readers, I have been a passenger many times!

14

A 'Touring' Rickshaw and a 'Stretcher'

'Why bother talking about those damned coolies!'

You will usually hear that expression being used by distinguished people—like you and me. We use that expression without thinking about it, because nobody considers it insulting when talking about labourers.

This is to say we despise those miserable creatures who, with their heads down, pull us around town to make 5 or 10 sous a journey.

You also think like me, I think like Mr X, Mr X thinks like Mr T.

And yet, there is a class of people who don't think like us.

What class is that?

The rickshaw coolies.

I am sure you are about to whisper in my ear: 'When a person sits and lets another person pull him around, the puller thinks it's inhuman, doesn't he?'

But let's not talk about humane principles. Here, I'm only speaking of the dignity and identity of the passenger.

How do passengers look through the eyes of coolies?

On this question, let's listen to another lecture from my teacher, Tu, who delivered it one day during a drinking session:

'Don't think that you are just paid to run fast with your head down. As you are running, you still have to use your head, as you watch the road and listen for car horns.

'Using your head, you will soon understand that in life people who appear in fine clothes and put on airs are posing as something they are not.

'Let me tell you about a summer afternoon I remember well when it was as hot as today, and I was pulling two people from Hang Dao who did not bargain.

'They got out of another rickshaw, waved me down, and said in a very confident manner: "Lend me 30 sous! We'll pay you back later." They wanted to borrow the change to pay off the other fellow before continuing the journey with me. I saw that the two people were well dressed—in satin, fine material, high-heeled shoes, and glasses—and thinking they would be good customers, I was happy to oblige. I lifted up the flap of my shirt and, pulling the 30 sous out of the hem, I gave it to them. I asked them where they wanted to go, and they said they wanted to hire the rickshaw for a few hours. They also offered to pay 25 sous an hour.

'I accepted. One of them took my money and gave it to the other coolie who was still waiting to be paid. The two people then got into my rickshaw.

'Going around from one street to another, I had to stop for them to look around and then start running again, my shirt dripping with sweat. Although I was tired, I listened to them as I was running to try to work out what was going on.

'Perhaps at that time they thought I was an animal or someone from one of the mountain tribes and so they ignored me as they sat back having a good time. Their talk, the likes of which you wouldn't have heard from the roughest coolies, turned my ears red.

'I kept on listening until it was one in the morning. Then I realized they were on a trip around town looking for a chance to make some money, and weren't able to dig up enough to pay for the fare. This was why we went around and around all night.

'I was getting impatient and had to ask what was happening. At first, they sweet-talked me. Then they became quarrelsome and tried to pick a fight with me.

'Would you believe that they could then open their mouths and say: "We're out of money; if you want to be paid, you'll have to pull us around 'till morning; if you're not happy, you can let us off here!"

'This stopped me dead. At two in the morning, I had to return the rickshaw. The rent would be 52 sous. From when I started in the afternoon to the time I picked these people up in the evening, I'd made 40 sous. They had borrowed 30, and so this left me with 10. I had no choice but to keep on pulling them. Otherwise, where would the money come from to pay for the rent, let alone for food? So I had to grit my teeth and go on pulling 'till morning, hoping that they would feel sorry for me and pay a bit extra. When I returned the rickshaw, I would pay for the extra hours.

'From then on, I continued to tramp down the road with my passengers not urging me to go faster as they had in the afternoon. It was clear that they had nowhere to go!

'That day was really such an unfortunate one that it was just as though the first person I saw at the gate was a woman. I was so tired after running all day and so sleepy when I stopped at Co Ngu, but I did not dare to close my eyes. As I was sitting there, my eyelids felt heavier and heavier. For fear of falling asleep and letting the bastards sneak away, I stood up again and pulled the rickshaw to stay awake. When I turned around, I saw my passengers leaning against each other, asleep. One of them had slipped his turban under his arm as if for fear that someone would steal it; the other held between his legs a useless walking stick that no one could be bothered picking up even if he had thrown it away!

'At times I was so furious, I wanted to throw them out of the rickshaw onto their backs: yes, I was so frustrated, dead on my feet, yet I couldn't lie down, and I hadn't eaten a thing since midday.'

'Why didn't you pull them straight to the police station?'

'Because I'd have to put up with more kicks in the arse! Because they were so well dressed, no policeman would have said they were cheats. They'd have said I was a troublemaker. The Police? Forget about them!'

'So what did they do the next morning?'

'The next morning! As soon as they'd opened their eyes, the bastards told me to take them to Sam Cong Alley and stop in front of an opium den belonging to an old Chinaman. Then the man with the coat on knocked on the door and went in. When he came out all he had left on was his white tunic.'

'Did he pawn his coat with the Chinaman?'

'I wouldn't know! But if he didn't, where would he have got the money? Yet, he was still haughty with me. When he came out, he pretended to take out his purse and pull out some money. I thought he was about to pay me at least over 1 piastre. But he only counted out 100 sous' change; in other words, for pulling them around between six in the evening and six in the morning, they paid me 70 sous.

'I intended to cause a scene when the other fellow started to admit the truth. He emptied his purse saying there wasn't a sou left in it. He asked me to take the 70 as a down payment, and said that he would give me more when we ran into each other again.

'What could I do? I had no choice but to wipe the sweat off my brow and take it. Fifty-two sous for the hire, and another 30 for the extra time, 82 in all; and yet when I went back to pay this sum to the Supervisor, he still scolded me mercilessly.

'I returned to the boarding-house. Since I was very late back from my shift, everyone gathered around to ask me what had happened. I intended to hide the truth, but before I opened my mouth, there was a commotion: "Tu must have been a victim of touring con men!" "Last night you pulled a stretcher, didn't you?"

'I now understood that those tricks had been played on many coolies before me. A touring rickshaw meant a rickshaw that pulled people around the streets who were looking for random opportunities to make money. A stretcher meant a rickshaw that pulled dead bodies. The con men who lay full-length sleeping in my rickshaw all night were certainly no different from dead bodies.'

I thought about this story and laughed under my breath.

I used to have a friend who called himself a romantic. He usually didn't have a coin in his pocket, but still jumped into a rickshaw whenever he saw one.

There were times when he took a trip that was only worth 10 sous, but by the time he had finished running around trying to borrow money to pay the fare, the distance he had covered came to a few piastres.

A rickshaw which pulled him around town to try 'to find

money', he jokingly called an economic rickshaw!

Then another day....

15
The Lining of the Snake-skin Shoes

'Another day, night had just fallen, and, although there were only a few scattered raindrops, it was extremely cold. It was January, and I was only dressed lightly in two thin garments through which the wind cut like a knife.

'Six o'clock, seven o'clock, eight o'clock; Hang Buom, Hang Dao, and the road beside the lake; the streets were deserted; not a soul called as I searched endlessly for a customer.

'As I turned out of Cau Go Street, I suddenly heard the sound of people quarrelling. It seemed to come from under the roof of a dark veranda some distance away. Stopping the rickshaw, I stood and listened, and realized that the voices came from only about ten paces away. I heard clearly the voices of a woman and a man. The woman said: "I'm not going anywhere; I'm standing here 'till morning." The man said: "You are being very difficult; you are going to stand here and die of the cold, are you?" They continued to argue: "If you are afraid of the cold, you can leave!" "It's no good talking like that. Nobody's going to eat you in there!" "I've already told you, many people know my father." "If you don't want to go in, we'll go somewhere else; standing here, we risk seeing someone we know, don't you think?" "Go where? Where are we going to go?" "Let's just go, can't you see, that rickshaw coolie over there is laughing at us."

'I stepped closer, putting the rickshaw down on the pavement and pulled the hood back as I invited the couple to get in. At that moment, a man suddenly appeared at the top end of Hang Dau Street. Hurrying towards the rickshaw, the woman raised the back panel of her tunic to cover her head. The man quickly followed her, jumped into the rickshaw, and urged me to get moving.

'I pulled the hood back over the rickshaw. Turning the shafts to the right, I ran straight down Hang Gai Street. By then, I suppose, the couple felt easier. They didn't bother to tell me where to go; they left it to me. Across Hang Lo to Cua Nam, from the Cua Nam Gardens straight on to Ong Bay Palace; the night was cold and rainy, but I was soaked with sweat.

'Along the way, from inside the cover, I occasionally heard giggling. From the French school, I ran slowly, and the slower I ran, the tighter I had to grip the shafts to control the rickshaw. At one point, I heard a long sigh, then the words: "Please keep it."

'My body had just cooled down, but it broke out in sweat again.

'The girl asked to get out at Hang Dau Gardens, and the young man told me to take him to Hang Hai. When he stepped down from the rickshaw, he gave me 30 sous and went into a big Chinese restaurant at the end of the street.

'I couldn't even be bothered rearranging the seat cushions. I put the shafts up under my armpits and went on with both hands in my pockets.

'Until then I wouldn't have known what a Hanoi girl really was, one with a velvet tunic and black pants, handbag, and ear-rings.'

'Would you say those girls come from good families or are just prostitutes?'

'Both. We know all classes of people when we pull a rickshaw at night. About the prostitutes, there's no point in saying much, because their trade requires them to sell their bodies to survive. But it's not the same for the young ladies of good families who also degrade themselves: by making a few piastres in a couple of hours, they can behave like boastful young women who display themselves with make-up, perfume, colourful tunics, snake-skin shoes. They are like glittering angels on the outside and rotten on the inside.

'As a group, we call those girls the *nouveau riche*.

'Nowadays, the *nouveau riche* scene spreads out like the jungle in Hanoi: the women come from the meat stalls, the vegetable stalls, the egg stalls, the prawn stalls, the typists, the clerks' wives, the daughters, and sisters of various government officials.

'When you see those women with their hair parted or wearing high heels, don't think they're rich. They haven't got a sou on them; if they knocked over a basket of cheap rice cakes, they'd probably have to take off their tunics to pay for the damage.

'They are no different from the shoes you drag along the street. Beneath the glass beads twinkling like diamonds on the velvet toe is a soiled inner lining.'

After a few cups of wine, my teacher was very eloquent today. After all, even though he had not met with good fortune, he had been a Confucian scholar for half his life!

In any case, he went on talking in that miserable setting; there were still many painful stories to tell. If we filter the stinking mud, we'll still find a few drops of water.

'One day it was so bad I sobbed, feeling sorry for the others and also for myself.

'That day I was on the night shift. It was after nine when a girl called me at the end of Hang Bat Street. The tart, who was fairly well dressed, got into the rickshaw without bargaining and told me to take her to Hang Buom Street. When we reached the end of Hang Buom, she didn't tell me to stop, but said to go on to the road along the river. Once we'd travelled down along the river to Don Thuy, we ran into a procession blocking the road. The procession had trumpets, drums, and lanterns, and once it passed, the girl told me to pull her along behind it.

'Passing the French Opera house, Trang Tien Street, Hang Trong, the road beside the lake, Hang Dao, Dong Xuan Market, the eastern entrance of Hang Ga, Mr Sau Vo's Palace, the procession entered the municipal gate. A French policeman told us to turn into Gio-Giep, but the girl was undecided and told me to continue slowly back towards the eastern gate of Hang Ga. After that, she told me to run around until 1 a.m., then asked me to take her back to Hang Bat. But when we got to the top end of Hang Bac Lane leading to the lake's side, she told me to let her down. Once she was down, she told me to follow her with the empty rickshaw along a dark, narrow lane, between high walls.'

'I suppose that once you entered that dark lane, she slipped away, didn't she?'

'If only she wanted to slip away! She grabbed me, then implored me: "Please, I beg you, have pity on me! Do anything you want with me! I honestly haven't got a single sou."

'I pulled my hand away, and grabbed the front panel of her tunic. She still begged me: "All right, you can search me, I honestly haven't got a sou."

'I brushed her hand away, searched her waistband for money, then the flap of her Bombay silk tunic from which a large piece of material now came off in my hand. Also searching the pockets in her undergarment, I only found a tin of rotten Co Ba grease and some coarse paper.

'I was speechless with anger. Seeing me like that, she came close to me, took my hands, and put them on her. In the darkness, I wrested myself away from her, feeling her ears and neck to see if she was wearing any jewellery. Naturally, she wasn't. I felt her hair which was done up with a comb. I pulled it out, found it was broken, and put it back. I pushed her arms up and searched her again. She didn't have any bracelets on her wrists, just a string of fake jewels that weren't worth half a sou. I lowered my head and lifted up her tunic to see what kind of pants she was wearing. Oh! What I saw was terrible! Front and back, they were a maze of patches.'

'Cotton or silk?'

'Silk, real black silk; it looked shiny when she first stepped into the rickshaw.'

'So after that, you had to let her go?'

'After searching her pants, I felt her legs. I saw a pair of pointed shoes and pulled them off her feet to have a close look: they were a pair of faked snake-skin high heels, with the torn skin peeling off.'

'Then why didn't you strip off her Bombay silk tunic?'

'Ah, that tunic? Bombay silk that disintegrated in your hands. All you could use it for were rags to wrap around a baby's backside!'

'What did you do after that?'

'What more could I do! I threw the shoes down on the ground, stood up, grabbed her, and intended to slap her, but seeing her as she was, I restrained myself. We were both in a pathetic situation. My life was miserable, and yet hers was worse. This thought brought tears to my eyes; I felt choked.

'I wiped my tears with the flap of my shirt. By the time I looked up, the girl had vanished, leaving me with the empty rickshaw.

'Perhaps, after she left, the girl laughed to herself that I was a silly old fool.

'I was a fool. But perhaps even more foolish, because I regretted that I had searched her from head to foot: I was the fellow who had pawned his long, dark tunic at the boarding-house in Ha Nam some years ago.'

16
More Dead than Alive

'But come to think about it, it was silly of me to shed so many tears.

'In life, we must deceive each other and be unscrupulous to survive. To be considerate to others and live an honest life will only make you a laughing-stock for city people.

'The rickshaw trade has kept me alive until now. But from the time I was beaten to within an inch of my life at the Supervisor's place, I began to take a torturous path, the dirty, dark one of an animal.

'At that time I thought: from the day I had my dark tunic stripped off me at Thai Binh, there was no further point in keeping my status as a scholar.

'Eating with dogs, one has to put one's head down with them. Although I'd pulled a rickshaw for seven years, it was only from the day I was beaten that I completely became a coolie.

'What happened that day? Let me give you some idea.

'One day a little over four years ago, I had just come out of Ba Ga eating stall with 72 sous' change in my pocket. I remember clearly that I'd just finished counting out the money when someone called me and asked me to take him to the Post Office beside the lake.

'We arrived at the Post Office, and my passenger told me to stop and wait for him. He went inside and soon came out, saying he wanted to borrow 50 sous to buy stamps. All he had was a 20-piastre note, and the postal clerk didn't have any change.

'I took 50 sous out of my purse and gave them to him.

'After that, I sat down and waited. Some passers-by called, but I said I was waiting for someone, and walked slowly to a nearby stall to have a cup of fresh tea. When I finished the tea, I asked for a toothpick and walked back to my rickshaw where I sat down picking my teeth.

'I waited from 8 a.m. to 9 a.m. and saw many people going in and out of the Post Office. However, the longer I waited for my passenger, the longer I didn't see him. I was becoming impatient and restless, and wanted to go inside to see what he was doing.

'I couldn't see him inside, and as the office was so crowded, I went back outside and waited restlessly for him.

'After ten o'clock, there were far fewer customers in the Post Office. I went in again to search for the fellow, but he must have vanished some time before.

'I could feel the cold in my bones, and yet I was sweating. Crying as I went along, I enquired after the passenger who had cheated me.

'Seeing me so distressed, passers-by and fellow coolies all gathered around. I told them the story and they said that he must have slipped through the gate of Paul Bert Park.

'I couldn't believe what they said and kept thinking: someone who looked so dignified, dressed up in a satin tunic and turban, how could he have the heart to cheat a poor rickshaw coolie? Then, after hanging around there until midday, I finally realized I was wrong, and that the others were right.

'I was so furious and frustrated, I cried out like someone who had gone crazy. How was I going to have enough money for the rent which I had to pay to the Supervisor at 1.30?

'From then until 1.30, I wasn't going to find another passenger.

'I was still thinking about whether I should continue working or return the rickshaw when the Supervisor loomed up in front of me on his bike.

'I was scared stiff. I couldn't see clearly, and my limbs began to tremble. The Supervisor jumped off his bike and yelled; he saw me begging him and guessed I didn't have enough money to pay for the hire. He rushed up to me, grabbed me around the chest, kneed me, pushed my head down, and beat me all over. Next, he ripped open both the outer and inner garments I was wearing and searched them thoroughly. Seeing I only had a water-pipe in my pocket and 22 sous, he threw the pipe away and, taking the money, put it in his own pocket. After searching my pants and hat, he also went through the mattresses and the roof of the rickshaw searching for money. Although it was cold, he didn't return my clothes, and the welts his beating left on my body turned blue and purple.

'Fuming with anger, he told me to pull the rickshaw back half-naked, and then jumped on his bike and rode along beside me.

'On the way, he cursed me fulsomely and accused me of giving the money to someone from my family. He threatened to thrash me again so that I would learn not to steal in the future.

'I wanted to speak, but was choked with anger. I didn't mind being cold and beaten up. But as he called me a thief, I was furious; I had never taken anything from anyone.

'Throwing the shafts of the rickshaw down, I rushed at him and punched him in the face, causing him to fall off his bike. He thought I would run away, and called out as he crawled to his feet, but I stood there grinding my teeth as I faced him.

'We were only twenty or thirty paces from the rickshaw yard. People there heard the Supervisor's calls and rushed out, but he had already grabbed my head, and was dragging me towards the yard. There was nothing I could do; with a body like mine, how could I compete with him. He was as strong as a horse; and, me, I had arms like reeds and couldn't even truss a chicken.

'The bashing I took from him in the yard that day, I think I still fear it. Can you imagine the things they did? They were really cruel.

'Throwing me into a narrow room and tying my elbows together, four of them beat me, one after the other. They kicked me to their heart's content and took it in turns to grab tufts of my hair so that they could pull my face up and slap it. Finally, they tied a rope around the one that bound my elbows, threw it up over one of the rafters, and hung me from the roof.

'At first, I was still so enraged, I couldn't feel anything. Later, I felt that my arms were being separated from my shoulder-blades, that my cheeks had been stripped of skin, and that my ribcage had collapsed.

'Hanging in the middle of the room, my face looked straight down to the floor. Beneath my legs, the bricks seemed to spin like pin-wheels. I closed my eyes tight. In my ears I could hear a whirring, like the sound of buzzing bees.

'I foamed at the mouth, my nose bled, and my eyes bulged. I gradually lost consciousness and passed out.

'When I opened my eyes, I saw that I was lying on a plank that was placed flat on the floor. My head was wet as though it had just been washed and felt feverish as though it was giving off steam.

'Looking around from side to side, I could see I was alone in the room. I intended to sit up, but then realized my arms were bound tightly together at the wrists.

'My gums were dry, as were my teeth. The saliva had dried up in my mouth. Lifting both my bound hands to touch my forehead, it felt very hot. I had a fever. My body was so hot, it was as though some madness was rising over me.

'A little later, the Supervisor appeared, and, seeing me with my eyes open, he stood there staring brazenly at me. After he'd seen all he wanted, he spat in my face and swore fiercely: "Son of a bitch, do you know who's boss now, or are you still a smart-arse?"

'With my throat extremely dry, I implored him to relieve my thirst, but he wouldn't give me even a mouthful of water. I didn't know whether it was morning or afternoon, and only saw the rain drizzling down outside in the courtyard.

'Then he ordered someone to untie me and threw into my face my brown shirt covered in mud. I grabbed the shirt and stood up, ran into the courtyard, and cleared out through the gate.

'I stooped and staggered along the street like a torn bag of bones. When a few spots of rain flew into my face and hit my back, I felt my fever subside.

'I was exhausted. I saw from a clock on a public building that it was 9 a.m., and this meant that the Supervisor had detained me for a day and a night. During that period in which I had been unconscious, I had neither eaten nor drunk a thing.

'Passing a water-pump at Ham Long, I dipped my mouth into a bucket of water and drank without listening to the curses of the woman who owned the bucket.

'With that beating, I returned home sick and lost twelve days. At first, my wife sold a bronze pot to pay for medicine and food. Later, with nothing else in the house to sell, she went off crying to sell to her friends the pair of pants made of good cloth from Buoi which she wore at New Year.

'From that day on, I regarded everyone around me as snakes and centipedes. I committed a serious crime,* I worked as a pimp, I became addicted to opium, I spoke obscenely, I opened my trousers and urinated in the street without

*This crime took place about ten years ago. The newspaper did publish the story and Tu himself has told me very clearly about it too. However, for special reasons, we don't think it is appropriate to record it here. (Tam Lang)

blushing, farted without embarrassment as I pulled the rickshaw. In sum, I was in a state where I didn't pay attention to anyone, like the louts who shit shamelessly in the fields with the dogs standing around them, waiting.'

17
The Fox in a Coolie's Clothes

'From that day, I only had eyes for one thing: money! There was nothing more important to me than money. Benevolence, virtue, rites—I tossed them all away.

'Before, when you had money, you would sit grandly in a rickshaw and scold the coolies who pulled you along the street. Now that you have no money, you must come down from the rickshaw and pull other people with your head down, listening to their abuse.

'In life, a fellow who does not value money is a fool. Those with money have the power to command us. However, even as we accept their orders and take their money, we still want to spit in their faces.

'So I now turned my hand to everything I had formerly thought was despicable. I did this without regret; regret had no meaning for me either.

'Just as with other trades, my rickshaw trade is only a cover for another. Automobile mechanics use their garages to deal in opium; some open photography shops to make counterfeit money; others work as interpreters and secretaries but prosper from keeping prostitutes; I work as a coolie, but also have another trade: that of a pimp.

'Dealing in froth and bubble, you don't waste any labour or capital. At night, I take up the shafts of the rickshaw and go to find some ill-bred braggarts and lead them to the girls, and so I make money both out of the girls and them. Out of each piastre, I get 20 sous' commission from the prostitutes, and if I bring a rich customer, I make even more, besides the rickshaw fares. If I can get two customers a night, it means I can gulp down as much wine as I want and smoke as much opium as I please.

'These last three or four years, I've hardly worked during the day when it's either freezing cold or boiling hot. At night, it's not so tiring, and it's also fairly easy to find customers; aside from the hire on the rickshaw, you can still put aside from 30 to 40 sous or even 1 piastre each day.'

'Why don't others do the same as you? The way you describe it, it doesn't seem particularly difficult to make a living.'

'Yes, it sounds easy, but you only know how difficult it is when you try it. Pimping has many devices, many tricks. It's not only a matter of cunning bluff, it's also a matter of knowing many gambling-houses and brothels, the places where the rich play, and those where the new prostitutes go. You certainly have to be familiar with those places, then know how to induce the girls to go there. The ones who won't listen to you, you have to threaten; the ones that are hungry for money, you must lure them with the promise of money.

'The street girls with loose morals, you must know how to catch them; those who sell their wares out of baskets on the side of the street, you have to know how to bait them; with country girls, you have to know how to "drug" them: each case requires a different approach.

'The few who master all those tricks are the old foxes, the old foxes who have been in the rickshaw trade for a long time.

'Let me tell you something that happened last year; it'll give you a good idea of what I'm talking about.

'A girl who lived in a certain street often left her house and took off with her lover to a hotel room in another part of town from about 7 p.m. to 9 p.m. Because I'd once followed her after she'd left the hotel and picked her up and taken her home, I found out her name and where she lived. Another time, I learned the name of her lover and who he was in the same way. So, knowing both of them well, I loitered around that street every night from then on. After coming across them unexpectedly many times as they came and went from their illicit meetings, one day, I hatched a scheme with the Hotel Supervisor to set her up. Having arranged everything, I went off with the rickshaw and waited around in the street where the girl lived. At nightfall, even though I wasn't sure where the girl was going, I still followed her with the rickshaw. As she turned into another street, I came up beside her on the sidewalk, called out her name and, adopting a familiar tone, I said: "Hello, Miss, Mr Z is waiting for you at the room in Y Street, and he asked me to bring a little boy here to give you a message. Today, Mr Z is in a hurry, and didn't have the time to send the message in advance. If you'd like to get into the rickshaw, I'll take you there."

'I invented that story, but it worked because I'd often pulled either the girl or the young man in my rickshaw while the other travelled in a rickshaw running beside, and I'd overheard all about how they arranged their meetings. For example: he would write to her in a woman's hand, differently each time, a poem in which he pretended to be a girlfriend inviting her over for a visit; no matter what kind of paper a letter was written on, it was always sealed with the mark of a water-pipe as a secret sign; each time, they paid a child, either a little boy or girl, who carried the letter while pretending to be a young maid or boy-servant, so that the people at her home would not be suspicious.

'When she heard me speak, the girl seemed to think it was

strange and looked sceptical. Immediately, I called a little boy walking along the other side of the street, told him to give me the letter, and said without giving the girl an opportunity to question me: "I wouldn't dare to lie, Mr Z instructed me to tell you if you didn't believe me: that he is in Y Street and that you would understand."'

'Where did the little boy come from?'

'He was the son of the Supervisor at the hotel. He was only about eleven or twelve. I told him to follow me and to do what I told him to do, and if the girl asked a question, all he had to do was say: "Mr Z hired me for 10 sous and told me to bring this message to you; I didn't know the way, so Mr Z told me to follow this rickshaw man."

'The girl took the letter and asked the boy a question to which he replied as I had instructed him. Going to the foot of a street lamp, looking around her to ensure that no one was watching, the girl opened the letter and read it three or four times, then put it into her pocket with some hesitation.

'I said again: "Please get into the rickshaw and let me take you, Mr Z instructed me to invite you to go there immediately."

'After again hesitating for a moment, the girl stepped into my rickshaw, gave the little boy 10 sous, told him to go straight home, and sat back as I started running.

'I pulled the girl into the courtyard of the hotel and took her straight up to the upper floor and called the boy. The boy opened the door of the room in which the light had already been switched on, and two bottles of lemon drink, one opened, one unopened, together with two glasses were standing on a table; a Western coat hung on a hook; an electric fan whirred above the fireplace.

'The room-boy knew what to say straight away because his boss, the Hotel Supervisor, had already told him. As he spoke, he pulled out a chair and invited the girl to sit down: "Mr Z has gone downstairs for a minute; please sit down for a minute and I'll go and let him know." The girl seemed worried and, to cover her embarrassment, she put her hand in her pocket and then must have remembered that she owed me money for the fare. Giving me 20 sous, she told me to go. I just sat there at the door, and said I was waiting for Mr Z to arrive to give me some more money as he promised.

'A moment later, a person looking very well dressed in Western clothes entered the girl's room. He was the Hotel Supervisor disguised as a rich young man. I followed him as he entered. The girl stood up quickly when she saw the stranger and tried to run out in a panic. But as he entered, the Supervisor had already locked the door. He laughed as he spoke, showing two gold front teeth: "Stop, sit down, we know each other already. Your father, the senior clerk and your brother, the junior one, how are they? The other day when I was in the south, I also met your mother." He spoke with such a confident air, because I had fed him the information obtained from my investigations. I persisted in asking for more money as though I had nothing to do with what they were talking about.

'Acting rich, the Supervisor tossed me a piastre, opened the door, and told me to go. As I was leaving, he stopped me and feigned a question: "You already know this girl's address don't you?" I answered: "Yes, I know it well, Sir." He said: "All right, you may go now."

'I went out, the Supervisor closed the door behind me, and I don't know what happened that night. I only know that as I left, I could hear the sound of the key as he double-locked the door.

'The next morning, I returned to see the Supervisor and found out that the scheme had worked. We then calculated our shares as follows: every time we had a customer and could get this girl over, apart from the money for the room and the girl, I would get 30 sous out of each piastre, he would get 30, and any tips would go to whomever pleased the customer.

'With a classy girl like this, we'd get rich customers. And with a few good deals like that, we'd be flush in a month.'

'But what if the girl refused to be involved?'

'If she didn't come, she'd go to jail! The Supervisor will act like a rich young man for a few more times, then tell her the truth. He bluffs her by saying that he knows all the family, and that if she does not obey him, he will threaten to cause a scandal. City girls, children of well-known families, have all the more to keep their secrets. They have to obey to avoid a scandal. After the first step comes the second. The first step is difficult, the second easier, and the third ... if you make one small slip, it's fatal. It's not difficult ... go past the limit, part the hair on one side, put on a flashy smile, draw on a pair of eyebrows, paint on a beauty spot, put on a corset, and you're gone: you've become a prostitute. Only the God of Thunder can save you.

'And so that's the world of the classy ones. As for the rough girls working in the market, each one needs to be handled differently, each has her own quirks; you can't anticipate them all, you have to work them out as you go along.

'But there's one other easy way of making a sou. If you are working in the early morning or at night and you realize you are pulling a girl from a good family who you suspect has been enjoying herself, when you get to her house, ask her for some extra money; if she doesn't give it to you, you make a fuss: say that she has been out with her lover in one house and with a rich man in a hotel. If you make up stories like this, the girls will pull out a few more sous, because they are afraid of being exposed in front of the neighbours.

'These last few years, although I've called myself a rickshaw coolie, I've lived off the girls. Those that leave home, those that are confined for medical examinations, I couldn't care less about them; I only know one rule: money! But they don't suffer great losses; they make money as prostitutes, sometimes their customers become lovers, and when they're picked up, they have lovers and pimps who help them by paying off the police. Life is money, virginity and humaneness are nothing, only money counts! Money is more important than anything.

'If I was like others, I'd already be wealthy. But with an opium addiction, life is miserable. There are days when you don't make any deals, and you have to suck in old residue.

'But it's such a miserable way of making a living, if you don't get addicted, there's nothing else to do.

'So I'll tell you the painful story of what happened after I was first addicted.'

18

The Black Queen's Brew

'I really didn't know until that day how strongly opium can slam you.

'One night I was waiting outside a French house in La Ga Hang Co, sitting and gossiping with a few other coolies. Suddenly, I went cold all over, then broke out in a sweat. My arms and legs were racked with shooting pains. Next, I couldn't help yawning. First, I had a few short yawns, and after that came the long ones that hurt my jaws, as my eyes and nose started running. I wiped them with my shirt-front until it was wet through, and still they kept running.

'At first, I made an effort to go on waiting for a fare. But after a few more yawns, I felt my body go limp, and my eyes began to bulge.

'Those that were sitting around with me first thought I had been caught in a draught. Then, one fellow, who saw me as he pulled a rickshaw past, stopped and laughed: "Go and beg the Black Queen at the southern Gate and you'll be all right." Once he had his joke, the bastard said I was an addict. I had a feeling he was probably right, but I still hadn't accepted it, and I tried to inhale some *lao* tobacco smoke.

'I did this, but it didn't have any effect, and I still felt unsteady. I began to believe him, but with only 7 sous in my pocket, I didn't know what to do. I went off pulling the rickshaw in no particular direction. After a while, I remembered a couple of fellows who ran dens and who had let me smoke a little free opium in the past. I went straight to Hai Phao's house.

'However, this time it wasn't like before. Phao told me that if I wanted to smoke, I had to pay 10 sous for it. I offered him all I had, but he wouldn't budge. I pleaded with him to let me smoke some residue, but he still wouldn't let me. He blew out the light and put away the implements.

'I had formerly gone to pick up some girls in his family and take them to customers on a few occasions, and he had invited me to smoke a few pipes. I refused, but he insisted and said: "Working at night, a few pipes will keep you from feeling tired; a few won't turn you into an addict."

'I gave in and had a smoke. It really kept me awake for a long time, and I didn't mind pulling. I became an addict because of that damned Hai Phao. That night, I thought that he would invite me as usual when I asked him for a smoke and didn't expect that he would chase me away like a demon for being 3 sous short. I had helped him out a lot, and for him to treat me so badly was really despicable.

'Leaving Hai Phao's house, I went to Cua Nam Street and asked for the house of the Black Queen. Some coolies sitting around on the sidewalk pointed to a small house in front of which was a tea stall.

'After listening to the fellow in Hang Co suggest that I consult the Black Queen, I thought the house would have an opium tray for coolies. As it turned out, this wasn't so. It only sold "liquid residue" at a low price for addicts.

'I asked how much it was and gave 5 sous to the Black Queen. Do you know what she gave me? An earthenware bowl full of black liquid like roasted rice water. This was the "liquid residue".

'I picked it up and sipped it; it tasted as bitter as insect poison. But I could smell opium in the bowl, and this woke me up a bit, and I emptied the bowl in one gulp. Having taken that medicine, I rinsed my mouth with fresh tea. After a while, I felt the medicine circulating through my whole body and, as it did, the pain went away. But, soon, my body turned hot, and my eyes went as red as a mad dog's. I was like a madman who only wanted to rip his clothes off and run around naked and hit and kick anyone to reduce the irritation in his arms and legs.

'I was like that for a while before I regained my strength. That night, I was able to pull the rickshaw strongly and keep awake for at least as long as when I had smoked opium. But although the medicine satisfied my addiction, I felt very queasy the next day. My body was so dry and hot that if someone had lit a match, it would have gone up in flames.

'After I'd been to the Black Queen a number of times, I knew from the ingredients of the liquid that it required a lot of effort to make. She would take the rags that are used to clean the opium tray, the lamp, and the pipe, and the rags that are wrapped around the implements. She would also take the pieces of broken or cracked pipes that people had thrown away and chopped into splinters like toothpicks, and the uncleaned bronze opium containers. The Black Queen took all of these, threw them into a huge earthenware pot, poured in some water and heated it. She heated it until it was just about to boil and removed it from the fire for fear that some of the liquid would be lost through evaporation.

'I forgot to mention, to the contents which already included the basic elements—metal, wood, stone, water, fire—the Black Queen added a spice: the dark opium residue! The very old residue was as black and as crumbled as coal dust. She took a pinch of it and sprinkled it carefully into the ingredients. You have to see it to know how terrible it is. Apart from the things we can see, there are also the things we can't see like lamp oil, spit, and sweat.

'Having taken the pot off the fire, the Black Queen pours off the water and, with a steel European ladle, scoops the foul scum off it. The residue at the bottom of the pot is dredged out and sold as medicine for scabies; the empty opium tins are sold for scrap metal; and the liquid drawn from this pot-pourri is sold to addicted coolies for 5 sous a bowl.

'The Black Queen! I don't know if her parents or someone else gave her that name. Her skin was very dark, and the fact that she sold that black brew only made her name more fitting!

'Addicted rickshaw coolies who are short of opium or who miss out on a pipe all have to go to her. If they are suffering from withdrawal and haven't been able to get a bowl of her brew, they are like possessed men and there's no way they will respond to calls from passing customers.

'For coolies like us that are already addicted, I think that if we had a bowl of that medicine each day, it would save both money and time.

'If you drink it and feel all right, there's nothing more to say. Many coolies who have drunk the brew as a substitute will die from one illness or another, the most feared of which is constipation followed by the passing of blood. When you take that brew and start passing blood, only Heaven can help you. Once you are an addict, you can smoke a lot of opium because the pipes only give you the smoke. But when you take the brew, it is absorbed into your entrails. With an addiction to that black brew, the skin does not just become discoloured, it gradually turns black, the eyes become sunken, the neck shrinks, you can't eat or sleep, and the blood eventually comes out in a watery brown liquid: you soon join your ancestors. Smoking opium is also harmful, but only to your lungs so that when you get old, it only gives you a bad cough. Look at me, I've been addicted to smoking opium for over four years, and, although I'm thin, I'm still strong and can stay awake for a long time. If I couldn't do that, how could I work in a trade that takes me out all night?'

Tu spoke and smoked and spoke again, and although he complained of an unquenchable addiction that kept him hard-pressed and poor, he still praised the drug for its many beneficial uses.

I had heard people sing the praises of Miss Phu Dung, the Opium Lady, many times before I met Tu. So I didn't feel like listening to his eulogy and let him rave on.

Of the three days I had to spend out at Co Xa, I only had half a day left. But I now knew the secrets of the rickshaw trade. Tu, my landlord for these three days, had unintentionally revealed them to me.

19

No Spoke in the Wheel

Now let me say to you here that perhaps there were times when you, Dear Readers, said to your friends: 'That's enough! Why bother arguing with those rickshaw coolies!'

I must also confess that there have been times when I said to my friends: 'Those coolies, why waste energy quarrelling with them!'

Dear Readers, I have been of the same mind as you: we have despised the class of people who pull other people.

But do they really deserve such contempt? Today, let us rethink this question.

Now, let's imagine that someone asked: 'Who is to blame for the class of people in our society that works like animals pulling other people?'

What would you say?

If you think carefully, I dare say you would answer honestly as follows: 'Society is to blame.'

According to its strict meaning, 'society' is all of the people who come from the same origins and who all live together under the same system, and that includes you and me.

Yes, you and me, all of us are equally at fault.

To lower a powerless person from his status as a human being to that of a horse, to give him two wooden shafts and say 'I will sit up here while you pull me' is the same as saying 'You are not a human being'.

Having been unjustly denied membership of the human race, why do rickshaw coolies need self-respect?

We take away their dignity without knowing it. Why do we scorn them for supposedly doing undignified things?

I've seen many stories in the paper: some rickshaw coolie has found a purse on the side of the road and taken it straight to the police; another has come across a woman giving birth in the street, taken off his shirt, and wrapped it around the new-born baby, then helped the mother and child into the rickshaw and taken them to their destination.

Journalists praise them: 'Hearts of gold in ragged shirts.'

Why can't rickshaw coolies have hearts of gold like any other people?

As he pulls us, one coolie farts in our faces as he runs; another coolie stands in the middle of the street changing his clothes or urinating in the street before our eyes. This is because we put them in this situation.

If society gave them back their dignity and treated them as human beings rather than as animals, then society would see!

I dare say that for a long time, most of those obscene stories about coolies arise from the way our middle- and high-class people and intellectuals treat them. Sitting up on their backs and crying 'Faster, faster!'; this is why they act like animals.

People who let other people pull them should share the shame.

Horses pull carts because they were born with four legs. Human beings shouldn't work like horses because they were born with two legs.

This is why I said 'people who let other people pull them should share the blame'.

If it hadn't been regarded as a shame, the League for the Rights of Man would not have intervened in the rickshaw issue at the Colonial Exposition at Vincennes, where up to forty rickshaws—among the 'Local Products of Indo-China'—were not displayed, but left lying about in disorder before the eyes of people from a thousand countries.

When I heard this news, I felt respect for the French, especially the French League for the Rights of Man.

Without distinction of colour or race, the French had taken away the shame of the Annamite people.

People in the imperial country think that the situation of people pulling people is a disgrace and try to do something about it.

How about us?

We still sit in rickshaws with our heads held high, regarding that disgraceful matter as commonplace, without anyone wanting to think about it.

Mr Phi Bang published in *Trung Lap Journal* an article

about the rickshaw problem in which he made the following comment: 'In life, people often give great consideration to big issues, but often neglect small ones, unaware that these insignificant matters have a big influence on our lives, our country, our race.'

In addition to this, E. Babut in the *Phap Viet Journal* asked the following question about the rickshaw trade: 'Can we expect this trade to disappear completely?'

Mr Phi Bang wrote on another occasion: 'If you want to abolish the rickshaw trade, first you must find jobs for the thousands of people who work like horses.'

In line with this, E. Babut also wrote in the *Phap Viet Journal*: 'When our country is more prosperous, I do not think that people would want to work at that trade any more. But unfortunately we have not reached that stage yet; the rickshaw trade is still a very necessary one for many people to make a living today.'

Make a living!

At present in Hanoi, there are up to fifteen hundred people who survive solely on the rickshaw trade.

Whether it's cold or hot, raining or fine, they hunch themselves between the shafts, grip the handles, and run all day streaming with sweat, and it's as though their clothes have been soaked in water.

They exhaust themselves like that to make what? Five or 10 sous a journey. Just enough money to buy a little rice to eat, low-grade rice mixed into a thin broth.

To eat to survive is fair enough! But they can't survive with dignity. They have to listen to the crude curses of the people who sit in their rickshaws, and bear the blows of police truncheons, as well as the bashings they take from the rickshaw Supervisors.

That means that you eat to survive, survive to run, run to digest the food, and eat again.

To relieve the misery of the people in this trade, somebody has recently made a suggestion: 'Ban the double rickshaws.'

But someone else in the trade has another view. To help them to attract customers, he says: 'The double rickshaws shouldn't be banned.'

Let me also join this discussion, for I have a different view from both of these: 'We should abolish the rickshaw trade!'

Saying that, I'm sure someone is about to say: he's putting a spoke in the wheel, he's only a troublemaker talking nonsense.

Not so! I'm not putting a spoke in the wheel, and I'm not a troublemaker talking nonsense!

Please let me explain why.

20
A Request

Yesterday afternoon, I was wandering around town when I unexpectedly found myself in Hang Dao Street. A red and white striped cloth roof cover which was stretched across a steel frame appeared before my eyes; I looked again and saw a tricycle which carried soft drinks with the Bear's Head trade mark around the streets.

The Bear's Head tricycle sped along the sealed road from the direction of the Opera House. At the same time, a tricycle carrying goods from the Huong Ky Photography Shop also appeared in Hang Dao, and the rider waved to the fellow on the Bear's Head tricycle. The two tricycles stopped beside each other and the riders got down. One gave the other 3 sous and the other busied himself with the preparation of a glass of grated ice water which he handed over in return. With the transaction finished, the two riders got back on their tricycles. The Huong Ky tricycle went in the direction of Hang Trong; the Bear's Head went in the other direction to Hang Dao.

Standing on the edge of the sidewalk, I looked again at the two tricycles as they sped away from each other, and just at that moment, an idea came into my mind: we could use these tricycles to replace the rickshaw.

Three rubber tyres placed on three steel rims, two wheels in front, one at the back. Place a rattan basket between the two front wheels. Behind the basket erect a long rod to support a roof; at the back edge of the basket, place handlebars so that the person pedalling the tricycle can drive it.

There, sketched out, that's all there is to it.

A few things set up skilfully to keep off the rain and sun; the makers will be able to manufacture a kind of carriage where people pedal people.

I don't dare accept credit for this initiative, because this kind of carriage which pedals people has already appeared in Shanghai where people go all over the city in them.

When people pedal a tricycle for others, it is a more respectful, more humane activity, because the person pedalling is also able to sit and does not have to lift his legs and run head first down the street.

If you have the money and are in a hurry, then sit up in the tricycle and I'll pedal you. I haven't got any money, so I'll pedal you and get you to your destination as fast as I can. In such a situation, there is nothing offensive to human dignity: you sit, and I also sit. You sit relaxed in front without wasting your energy, because you have paid me the fare; I sit behind raising and lowering my knees, because I have accepted your money. If the pedalling makes me sweat, I'm still happy because I'm doing that work of my own free will, and because you don't have the right to call me a horse when my occupation is one of pedalling people rather than pulling people.

In discussing the abolition of rickshaws, I'm sure some rickshaw owner is about to whisper in my ear: who do you want to kill?

I wouldn't dare to answer those people who think more of money than flesh and blood. Here I address my comments to those who have wider vision, people who have a desire to resolve social issues.

In our country, the rickshaw trade began over half a century ago. Before the French came here, the primitive road system did not facilitate communications, and the only kinds of carriage we had were palanquins and hammocks with which two people carried one. When roads were opened that were sufficiently wide and smooth, the rickshaw came here from its home country, Japan, after passing through China. Next came the horse-drawn wagon which left its wheel marks imprinted on every road and track. In fifty years, the imprint of the wagon wheels has faded as the rickshaw advanced to a point where it runs on two wheels with rubber tyres that are pumped up with air. It has advanced as slowly as that because it never ran in front of the person, but followed obediently behind the person running.

Perhaps the rickshaw cannot progress beyond its present level of development, because the rickshaw trade has not changed one bit in the last ten years and a rickshaw with rubber tyres is still only a rickshaw with rubber tyres.

In this era of evolutionary competition, anything that doesn't advance must fall into obsolescence one day. Sooner or later, the rickshaw trade will also come to an end.

Must we let it eliminate itself, or must we eliminate it before it does?

With a trade that is such a national disgrace, we shouldn't let it prolong its life. We must kill it off immediately. As long as it lives, it will be a source of shame for us.

If we abolish the rickshaw which pulls people and introduce the tricycle which pedals people, we will still have enough work for the rickshaw coolies. Fifteen hundred people in Hanoi make a living each day from fifteen hundred two-wheeled rickshaws, and so fifteen hundred tricycles will also allow that number of people to make a living.

To call for the banning of two in a rickshaw, to call for an abolition of that ban; the members of the Hanoi and Haiphong city councils should not waste their energy on such a peripheral matter.

First, the members must realize that the issue is one of abolishing rickshaws and then proceed to abolish them, not grope for the moon's reflection in a lake or pluck stars out of the sky.

Having said that, I would not dare advocate that the members ask their city councils to do away with rickshaws immediately. No matter how cleverly the councillors act, they have not got a magic wand that will convert over a thousand rickshaws in a flash.

We merely wish to discuss one matter with council members: that Mayors be requested to order the following change. Each time they inspect rickshaw repair shops in the city, the police should take the number of broken-down rickshaws and prohibit their repair; those rickshaws will not be able to transport people, only goods. A rickshaw owner who wants more carriages to transport people must fabricate tricycles in accordance with the model that city councils approve of; this new model must be simple so that the amount of money which the owners spend on the fabrication of it is similar to the amount they spent on the fabrication of the old one.

There is nothing difficult or unusual about that method.

It is very much like other regulations that are currently being enforced in the city: the repair of thatched houses or old houses that are broken-down is now prohibited; owners have to demolish them and build new houses according to regulations made by the city's hygiene office.

By employing such means, I dare think that, in three years, you would not be able to find a rickshaw in the city. In that time, the rickshaw coolies would still be able to make enough for two meals a day, the rickshaw owners would still make a profit, and the city would still be able to collect rickshaw taxes.

By doing away gradually with the rickshaw trade, we will be able to create a decent life for the coolies; they will live without their occupation stripping them of their dignity; although they will always work with their legs, that work will no longer be that of a buffalo or a horse.

How can a request that does no harm to any one but is able to elevate the body and soul of a class of people be discarded?

The lock on the enclosure which traps the horse-people has always had a key: the one I found at Tu's house out at Co Xa Nam.

It is very old.

But even though that is the case, it is not completely useless, and so I want to hand it over to our councillors today.

Household Servants

VU TRONG PHUNG

VU TRONG PHUNG was born in Hanoi on 20 December 1912 and before he died at the age of twenty-seven, he had written some twenty works of modern realism. These included eleven novels, four long works of reportage, two long plays, at least twenty short stories, and a translation of Victor Hugo's play, *Lucrece Borgia* (1833). He also drew, played music, and wrote some poetry.

His mother, Pham Thi Khach, was from Hoai Duc in present-day Hanoi. Originally from Hung Yen (presently Hai Hung) Province, his father, Vu Van Lan, was an electrician at the Charles Boillot Garage in Hanoi. He died from tuberculosis seven months after Vu Trong Phung was born. As his poor mother then nurtured him with great devotion, three main obsessions soon combined to shape Vu Trong Phung's life and writing: his love for his mother, his bitter sense of injustice at his poverty, and his belief that he would die young from tuberculosis.

He completed first grade at Hanh Voi Junior High School, but failed the entrance examinations for elementary teacher training. At the age of fifteen or sixteen, he found work as a clerk in the Goda Company, and later at the Far East Printing House [Imprimerie D'Extrême Orient] where he learnt to type. When he lost his job in 1929 or 1930, some say it was because he typed his stories during working hours. However, at the time of the Great Depression, many companies were laying off employees. In 1930, Tam Lang gave him a start on the *Ha thanh ngo bao* [Hanoi Midday News], and thereafter he devoted himself to writing. He was a good husband and father.

By 1934, he had published many newspaper articles, two works of reportage, and his first novel, *Dut tinh* [Broken Love]. Around this time, his friend, the writer, Lan Khai, said that 'the reporter and novelist was a thin, unhappy youth about 1.6 metres tall with … a slightly hunched back'. The idiosyncrasies of his dress included the turban which he wore down to his bushy eyebrows, and a strange satin jacket. When not wearing the turban, he often placed experimental parts in his hair. Then, in 1936, he astonished many with the publication of three novels which are among the highest achievements of modern Vietnamese literature: *Giong to* [The Tempest], *So do* [A Fortunate Life], and *Vo de* [The Broken Dike]. *Com thay com co* [Household Servants], which is usually regarded as his best work of reportage, was also published in the *Hanoi bao* [Hanoi News] in the same year. He died on 13 October 1939 of tuberculosis after becoming an opium addict in the hope that the drug would prolong his life.

1
Introduction

DEAR Sirs, for a long time I have parted my hair on the side.

Then, a month ago, I let it grow really long to cover the back of my head and reach the nape of my neck. My sideburns came down like two chicken tails.

That means I have a fashionable hair-style, one that people who aren't up to date vaguely call the 'Philosophe' fashion! But upper-class people who are familiar with this fashion, they would know that I have the hair-style of a 'humble servant'.

I bought my shirt from an Indian shop for 15 sous, but it looks really good on me. It has short sleeves and is the colour of peach blossoms. I wear black trousers, but they are made of thick shiny satin.

For quite a while now, I've always worn dark glasses. I wear them in the morning, at noon, and also at night. I'm only lacking the big chest, strong wrists, and pock-marks which would have ensured me the respect of other humble servants and elevation by them to the position of 'Big Brother'.

So, I've wandered around visiting eating houses, cinemas, and water-pumps for a couple of weeks. I have been mixed up with three or four street girls and had an affair with a wet-nurse. I have become friendly with a few Madams and called one of them my adopted mother.

One clerk's wife wanted to keep me for 80 sous a month, but I didn't accept the offer. Next, a modern young lady offered me 12 piastres a year, two sets of clothes, and a sash. But she didn't go ahead with the deal, because I wasn't tricky enough to conceal my bad manners and rough ways.

Oh dear me, my path to wealth and honours has been full of obstacles! So after a few weeks of looking for work, I've gone back to my previous form! Assuredly, my destiny is not that of a household servant.

But what about a long work of reportage on household servants?

Why not! Not long ago, Maryse Choisy donned the garb of a maid, and wrote a long reportage, *Carnet d'une femme de chambre* [Notebook of a Chambermaid], 1933, which was not without value for social scientists.

2

One Night in the Eating House

I don't need to tell you either the name of the eating house or the street in which it was located. I can assure you, Dear Readers, it was the sort of eating house like thousands of others, where you felt like vomiting as soon as you entered. There was the smell of cheap fish, buffalo meat, tainted pork, pig and cow offal, sour tamarinds, and bad pickled vegetables. OK, that's enough of the unbearable smells, although it was very strange that they didn't seem to bother the woman in charge who held a bamboo fan in her hand and was stripped naked to the waist. She occasionally felt the need to pull her pants up to her crotch and, without any inhibitions, scratch herself vigorously like a man.

It was very late at night.

An old woman whose occupation it was to find jobs for servants brought me to this place and said to the woman in charge: 'Let him sleep here a few nights; when he's got work, I'll give you the money for his lodging.' The woman in charge didn't deign to look at me, slapped a mosquito on her neck, scratched the area, scratched her back with the fan, and waved me inside to lie down. Before she left, the old woman reminded me: 'Make sure you are at the T-junction early tomorrow morning!'

'Yes, ma'am.'

I finished my reply, then tiptoed inside. Really, my feet had never trodden on such a sticky muddy floor as that. When I reached the sleeping area, I didn't know where to lie down because all the beds were full of people lying higgledy-piggledy all over them. As I hesitated, the woman in charge of the eating house shouted: 'Hai, where are you! Tell him to go up to the attic where the servants sleep!'

Then a young man ran out and led me across a courtyard

to a bamboo ladder and said: 'Up there.'

Following his instructions, I climbed the ladder. When I got to the top, I saw a fairly wide space. There were only a few sleeping mats spread out, and the wall was very yellow with smoke that came out of the kitchen nearby.

A number of people lay around like pigs; males on one side, females on the other. There were four young men the same age as me, and three young maids: one about ten, one fifteen, and one who was much older. While the two younger ones lay around carelessly, the older one lay modestly in a corner, quietly holding a fan as she looked at me.

I moved in the direction of the young men and sat on a corner of a sleeping mat. I looked around and, seeing no one from the eating house there, I permitted myself to turn up the lamp. I picked up a long bamboo match container and, intending to use it as a pipe, put some tobacco into a hole on the side of it, raised it to my lips, and lit it with the lamp.

Suddenly, one of the boys said: 'Why smoke like that? It's very hot. Use that bamboo pipe over there.'

I turned around and saw the boy sit up and go and get the pipe for me. After I had a smoke, I gave it to him and let him finish it, and so we became friends.

He said: 'You look very experienced. You must have been in the city a long time.'

'That's for sure.'

Just those few words made him afraid of me. From then on, he always called me 'Big Brother'.

'You still look very inexperienced. You've just come from the country, haven't you?'

'Yes.'

'Have you found any work yet?'

'Just for a month in a house in B Street. But I couldn't bear it and left. The master was too cruel.'

'In what way?'

'He cursed me continuously.'

'You certainly haven't got the right attitude to fill your belly! Don't stand on one mountain top and look to another, or you'll soon find yourself without any support.'

The bustling sounds of people running in and out could still be heard in the eating house. Nearby we could hear the sounds of people closing their windows and doors for the night, and yet inside the eating house, it seemed that people had just begun cooking. The clatter of chopsticks hitting bowls, the sounds of running water rushing into the courtyard, and fat sizzling in the frying-pan could all be heard. Perhaps the servants in the eating house couldn't distinguish between night and day. One fellow sang loudly, while all the others cracked jokes to stay awake.

I continued to advise my new companion: 'Block your ears, when you get a job, let your masters listen to their own curses. As long as you keep your job, you won't starve!'

He blinked fearfully and argued meekly: 'Forty sous a month and not a day when there are enough leftovers to eat, is that sort of job worth keeping?'

But I didn't want to hear that. I was going to talk big to impress him.

'Now look at me; wait until you are like me, then you can stand on one mountain and look to another. Got it?'

He echoed my ideas: 'Yes, indeed, you are very experienced.'

'You bet, when I go to the water-pump, I just raise my voice and I get two buckets of water. I'm also good at cooking any kind of food, French food or ours.'

'So why did you lose your job?'

I opened my eyes wide and glared at him: 'What do you mean, lose my job? I got 2½ piastres last month, then I asked for 50 sous more and didn't get it, so I left!'

The look on his face showed how much admiration he had for me. But the purpose of saying all that was to make the young girl who was lying there glancing at me think I was a general among servants. I had taken the opportunity to 'spread my wings' and succeeded, because from then on the girl continued to regard me with interest and did not go to sleep.

I thought it prudent not to continue boasting, so I quickly asked the boy: 'So how about you, what kind of people do you like to work for?'

He answered: 'Poor me, what skill do I have to dare to make demands on anyone! I only want to go into a household where people treat me fairly, don't work me to the bone, don't beat or curse me, unlike the house I just left. Poor me, there were too many masters and mistresses and everyone beat and cursed me! One person ordered me to do something, and before I had finished it, somebody else called me. I was treated like rubbish.'

He claimed that he'd never seen a house as bad as that before. So his experience as a servant led him to despise his masters. He's only the child of ordinary parents, and, if what he said is true, he wouldn't behave as badly as his masters.

After I heard his story, I reconstructed the story of a family that no one could have imagined existed on earth.

There were six people in the family: a father with an old wife, and an eldest son who worked as a messenger for a government office, together with his wife and their two daughters.

Six people closely related by blood or, at least, by marriage, and yet every day they each go into the kitchen to cook their own pot of rice. When they eat, they sit together, but each one eats his or her own dish. Generally, the father eats a dish of minced pork; the mother, one of fried bean curd; the son and daughter-in-law eat sautéd meat and vegetables, while the daughters eat pickled vegetables and soup. Everybody sits and eats together, but if a person is tempted to put his or her chopsticks into another's dish, a fearful look will immediately come that person's way.

That is a rough sketch of how that family lives.

So, one day, when the daughter-in-law kept a plate of freshly cooked meat paste aside for her husband, the husband's father unfortunately ate early and dipped into that dish.

On coming home from work, the son lifted the cover off the food and, seeing that his delicacy had been touched, instantly shouted: 'Who ate my food? I come home exhausted from working all day and haven't eaten, and someone has already eaten some of my food. Who was it?'

The father was quick to respond in a soft voice: 'Dear son, it was me. I thought your wife had just made the paste for me, so I have tasted some of it by mistake.'

Can you guess what the son replied? I'd rather leave it to you, Dear Readers, to guess, but I don't think you can. Victor Hugo would not have been able to imagine someone as miserable as that.

Before I tell you the answer, I should tell you something else which the young servant told me: the father rented the back room, the son rented the front room. Consequently, the son had this to say to his father: 'You made a mistake? You live in the back, I live in the front, and my wife keeps food aside for me in the front, and you make a mistake! That's a very strange mistake!'

Then the young boy concluded with self-respect: 'I would be proud to serve a good master, but working for someone like that is very shameful!'

I nodded my agreement and gave him a cigarette and a match, but took advantage of the hearty laughter of the older girl lying in the corner. Her laugh encouraged me to pick up the lamp and shine it on her face.

3
Sixteen People for Sale

If these words were written beautifully on a blackboard and placed in front of where we sat on the footpath, perhaps people going along the street would pay more attention to us, and we would be able to avoid the situation where we just offered our faces to the flies. Following the instructions of the old woman who found places for servants, I was at Admiral Courbet Street from 7 a.m. At first, there were only seven of us there from the eating house. Gradually, more people joined us, and I didn't know where they came from. They could easily have come up from under the ground or dropped from the sky, as they all gathered at the crossroads like flies attracted by the smell of honey. Because I didn't need work, I was able to watch with calm detachment the people who came to compete with each other. But the young boy I stayed up with all the previous night in the eating house could not be so calm. Every time he saw someone, either male or female, come to stand in line, he complained: 'Good heavens, more and more keep coming, when will I ever get chosen to work!'

It is true at whatever level in society, a workmate is someone you have to watch out for. An old wet-nurse started to damn the air: 'A curse on their ancestors! They are all coming at once!'

The crowd sat around in little groups of young people, old people, women, boys, and girls. The old woman who was trying to place us didn't sit down, but walked up and down looking first at one person and then another like a general reviewing his troops. While walking, she mumbled something, perhaps counting or evaluating those people who depended on her. Some were whispering, others talking loudly. Others also cursed each other jokingly, picked off each other's head lice and bit them to ward off their hunger.

I saw the old woman had no customers and worried about her miserable mob. But the woman herself, she looked pleased for some reason which I did not yet understand. Then I thought of the unemployed workers at the Port who agreed to meet at a predetermined place, and were able to assemble there in a large demonstration. But these servants, there is not yet any organization for them. This throng of low-class people splits up and disperses everywhere in the city so that sophisticated people think it is civilized. Even social scientists think there is no adversity there.

But, in fact, it's very tragic.

The city lures people from the countryside who leave dry fields and dead grass, and who starve a second time after they have abandoned their homes. It reduces people to the level of animals; it often drives young men into prison and young women into prostitution!

Sixteen people for sale!

Not one customer wanted to buy that morning.

So how much were those sixteen individuals worth? The fact that there were no customers, was it because the price was too high or too low?

4

A Person's Value

Sometimes a person's value is lower than an animal's. In fact, I have seen dogs who were able to eat beef which their masters had bought for them. Sometimes, dogs make their masters spend more on them each month than they spend on a household servant.

These sixteen people of all sorts—big, small, young, old—

each one of them could hope for no more than a dog, often less than a dog. And even though they could use their legs and arms to perform many useful functions and very heavy tasks, they still couldn't get work.

I pointed at the group of young boys and girls who were still under twelve years of age and asked the old woman: 'This group, what sort of wage do you expect to get for them each month?'

The old woman looked me up and down disdainfully and, as she turned her head away, she eventually answered: 'Today, those brats will be lucky if they can be hired by someone who still has some food left over for them to eat!'

'And your commission, I suppose it's not much?'

'That's obvious! But 5 or 10 sous is enough. It's better to have a little rather than nothing.'

I pointed at the group of youths the same age as me and asked: 'What about this group?'

'Fifty sous for some, 30 for others.'

'And how much do you expect for those old servants who are munching corn over there at the foot of the tree?'

'About the same price.'

I pointed to another woman who was a wet-nurse and asked: 'And what about that one?'

The old woman changed her tone of voice and replied: 'Ah, for that one I'd have to find a place that offered at least 2 piastres in wages! And for commission, I'd also have to ask at least 1 piastre! She's very clean! Her milk is of the highest quality.'

At this moment, the old woman looked into the distance and returned to the sidewalk where she sat down. Then, just after that, I saw another old woman wearing a white silk blouse and large ear-rings waving as she approached her.

'Hey, you! The wet-nurse I had last month for my daughter-in-law has already asked to leave!'

Moving as though she had a spring inside her, the old woman jumped up and gasped: 'Oh dear! What happened?'

'Her husband died and she asked to go home for fifteen days. So I decided it was best to tell her not to come back.'

'Thank God, I thought it might have been something else.'

So, having heard the sad news that some person had died, she sighed, then looked relieved and quite cheerful. The other woman went on asking: 'The clerk's wife is still very tired from the birth. Have you got anyone right now?'

The old woman put on a thoughtful expression before answering: 'Dear Madam, I've got someone here. But I've already promised her to someone else. I don't know whether I should let her go with you straight away or have her wait here. . . .'

The other woman cut her short: 'Let me see if she is good enough to hire straight away. The clerk's wife is tired and still recovering.'

'Dear Madam, I have the greatest respect for you.'

'Come on! There are plenty of people available these days. It's not as difficult to get them as before. You'll still be able to find another one for the other person.'

The old woman turned around to address the wet-nurse: 'Stand up, come up here, quick. It's no good just sitting there looking dumb, is it?'

The other woman looked the wet-nurse up and down then nodded and said: 'Mm, she looks clean enough. Let me see what her milk is like.'

The old woman said quickly: 'Dear Madam, she's from the country where she's the wife of a deputy village chief. She's never been muddied by working in the fields!'

The wet-nurse undid her bib and, uncovering her soft white breasts, squeezed some milk into the palm of one hand. The other woman had a quick look and said: 'Not too bad.'

The old woman immediately sprang up to her full height

and snapped: 'Good heavens! Milk like that and all you can say is "Not too bad". It's the best quality you've got there, Madam.'

The other woman pursed her lips: 'Right, that's first quality, I suppose.'

'Of course. She's just had her first child, she has never dirtied herself working in the fields, and she is also the wife of a deputy village chief. She's never toiled like others, so how can her milk not be good?'

'All right, how much?'

Before the wet-nurse had time to open her mouth, the old woman jumped in: 'Please, Madam, the same amount as the other person offered for her.'

'So how much is that?'

'Well, the other person asked me to help her by finding a clean girl with good milk for about 3 piastres a month. Because I've been busy, I haven't had the chance to take her to the other person yet.'

The woman who had come to hire a wet-nurse pursed her lips and said: 'No, I'll pay as much as I paid for the last one: 2 piastres.'

With this, the old woman joined her hands in front of her chest and bowed repeatedly as though she were standing before some temple, then turned her head away without answering.

'Well, what about it?'

'I beg you, Madam, offer her 2 piastres and 99 sous, and see if she accepts it.'

The other woman replied angrily: 'What's this got to do with you? Your job is only to get the commission, isn't it? So why are you involved in setting peoples' wages?'

The wet-nurse looked timidly at the old woman and spoke softly: 'Dear Madam, if you could give me the same wages as the other person offered, I'll break my other appointment.'

The other woman just stood there saying nothing, then turned on her heel, and walked away. I asked the old woman: 'But I heard you say before that you only needed 2 piastres a month for the wet-nurse.'

'That's right. But you can squeeze more out of a customer like this. You'll see, she'll be back before long.'

As expected, about half an hour later, the other woman reappeared and said: 'All right, I agree to pay 3 piastres a month for her, and, for your part, come and get your commission when you are free.'

Despicably, the old woman scratched her head, frowned, and complained: 'Dear Madam, I really have great respect for you! I now have to find another wet-nurse for the other person straight away. Therefore, I'll have to ask for half of my commission now.'

On receiving 50 sous, the old woman turned to the wet-nurse and said: 'All right, go with this lady, and this afternoon I'll collect the rest of my commission when I come by the house with your clothes. Your mistress is a generous woman, the clerk and his wife are also people who care for others, so when you live with them, you must be polite, show your gratitude, and look after the little one. Understand?'

They parted: the old woman had succeeded in her business of 'squeezing' those whose lives she dealt in. Meanwhile, with respect to servants, the value of a person has nothing to do with their capacity for work, but hangs on the tongue of a coarse old woman who trades in people, is as slippery as a snake, and never speaks the truth.

A morning's trading had passed and afternoon was upon us. The old woman had only been able to 'consume' one wet-nurse, but had made some money. It didn't matter to her that the other fifteen were hungry, because she didn't have to be hungry for the others. They just continued to sit there on display, in a line with their legs stretched straight out or spread apart with their pants pulled up to their thighs so that they could 'investigate' the hair on their legs, or nod off to sleep.

But later when I began to question the young girl I had spoken with the night before in the eating house, I found that she didn't really want to work.

Oh, how strange! A maid who loses her job, yet doesn't want to work! What's the reason for this? Now, I had to get to the bottom of that, and in the course of our conversations I got quite close to Miss Dui.

5
Miss Dui's Novel

This story came from a young maid's heart, and so, while I was sitting in front of the lamp recording it, I wanted to dream that it contained a little poetry. But how wretched it was! Her name was so unattractive and her confidences were not revealed in a beautiful setting such as the beach at Do Son or Co Ngu Road. Oh dear, we were not fortunate enough to be like the lovers in romantic novels: Dam Thuy and To Tam, Mong Ha and Le Anh. Dear Readers, our courtship took place one afternoon on a sidewalk near a pile of rubbish amid the bustle of the capital's passing parade. Most assuredly, we were not noticed in 'the rush of wheels and steeds, the crush of clothes in the cavalcade'. Members of society's upper stream never have any desire to look down at the lower one, and, as a result, the things that high-class people do in the dark, humble servants like us dare to do in the light of the sun.

And inseparable lovers like us didn't know how to put on

deceptive airs: when we talked, we forgot completely that both of us had our pants pulled up to our thighs! Because of that, I was able to believe that Miss Dui's confession was sincere, even though it was not made in the solemn surroundings of a church before the face of a stern missionary whose every gesture is a sacred sign. And me, the 'baptist', I only had the face of a small, unemployed fellow.

Miss Dui had feared becoming a servant, because of prejudice in the village which held that such a calling was not respectable. The year she turned ten, her father had an important position; the year she turned twelve, he was a well-established village chief. From then on, however, her father revealed some quite ordinary human weaknesses as his success went to his head. His wealth began to disappear. Eventually, his fields and ponds were completely sold off, and Miss Dui had to go to the city to work as a servant!

'My mother still ploughed the fields for other people in the village, and my father now pulled a rickshaw! Really, he brought it on himself, he had a good reputation but lost his position, making his wife and children suffer. Nowadays, he's kicked by the Supervisor at times when he can't pay for the hire of the rickshaw. But I don't feel sorry for him! He can die! That'll teach him.'

Miss Dui was very contented to talk like that. I asked her: 'Does anyone in the village still call him Mr Village Chief?'

She smacked her lips and said: 'Fortunately, no one in the village knows that he pulls a rickshaw in the city, so every time he returns home, the villagers still call him Mr Ex-Village Chief!'

'Tell me about your master when you first became a servant, and also about your thoughts at that time.'

'Oh God! I've never suffered so much in my life. I thought I'd die straight away!'

The first step: Dui worked for an old prostitute who had

formerly lived with a foreigner. Dui didn't have enough to eat, and yet she had to work very hard. Every day she had to wash three big tubs of dirty, bad-smelling clothes. Whenever the old mistress called her—about three hundred times each day—she made herself important by cursing Dui's ancestors before she called her name. During the first few days, Dui thought of her mother, resented her father, and wanted to kill herself.

When she reached this point in her story, Dui suddenly burst out laughing: 'But then every afternoon I could also go for a walk in Paul Bert Gardens! The way my old mistress dressed herself up looked so funny: high-heeled shoes, her hair done up in chicken tails, and a Chinese blouse and trousers! Seeing any African, she would ogle him and start flirting with him straight away. She made me follow her closely as though she wanted to force me to learn the prostitute's trade. Her cheeks were so wrinkled and heavily powdered all over that her face looked stupid and ugly. Yet she managed to catch a man, and everyone knew that such a person would have to be a foreigner. And what happened next damned her ancestors! It was she who made me lose my virginity! Oh, Big Brother, I had just turned thirteen when she stuffed a rag into my mouth and held my legs so that an Indian could rape me!'

Looking carefully at Dui, I could see that she had something attractive about her, and listening to her recount this dreadful event from her past, my face was hot with anger and my eyebrows rose as though I was witnessing it before my eyes. I quickly asked her: 'Didn't you take them to court?

'But after he'd finished, she coaxed and threatened me a lot, then gave me 2 piastres.'

'You wretch! For 2 piastres, you could. . . '

Dui brushed my indignation aside: 'No. No. No. Don't be so quick to scold me like that. After it happened, it was as though I was about to die. I lay paralysed for half a day. And in the middle of it, remember that she shoved a cotton bath towel into my mouth, so how could I scream? I refused to accept the money, I went out into the street to tell a policeman, and was about to burst out crying in front of one. But before I'd had a chance to tell him the whole story, the old woman ran out and stood between us, and said something in French to the policeman I didn't understand. Then I heard the policeman's tone of voice change as he scolded me and warned me against false slander and said that, if I lied and went to court without evidence, I'd be thrown into the stocks! After that I became scared and didn't dare to think about going to the police station any more, and had to accept the 2 piastres as compensation. Three days later, I recovered, and following her old ways, she forced me to take customers again. Curse her ancestors. It really was heaven's retribution. A few days later, she was hit by a car and broke a leg. Ah, you know, I think heaven exists.'

Dui continued to talk at length about her terrible mistress and in praise of God whose eyes are not closed. She vilified her old mistress to the point that it made me lose all pity for her and not want to hear any more. I had to ask her to end that story and tell me about the work she had with other masters and mistresses after that.

'After that, I was able to go and work as a maid in a rich house. I was very pleased with myself, thinking that people there would certainly treat me kindly. But, good heavens, you wouldn't believe it! The richer people are, the meaner they are: they behave like dogs.'

At first, when she stood at the door, Dui hesitated behind the old woman who had brought her there, and just looked at the tea chest inlaid with mother-of-pearl, the parallel sentences inscribed in gold characters on lacquered panels, the porcelain bowls on porcelain stands, the mirror-wardrobes, the brass incense-burners: it was overwhelming! Her mistress told her solemnly that she would be paid 50 sous each month. Dui started working with joy in her heart.

Fortunately, on the first day, there was no incident to report. The following night because the dinner was late and there wasn't enough food, Dui got three pieces of duck from the larder. Unfortunately, however, the mistress became aware of the missing duck the next morning and dragged Dui out and beat her and said with calm cruelty: 'Damn all your ancestors, you've already revealed your penchant for stealing. There were twelve pieces of duck in my meat container and you dare to slip your chopsticks in and take out three pieces to eat! I counted them before I put them away. You thought I didn't know, didn't you?'

From that day, the mistress always cursed Dui's ancestors, no matter what she had done. One day she had sent Dui out to buy 10 sous' worth of roasted pork and, as soon as Dui came back and put the meat on the table, a big argument started between the mistress and her husband. He called her animal names, and she used the private parts of a woman's body as nouns and adjectives to refer to his face. The master spat angry words at the mistress asking her why she didn't tell the maid to go out twice instead of once to buy the 10 sous' worth of meat. If she had gone twice, each time she could have bought 5 sous' worth and asked for a little extra, and that way they would have got more meat for the same price. He was in such a fury that, as we say, angry with the fish he struck the chopping board: he proceeded to call Dui out and slapped her twelve times across the ear, even though she hadn't done anything wrong.

I interrupted her story and said: 'So why didn't you leave straight away?'

She looked at me for some time as though she were mocking me and replied: 'At first I wanted to leave straight away.

But I wanted revenge. I would not be satisfied until I got my revenge, and so I was resigned to working there.'

Then it happened: her revenge: it was so wicked that one could only take one's hat off to her. The mistress had a daughter of thirteen who had just reached puberty, but in whom the flame of passion had flared early so that she was very easy to excite. The young lady who often sat around down in the kitchen talking loosely was further stimulated to chase boys by the collection of dirty stories which Dui told her. Before long, the young lady had quite a few liaisons for which Dui acted as a go-between. For each letter she carried, Dui was able to make 10 sous, and with all the letters going to and fro, she was able to eat snacks until her teeth hurt and still she didn't spend all her money.

But that wasn't all.

The mistress also had a twelve-year-old son whose school-bag was always full of pornographic photographs. Knowing this, Dui spied on him in the middle of the night. Then, one night, when he took the lamp and went out the back for a pee, he saw on the bamboo bench the two very white, tender thighs of the maid stretched out before him! From that night on, he went out far more frequently than before. Finally, after the hundredth time, he held his breath and tiptoed up to put his hand on one of the maid's soft thighs, whereupon she unexpectedly woke and sat straight up.

To keep her mouth closed, the son gave her 1 piastre. After he'd paid the money, he looked as though he would go crazy and threw himself down on the bench and hugged the maid tight. And that's how things went on for a long time.

At this point, Dui kissed me very affectionately and laughed: 'Hey there! No qualms at all. I went on screwing the money out of him, and in a couple of weeks, I'd made 9 piastres. And he only ever touched me on the outside!'

'So why didn't you stay there for the rest of your life?'

'Ah, simply because I wanted to be a singing girl.'

'A singing girl?'

'Yes, if I'd stayed there, I'd have been a maid for the rest of my life.'

Oh! The far-reaching influence of rape! If Dui becomes a Madam, I'll have to go and thank the Indian who raped her!

6
The Light of the Capital

The following night, I returned to the eating house.

This time, instead of telling me to go up to the attic where I had previously slept, they shouted out loudly that I was a pimp, that the old woman who placed servants had forgotten to come back and pay the 2 sous for my lodging, that today I was lucky enough to be allowed to sleep 'out the back', and that they would get the old woman to come back and pay.

I didn't argue with them.

I went on as though I hadn't heard a word. I put my head down and quickened my pace as I passed the kitchen and arrived at the courtyard which they called 'out the back'. Fortunately, I wasn't by myself. Over ten people were there. They lay or sat in the bright moonlight on sleeping mats that were spread out on planks of hardwood. It seemed that the courtyard of the eating house had connections with a timber yard.

There was nothing attractive about this scene. There were just some filthy, high, thin walls with black roof-tops all around. On the right-hand side near where we lay was a chicken coop; in front of us was a blocked drain full of stagnant pitch-black water; on the left was the toilet where people from everywhere emptied their bowels. I regretted the moonlight.

Once I'd merged into the group of ten people, I saw three of the young boys I'd slept with up in the attic two nights before. Their childish faces showed no worry or sadness at all. Meanwhile, the others really looked miserable; their clothes were enough to suggest all the suffering of humanity from the time life began.

There was one bald fellow with a very pale face. But he was fat enough for his body to look normal, and I guessed that he'd just left hospital or prison, as he sat there running his tongue across a piece of paper with some very black substance on it. At first I didn't know what he was doing, but then realized he was licking opium residue. One other fellow had a very long neck with three or four medicinal plasters stuck on it. He was sitting with his head turned upwards, like an astronomer observing the stars. A third young boy was scratching himself noisily as he sat up to cough and spit. An old woman who was dressed neatly had a meaningless, washed out expression on her face. She sat holding a bamboo fan which she waved across the face of one person after another as though they were all her children. The other six, all males wearing rough peasant clothes, slept soundly.

When I jumped up on to the sleeping mats, none of them bothered even to look at me. I was sure that not one of them had a sou in his pocket—which was why they had to sleep here—and that, likewise, their stomachs were as empty as their pockets. Meanwhile, they were able to stay there, not because the owner of the eating house was benevolent, but because of the possibility that these ragged sick people would be able to go out and make or beg a few sous and surely come back to the eating house and buy their food there. And if they were able to steal something, the owner would certainly be ready to take it too. It wasn't that the owner had suddenly turned her establishment into a house of charity.

Based on their appearances and clothes, these thirteen

people were not from the city. They came from the country because they couldn't find enough work there to have two meals a day. The capital attracts and corrupts them. When they left the country, they did not realize that they would find themselves in such a plight. They were confident that they would get work they could be proud of. They must have exposed themselves to the sun and rain as they begged for a sou or a bowl of rice on the road before they reached Hanoi.

Dear Readers, just imagine Hanoi: street after street. And think of a very clumsy peasant lost in its labyrinth. Each street has houses, sidewalks, and footpaths, which means they all look alike and the roads appear to be never-ending. A peasant goes on and on and on; he feels exhausted and stops. He's hungry but he can't eat, because he has no money. He wants to rest but can't lie down, because he can't pay for shelter.

He is tired but he must go on. Gradually, he can't go any further. Unfortunately, he is not allowed to stop in the city, and he must go on, wandering from one street to the next, sometimes going around in circles without knowing it. Reaching an intersection, he sees a crowd of people. Seeing that most in the crowd are originally from the country, he stops. A smart-looking old woman, her ears heavy with golden ear-rings, has the appearance of someone who is very 'powerful', as she waves her arms, beckoning the peasant to stop. She speaks in a loud voice: 'Hey, where are you going, looking so haggard like that? Do you want some work? Come over here, hurry up!'

The peasant is very pleased, because it's the first time he's met a city person who wants to talk to him. But to talk about what? She says compassionately that she'll get him some work! Then, for the first few days, he has some food as he lies around waiting in the courtyard of an eating house or at the side of a theatre. Generally speaking, all the peasants who come to the city have a story like that. How many intersections does the capital have? How many positions does it have for the destitute people who want to join the servants' trade? How many similar tragedies could one count in the capital each day?

These thirteen people, the reason they've ended up here is because they are like moths to a flame who have been dazzled by the light of the capital.

The owner of the eating house has taken them in illicitly and let them stay in a corner of the courtyard. During the day, they go and display themselves at the crossroads. While they are waiting for work, they gradually eat the few sous they have left. Then comes the day when their pockets are empty: they still haven't got work; no one has given them half a sou or a bowl of rice gruel as alms. It's now necessary for them to risk their lives, and some will take big risks. The women fall into the abyss of lust, the men into the punishment of the law. And, now, before going that far, they lie waiting calmly for the tempest of tomorrow.

If they never get any work, the fault doesn't lie in heaven, in you, Dear Readers, or in me. In fact, no one is to blame! There is no reason why people have to keep a servant.

The light of the capital.

Perhaps on nights when there are no moon and stars, the peasants in Nam Dinh, Thai Binh, Hai Duong, Bac Ninh, Son Tay, and Hoa Binh go out into their courtyards and see a shining halo each time they turn their heads and look far-off into a corner of the sky. There, hovering over a thousand years of culture and glowing with easy riches, what the peasants see is the halo over Hanoi, and they are still leaving their villages for it! Soon they too will be able to lie in the corner of a courtyard with a stinking drain, with the smell of chicken shit, and human shit. They too will have to lie curled up starving as they look into the heavens on a night like tonight when bright moonbeams fill the sky.

7
A Tragicomedy

While I was deep in thought about such stupid peasants, I suddenly saw another two young maids arrive. One was wearing a short skirt and carrying a small basket, her short hair was dishevelled, and she waddled like a fat duck. Although the other one was more properly dressed and her face looked cleaner, she had the air of a simpleton. She didn't look as if she had lived in the city before.

The two of them were moving around, not knowing where to sit. I said to the old woman: 'Please make room for those two to lie down.'

The old woman did this and started to fan them like a mother who is spoiling her children.

It came to my mind that I should entertain this 'audience' to keep them awake, by singing folk-songs and reciting popular poems. This seemed to interest them very much, and make them laugh.

The two girls laughed more loudly than anyone else, like silly women, reminding me of French Fou Rire [Mad Laughter] comedy records.

However, the simple-looking one suddenly released her arms from around the shoulder of her friend and fell down face up. It was as though she had been thunderstruck.

Dear Readers, I thought she had fallen in love with me. This is what people call *le coup de foudre* [the thunderbolt or love at first sight].

I was waiting for her to sit up, blushing and embarrassed.

The others were expecting the same.

But after she fell, she didn't move.

She looked dead!

A few people ran up to her to see what had happened. I did too. Alas, it turned out she was having an epileptic fit!

Her eyes rolled so you could only see their whites. Her arms and legs trembled violently. She frothed at the mouth. The laughing had affected her nervous system.

I was very worried and alarmed. Around me, people were making suggestions: she's caught a cold, food poisoning, a heart attack, death. The old woman was on the point of crying out also. I tried to explain what was happening and told everyone to remain calm. I chased two of the young boys down off the hardwood planks to make space for the girl who was having a fit to lie down.

'It's nothing, in a moment she'll be over her fit!' So saying, I sat down beside her, undecided about what to do next next.

The maid wearing the skirt explained: 'She's acted like this since the time she was electrocuted.'

'When was she electrocuted?'

'About four or five months ago.'

'How do you know?'

'I'm related to her.'

'How was she electrocuted?'

'She hung some clothes out to dry on a balcony.'

'And what happened?'

'She actually hung them wet on a power line.'

Hearing this, my hair stood on end. I quickly asked: 'How could she be so stupid?'

'She'd just come from the country and didn't know anything.'

'Why didn't her master or mistress warn her to be careful?'

'I don't know.'

'How strong was the electric shock?'

The young girl's tongue slipped out of her mouth in fright. She waited for a moment and said: 'Once she'd put her hands on the power line, she couldn't release her grip. She was hanging half over the balcony, dangling half inside it. It took people a while to get her off the power line.'

Suddenly, a feeling of great sorrow came over me. I turned and looked down at the face of that poor little girl, then sighed and asked: 'Did the master dismiss her when she began to have the fits?'

'Naturally.'

'I suppose that means she hasn't been working since then?'

'No. After that, she went to work in another house which she only left two days ago.'

'Why did she leave?'

'She had a fit when she was carrying a precious vase. She dropped and broke it, and, when the master demanded compensation, she took fright and ran away.'

'What an idiot. If her master demanded compensation, she could have had it deducted from her wages, couldn't she? Running away like that, she could be sued and end up in jail.'

'The vase was worth over 100 piastres, and, even if she worked herself to the bone, she still couldn't pay it back. Also, if she didn't have any wages, she'd have no money to send back to the village.'

I felt disgusted and said vaguely: 'Ah, the damned fate of a servant! What a miserable life!'

The fellow with the bald head said: 'That's for sure!'

'And you! Are you a servant too?'

'Of course!'

'Have you just come out of jail or have you just returned from some pestilent region with an illness that's sent you as bald as that?'

'Out of jail.'

'Why did you go to jail?'

'My boss told me to carry some illegal opium, a French policeman caught me, and the boss didn't acknowledge his part.'

'Why did you become a servant?'

'A dike burst, my house and belongings and buffaloes and

bulls were all washed away. My wife went to work as a wet-nurse and didn't return. I went out looking for her for a long time but couldn't find her, and I had to pull a rickshaw. I eventually found her, but, then, unfortunately, I had to go to prison.'

Next came the turn of the fellow with the plasters on his neck: 'I became a servant because my family was poor.'

The little boy coughing with tuberculosis chimed in: 'I've also been a servant these last four or five years. My father died, my mother married again, and I lived with my aunt who scolded me too much, so it was better I went out to make a living. My aunt was very rich with three or four brick houses. If she'd been kind, I could have depended on her, but she wasn't, so that was it.'

Next, turning to the old woman, I asked: 'And you, Madam, do you have any children here?'

She pointed to three young boys sitting beside her and said: 'These are my three grandchildren here. I've been taking them around looking for their father who also pulls a rickshaw. I heard he was in Hanoi, but after looking all around for him, we didn't see him. We also went up to Quanh Thanh and were told to go down to Hang Bo, and when we asked there, they said to go down to Bach Mai.'

'And how much money do you have on you, Madam?'

'I've still got 6 sous.'

The old woman said that calmly, as though she wasn't worried about a thing. I suppose that people like her who had reached such a state had to be philosophical to survive. Only others worried for them and thought that their suffering was worthy of compassion.

I asked another little boy: 'And you, why did you also become a servant?'

'My mother made me.'

'And what about you, you little devil, who hired you?'

'Many masters. I've only been a servant for three months, but I've already tasted rice in eight or nine houses.'

'And what about you over there, my boy, are you poor too?'

'I don't know.'

'Where is your father?'

'I don't know.'

'Where's your mother?'

'I don't know.'

'Where's your village?'

'I've never had one!'

He didn't know anything. He was only about eight years old at the most.

'So have you been a servant yet?'

'Once. The master thought I was a brat, and after hiring me for five days sent me away.'

'When are you going to work again?'

'Who knows; it depends on the old woman.'

'Which old woman?'

'The one who takes people to sit out at the crossroads.'

At this point, the girl who had the fit woke up. She forced herself to sit up and spat out all over the place the stagnant saliva she had in her mouth. She lay down again looking very tired.

A moment later, we could hear the sound of sharp footsteps approaching us in the courtyard.

A police inspector wearing a shirt made of local silk, a felt hat, Western shoes, and with bicycle clips around his trouser legs, stepped briskly towards us. A 'modern' woman wearing golden bracelets followed behind him.

The policeman came up to us, switched on a torch, and shone it on each of our faces. The 'modern' woman then called out: 'That's her there.'

The policeman said: 'Which one?'

'The young one wearing those trousers.'

The girl cried out: 'I beg you, Miss, I have been very stupid, please forgive me.'

The policeman snapped: 'Stand up and come with us.'

The modern woman grumbled: 'So you think 200 or 300 piastres is nothing, do you?'

The policeman asked: 'Why did you tell me it was only a few piastres?'

'That's what she stole. As well as that, she broke an antique vase.'

The girl cried out: 'I beg you, Miss, I haven't stolen so much as a sou.'

'Be quiet! Shut up! If you didn't steal anything, why did you run away?'

The policeman put a pair of handcuffs on the girl, and the modern woman said to him: 'Here, search in this basket.'

'No. It's mine,' I said.

'Go ahead and search it!'

At this point, I stood up, with my face probably revealing my indignation. The policeman said: 'Show me your identity card.'

I hesitated before giving it to him. After he had finished looking at my photo—fortuitously, the office issuing identity cards in Hanoi photographs everyone, as though they are prisoners—he was a little sceptical. He stood with his head down thinking, as though trying to remember something, then returned my card after he'd looked me over a few times.

I will never be able to forget the moment the young epileptic was handcuffed and the slap she got in the back of the neck from the modern woman.

When the young girl was dragged off, the people in the eating house ran out to see what was going on.

I turned around and, looking at the group of humble servants behind me, I saw that they had all gone pale and were scared for their lives.

8

The Servants Denounce Their Masters

The matter of a stupid girl being electrocuted, having epileptic fits, breaking a vase, being unjustly accused of stealing, and also being arrested was imprinted deeply in my thoughts.

At such a time, the little people who lived the lives of bees and ants did not feel discouraged about crying out over injustice. These people who were contented with the leftovers and soup dregs still felt that they were human beings. A young boy who had been beaten to the extent that he no longer had daydreams, when he went to the water-pump to collect water, he could still be angry and cry out roughly at the thought that he was treated as worthless.

The God who created the myriad species couldn't have told quacks not to boast, those smitten with syphilis not to cry and moan, room-boys not to despise guests as rubbish, monks not to dream of dog meat, and, just so, he could not have told the servants to refrain from denouncing their masters.

The boy with tuberculosis described the following scene: 'The first time I went to work as a servant, it was an unfortunate experience. When the mistress haggled over the wage, she agreed to pay me 50 sous a month. I had to fill three water-tanks and cut a lot of firewood. I filled the tanks, piled the fire wood up in the kitchen, yet the mistress looked for excuses to scold me all day. She did it to make me quit, and it was so unbearable. I asked to leave. Then the mistress conveniently complained: "There have been no problems and you ask to leave!" She continued saying that people like me could never advance, even if we worked all our lives. Of course, she didn't pay me. You know, all the masters are the same. When they need you, they look for you, when there's no more work, they find an excuse to kick you out without paying you.'

I asked him if there had been any happy days during the time he was a servant.

'Only once. Last year I worked for a young couple. The husband was a clerk. He never came home before 3 a.m. Each night when he came back late, and I had opened the door to let him in, he instructed me to break a bowl or a plate, so that he had an excuse to shout noisily at me. He did that to deflect his wife's complaints. At the end of the month, when his wife deducted the money from my salary to pay for the breakages, the husband reimbursed me. Later on, the wife started gambling. She went out all day. Before her husband came back from work, she gave me the money to buy rice soup and other dishes from the Chinese restaurant. This included anniversary and memorial days, when she told me to go out to buy food from the restaurant, even such special ritual offerings as sticky rice and the green bean sweets. Therefore, I slept all day and didn't have to do anything. Working with masters and mistresses like that was very pleasant.'

The man with the bald head interrupted him. 'That was pleasant enough, I suppose, but not as pleasant as in my case. When I first came to the city, I worked for an old building contractor. When we discussed the job, I was supposed to pull a rickshaw, but later on I didn't have to pull it much. I only had to walk his dogs in the street. He bought three Japanese dogs, each costing about 100 piastres and they had to be fed on beef and soup. All I had to do all day was bathe them. The only problem was that, being too eccentric, the old bastard told me to wipe the dogs' arses with paper.'

The young boy with tuberculosis said: 'But that wasn't a good job at all!'

The bald man kept us waiting for some time as he considered

his reply, then continued: 'The old man took good care of the dog, but didn't treat his father kindly. His father was dressed in poor brown peasant clothes like me, and he also had to bend over all day, working in the garden. Once, when the old contractor cursed and beat me, I was so angry, I thought of a way to get back at him: I put dog shit on the bench in the kitchen where his father slept. The old father was caught in the trap and, taking a long pipe, he immediately lashed out at the dogs. I reported this to my master, who cursed his father and his father's ancestors. From that day, I could totally ignore my master's father. Don't you think it was a good job?'

I asked: 'Why didn't you stay at that house for the rest of your life?'

The bald man replied: 'Well, I told you that the old master sent me to carry illegal opium and I was caught.'

'Because your master didn't acknowledge his part, you had to go to prison, didn't you?'

'Yes. If he'd owned up, it would have been the end of him. Prison would have killed him. Unfortunately, it was my fate. Without that incident, I could have stayed on; the master was kind enough to me.'

The man with the plasters on his neck joined in: 'Yes, your job was quite good, but not as good as mine. Nowadays, I look ugly because I'm not well, but when I started as a servant, I was very handsome, and I had a better lot than all of you. All the fortune-tellers had predicted that I would have a rich love life, and it was true. I was in a better position than all of you, because occasionally the mistress or her daughter fell in love with me.'

He then gave us a very detailed account of all his luck in an extremely sincere voice.

A few hours before that, I had been standing there hesitantly asking myself what I was going to do with this mob.

Now I am wondering what I am going to do with their stories.

Really, they are all very bizarre, all so crude and senseless that no one will dare to believe them.

The little boy didn't know how to invent his story like a writer, and so his story should be 90 per cent true.

Facing truth that is not normally considered worth writing down on paper, we find ourselves frightened and astounded by humanity.

Novels tell us things that people say is fiction.

In life, on the other hand, there are things that a novel wouldn't want to report.

And so I started despising humanity, because I came to believe that not one of us is able to see clearly the reality of life.

There are really so many books about human beings which aim to teach us about each other, and, yet, they are all to no avail. All the things people learn from books.... They are vague, mistaken, literary. Literature is one thing, life is another.

So now I would like to become a sociologist, a psychologist, a philosopher, but first I should become a humble servant! A rickshaw puller knows all the cruelty of human beings far better than a scholar. A room-boy knows more about the debauchery of humanity than a surgeon. A servant understands more clearly the behaviour of human beings than a realist writer.

If anyone wants to curse me for the above thoughts, then I can tell you that before he became a great thinker, a great writer, and a great man, Jean Jacques Rousseau had lived the life of a humble servant.

Perhaps his greatness comes from that?

9
I Am Me

Dear Readers, I'm now myself again.

Giving up the short-sleeved peach-coloured shirt, the local satin trousers, dark glasses, and long hair with side-burns, I'm now wearing my own clothes, and I can converse with you as a 'decent' person.

Now I am in the master's position, judging the servants.

I can invent stories that you will believe, or I can tell you true stories that you will think I have made up.

I can tell the story of my wet-nurse, the one who often reported me to my parents, beat me, and threatened me with ghost stories, but, fortunately, she died a long time ago.

I can also tell you the story of a young boy servant that I used to keep, because I liked his amusing manner. Whenever visitors came, I would call him out to give them the opportunity to hear his funny staccato speech.

'You don't have any brothers and sisters, do you?'

'Me only!'

'Do you still have your parents, uncles, and aunts?'

'No one!'

'Before they died, why didn't your parents get you a wife?'

'Not married.'

All my friends split their sides laughing as though they were watching a Charlie Chaplin film.

I was able to berate him for the fact that when he first came to the city, he looked so dumb, but a few months later he became a petty thief and cheated like a devil.

So, you see, I am able to provide you, Dear Readers, with any number of examples of what happens in the world of your humble servants.

But after he'd finished reading this thick manuscript, the editor, Le Trang Kieu, wrinkled his face.

He said: 'If you go on like this, you'll be lost.'

'Lost?'

He said: 'Yes, you're describing the seamy side of life here. This kind of writing was in vọgue a few years ago in the period when Hoang Tich Chu was famous.'

I didn't know what to say.

'The only difference now is in the new form of reportage. And the things you denounce in this story, they are the truths we should avoid.'

'But we have promised the readers that we will. . . .'

'That promise has already been fulfilled in what you've written. To publish more is to exceed the promise. Also, when one accepts that one is a realist writer, it already means promising a lot. And it is not only in one reportage that one can keep one's promise.'

So, then, we kept hesitating about whether or not we should publish all the truthful passages in the story.

Fortunately, we met the well-known writer, Mr Nguyen Cong Hoan.

He talked about literature and he touched on this reportage about humble servants.

He talked about both bad masters and bad servants.

During the conversation, I said that to write a reportage about the way the masters treat their servants is easy because there is a lot of material, especially about when the masters are cruel.

I hadn't finished talking when Mr Nguyen Cong Hoan laughed cunningly and said: 'We should investigate ourselves!'

At that stage, I didn't know what else to say to Mr Hoan.

But, now, I can tell all of you, my Dear Readers, that you should investigate yourselves.

If I have forgotten something, then please write your own reportage.

Days of Childhood

NGUYEN HONG

NGUYEN HONG is the pen-name of Nguyen Nguyen Hong, who was born into a petty bourgeois family in Nam Dinh on 5 November 1918. His father died early and left the family in great poverty. Hong had to leave school and, while his young mother went away to try and earn a living, he became a hungry orphan who hung around the markets and fell in with vagabonds. This life led to trouble and to ill-treatment in various jails in Nam Dinh, Hanoi, and the Tri Cu Children's Prison at Phuc Yen.

Unemployed for much of his youth, he often expected to die. At the same time, he started to write obsessively, day and night, regardless of 'the exhausting, extremely penetrating hunger on cold deserted rainy nights'. The two works that established his reputation as a major exponent of the realist trend were *Bi vo* [The Down-and-Out], which won the Self-reliance Literary Group's award for the best 'reportage novel' in 1937, and the remarkable autobiography *Nhung ngay tho au* [Days of Childhood], which was first published in *Ngay Nay* [Today] in 1938. In these works, humanism and Christianity already shape his social critique. He understood and empathized with the lower classes, but petty bourgeois characters played a central role in his work. This reflected his early family background and was necessary for him to play out the theme that haunted him most: not simply the poverty about which many had written, but the actual process of downward social mobility.

Around 1937, he became involved in left-wing political activities and in 1938, he joined a Democratic Youth Group. He wrote for the left-wing papers *The gioi* [The World] and *Nguoi moi* [The New Person] and was an early member of the radical National Salvation Culture Association. In 1939, he was arrested for political activities, and a 300-page manuscript novel about his life in Tri Cu Children's Prison was confiscated by the secret police. He somehow continued to write in the Bac Me concentration camp in Ha Giang. This was at the foot of a tamarind tree which overlooked a deserted landscape of mountains and valleys through which the wind howled.

During the Franco-Viet Minh War, he followed the Viet Minh, and a number of short stories in his 1946 anthology, *Lo lua va dia nguc* [Hell and Flames], tell of mass struggles which preceded the August 1945 uprising. After 1954, he stayed in the north and, still obsessed with the process of downward social mobility, continued to write about the old society, most notably in his 1961 novel, *Song gam* [The Roar of the Waves]. He published his memoirs, *Buoc duong viet van cua toi* [My Path to Writing], in 1971. He died in 1982.

For my mother

The Sound of the Bugle

My father was a prison warder, and my mother came from a family of traders. When they met, my father was over thirty, twice my mother's age. They did not marry because they knew each other and were in love, but because of their parents. On one side, my father's family had money and few grandchildren. On the other, my mother's parents were afraid of the danger of keeping a beautiful girl who had reached the age of marriage in their house. Rather than see her run away with a lover, they wanted her to have a secure position in a family that would treat her well if she had children.

I was born, and many parents and relations of well-known criminals came to welcome me into the world; so many people who were dependent on my grandparents came to visit too. Gold and silver objects, pieces of silk, fragrant rice, fat chickens, fresh eggs, fresh fish from the ocean, trays and bundles and baskets and dozens of things that were jammed into the closet and the pantry. The servants were satisfied and pleased at the good fate that saw them employed in such a rich and powerful household.

Later, each time my grandmother recalled my happy birthday in a rasping voice that was sometimes interrupted by the sound of her dry coughing, I felt very moved.

This was because I remembered the past with regret. My mother and father had not married because of love for each other: I understood that bitter incongruity well and was deeply aware of it from the age of seven or eight, that is to say, the age when one's curiosity is very easily excited, when images and sentiments are indelibly printed on a child's impressionable mind.

It was on cold wintry afternoons, afternoons when the rain fell in a fine drizzle and seemed to be whispering an entreaty to the whirr of the wind, that the flames leapt brilliantly from the charcoal brazier at the foot of the wall, sparkling red and drawing our minds into a region of sadness that was most desolate for my mother. This was even when she had me sitting on her lap, playing happily with my dolls; even when she could smell the aroma of various dishes commingling in the steam of the fragrant rice that wafted up in front of her face; even when she occasionally smiled warmly and always talked with graceful respect to my father.

At that time, how could my father know what thoughts and images tormented my mother's mind! Her pretty face, her clear voice, her sweetness and deference, how could they belong to a woman whose thoughts were always frozen by grief and the bitterest, blackest sorrow?

Perhaps my father was acting the same as my mother: being warm and attentive to hide a suffering soul. Perhaps that was the right thing to do! If my father had been a person without a conscience, one who acted lightly and only enjoyed the beauty and softness of my mother, then he would not have suffered in silence and looked at me with his mouth slanted to one side when I clung to his shoulders and shook him and asked: 'Father, my little sister, Que, is not your child, is she? She's the child of the Superintendent, Mr H, isn't she?' When she heard me ask that question, my mother's eyes would suddenly become bright, and her cheeks would flush a little. She would look around at my father, then turn her face away, or lower her head and look down at me.

Good heavens! That was a foolish question. What would have happened if my father were a cruel, jealous, or indignant man, and my mother had suddenly become ashamed and afraid because someone had prompted her child to utter words that sullied her life and her role as a wife!

Nothing happened! My mother and father only looked at each other quietly, while I continued to wheedle my mother, pushing myself on to her warm lap.

* * *

My suspicion that Que was the child of another man, Superintendent H, was never explained.

When I asked my father, he kept silent. The times I was being hugged and petted by my mother were the ones when I was prompted to ask her that question, and, just like my father, she only looked at me silently. But her eyes glowed and seemed to light up her egg-shell-smooth complexion with an effect that was completely different from the flicker in my father's deep dark eyes. And, at those times, my mother would put her cheek against my hair and lightly stroke a strand of it between two fingers.

Not feeling deterred, I continued to put the question to my two aunts and two cousins, my grandmother, and the neighbours. My aunts and cousins didn't answer, although that made sense. But what really didn't make sense was that, while they heard me ask so often, my grandmother and the people next door either ignored or scolded me: it was those same people who had put the idea into my mind.

Once my grandmother called me to her, hugged me, rubbed her head against mine, and asked: 'Who gave birth to you?'

Seeing a red paper bag full of cakes and sweet-smelling lollies in my grandmother's hand, I replied endearingly: 'Grandmother gave birth to me.'

My grandmother smiled and slapped me lightly on the cheek: 'Damn you, you are being cheeky. No!'

'All right, I'm my father's child, aren't I, Grandmother?'

My grandmother scowled at me affectionately for a long moment, then asked: 'What does your father do?'

'He is a warder at the jail.'

Still with a sweet tone, my grandmother asked: 'And Que, whose child is she?'

I was a little angry because I wanted very much to sample my grandmother's sweets, but had not yet been able to. I turned my head to one side, tilted my neck, and said in a sulky voice: 'I don't know.'

My grandmother tapped me lightly on the cheek: 'Don't be silly! Tell me, you naughty little boy, then I'll give you a lolly.'

But I wasn't foolish enough to hold back and get nothing to eat. I immediately pulled down a little the hand in which my grandmother held a cake and said: 'Que is also my father's child.'

But I was disappointed. My grandmother snorted and changed her expression: 'Not so.'

Feeling extremely angry, I screamed: 'If she's not Father's child, whose child is she? You don't give me anything; I don't care.'

With this, I pulled myself from my grandmother's arms and was on the point of running off when she took out a cake, broke off half, and gave it to me, and then held me tightly between her knees.

'I said she's not your father's child, and that's the case.'

I was not in a hurry to take a bite of the cake and tried to provoke my grandmother into saying more. My suspicions had been greatly aroused.

I said that Que was my father's daughter because she had a nanny who looked after her and gave her cow's milk which was an honour and a great treat for her. I had no idea that my grandmother arranged for the nanny because she did not want my mother to have to look after my little sister. She wanted her to devote herself slavishly to me and be a mother who was imprisoned by the austerity of old family customs. My grandmother again rubbed my head and smiled. The smile made her dry flabby lips move and split open without any hint of happiness.

'No, Que is the child of that fellow. . . .'

I was astounded. I opened my eyes wide, and shook my grandmother's arm: 'You're telling fibs, Grandmother, so you won't have to give me the rest of those lollies. She is the child of my father.'

My grandmother's eyebrows knitted sluggishly above her brown eyes, but her voice was still sweet and graceful: 'No, I've told you the truth about that, she's not the child of your father, she's the child of. . . .'

My grandmother hesitated for a moment and stared into my eyes: 'Do you know the Superintendent, Mr H?'

I shook my head. My grandmother looked severe: 'He's the person who leads the soldiers to the prison every afternoon and blows that bugle.'

I called out noisily: 'I know the one!'

But I didn't want to know any more about whether my little sister was really the child of my father or the child of the man who blew that bugle. Seeing that my grandmother's attention had lapsed, I immediately snatched a cake and ran out of the house.

Another time, I was at the foot of the lilac tree, in front of the kitchen built with broken bricks and burning firewood that came from the branches of that tree and dried leaves nearby. I was being held in the arms of a woman who had come to borrow some money from my mother. At first, I was absorbed in playing with a small cat in front of me and did not pay attention to the conversation between that woman and the other one, a neighbour, who was many years older, wearing shantung silk pants, a white bib, a torn silk blouse, and a blue belt. When the cat got angry because I had twisted its tail too hard, it clawed me and ran off, and I began to listen to the women. As she spoke, the woman holding me laughed all the time. The other woman did the same. Many times they looked at me together, with their eyes shining, and laughed heartily.

Although I was small, I still knew how to feel anger, and their conversation made me feel it to the point of pain. Yet I had to be quiet. I don't know what force kept hold of me and stopped me from jumping up and arguing with them or cursing them. These two women criticized all the neighbours and dug up dirt about them until they were bored with that. Then, they slowly analysed all the trifling details of my parents' lives. On the one hand, my father was harsh with a very cunning appearance. On the other hand, my mother was too quick to condemn my grandmother's unavoidable vices: wasn't it because women of my grandmother's age had learned to live with prejudices and cruel customs, and wasn't it because they thought education was unsuitable for women and freedom was sinful, that they tended to oppress and persecute others when they had the power and opportunity to do so?

Finally, the voice of one of the women was suddenly lowered. She pointed to a soldier not carrying a rifle who was walking backwards and forwards in front of the prison. Then she whispered to her old friend who was chewing on a mouthful of betel-nut: 'This boy's little sister is *his* child.'

* * *

Each afternoon it was the same, whether it was boiling hot or wet and cold: that soldier's blue-belted squad would pass my house. Exactly twenty men would pass, wearing yellow uniforms in summer, purple woollen ones in winter. They went barefoot with leggings, and wore peaked brass helmets. The three men at the head of each file in the column all wore stripes the colour of plum flowers on their sleeves. The stripes were wider than chopsticks. Going along in the same rank as these three men, a pace to the right, was a man of medium height, with a healthy complexion, bright eyes, and a slightly high bridge on his nose. His teeth were as white as snow.

He was dressed most neatly of all. He wore two golden stripes on a large red embroidered patch. Not carrying a rifle, he held with poise a tasselled bugle, and, each time he raised it, golden rays shimmered in the brilliant sunlight of the summer afternoon.

Each time the squad approached my house near the gate of the jail, the bugle would play happily, grandiosely. Drowning out all the noise of the bayonet scabbards slapping on thighs and the stamping of marching feet, the sound of the bugle rose higher each minute into a resounding blast that shook the calm air in our corner of the sky. Then, leaning on the sound of the wind rustling in the clumps of sparse lilac, the exciting sound of the bugle rolled higher and higher, and spread further and further to remote shining regions. It became warmer and warmer like longing, touching words. In a second, it reached its crescendo. Silence.

A moment later, a different group of soldiers marched out of the prison gate, and the same bugler led them. This time, the rhythm of the bugle's sound was faster than before, in time with the step of the retiring squad that was very hungry and looking forward to food and rest.

Marching on, footsteps, footsteps, like a wave of small leaves born on the wind. The eager sound of the bugle was still clear, vibrating in the wide open sky.

Behind the squad of soldiers, a group of women and children ran with short steps. On their backs, babies bobbed up and down as though they were riding horses.

A little way past my house, the sound of the bugle gradually built up again and rose high into the air. By the time the squad and the band of women and children had passed the thick garden on the corner, we could no longer see them and the sound of the bugle also stopped completely.

The afternoon wind suddenly rose in long shrieks, and the clouds hurtled across the dome of the sky where the clear sound of the bugle no longer rippled.

My mother, who had been holding my hand, suddenly released it and stepped down off the brick veranda and went out into the street.

In my surprise, I clung to the panel of my mother's tunic and called out in alarm: 'Mother, Mother, wait for me... Mother!'

* * *

How many afternoons were like that? There were hundreds! I can't say exactly how many; I only remember that there were many times when my mother led me into the front courtyard to greet the passing squads of soldiers who made noisy bustling sounds. Then, quite a while later, she would lead me back inside.

My mother stood in the bright warm light outside, or in the cold wind with the rain flying under the roof of the veranda. How many gentle afternoons passed; ones which somehow left an impression on my innocent mind, although without exact details? But in my heart and soul, always, always very vivid was the clear image of my mother's sparkling eyes and blushing cheeks as she looked at the man who blew the bugle, and his shining eyes looked back. And how will I ever be able to forget the strange sensation it caused me when my mother's trembling hand slipped from my shoulder, and a delicate chill dimmed her eyes, suddenly turning my chest cold. Then, the pleading voice: 'Don't get in Mother's way all the time! OK ... you go on, I'll follow you ... child.'

* * *

But one afternoon, I can't remember clearly whether it was a bright or a dark one, my mother did not take me into the courtyard. From that afternoon, there was only me running out in short steps to see the squad of soldiers going past with a different bugler. Many times, hearing the joyous sound of the bugle, I ran into the house, grabbed my mother's hand, and tugged it hard, trying to pull her outside. But my mother either released my hand and turned her face to the wall, or, if it suited her mood, pulled me to her bosom and hugged me tight, with her heartbeat strongly pounding my ear-drum, and the heat from her heaving chest transmitting some pleasant warm sensations to my flesh.

At those times, my eyes were dimmed by my mother's hot breath.

* * *

Que was my father's child—my cousins, my aunts, my grandmother, and the neighbours all said that. After the day the bugler was transferred to a place we did not know, my mother served my grandmother all the more respectfully, treated my father all the more considerately, and took good care of me and my sister. But from that day, I rarely saw my parents having a happy discussion together, except those times in front of my grandmother or some other very close person.

Until the time my little sister grew up, it was the same: my mother and father never looked affectionately at each other, never spoke warmly, or laughed happily together with bright smiles. The looks, words, and laughter of my parents were always tinged with subtle bitterness. Quiet pain always accompanied their memory of those ridiculous, shameful nights—I believe it wasn't many—when they had unwillingly slept together to continue a family line which had been maintained in obscurity for so many generations under an oppressive regime of rites and customs. In order to avoid hurting two children, one boy, one girl, who had the good fortune of being born into a wealthy family with few children, the parents also had to appear to be all the more close and fond of each other, and so lived lives of great hypocrisy.

Lord Have Mercy on Us!

The house was sold! My grandfather's two-storey brick house in Jules Ferry Street, Nam Dinh, which he had left to my father as the ancestral house was now gone.

That year, back in the twenties, I remember it clearly. Money was still easy and so the house was sold for a good price: 1,900 piastres. This was also because it was in the centre of a busy commercial area with pawnshops, numerous enterprises importing and exporting rice, and many of the most crowded restaurants. If it had not been so well located, its value would have been lower, and we would have found it harder to sell. It was a narrow house with few windows and no courtyard, the parapet on the second floor was made of wood, and its owner, who didn't eat or sleep, was being driven to despair by a looming deadline on some huge debts he had to pay.

My grandfather died early, the year in which my father had not yet married my mother. My grandmother had given birth to eighteen children. But, one by one, almost all of them had died.

Some were stillborn! Some died when they could jabber 'ba ba'; some when they were running around naked in the street, neglected by an overworked mother with so much to do! With more children than a flock of ducks, only three survived: my father and my two aunts.

So it only took two weeks to arrange the sale, and the house fell into the hands of different people. However, even before the day that my father's older and younger sisters had to sign the final deed with my grandmother before receiving 150 piastres each from the lawyer, my family had never been in agreement.

My father said with feeling to my grandmother: 'Those two are crafty. They are girls who are fortunate to have been born in this era. I have already given each of them about 100 piastres, and so I have not been unjust. Yet they still find fault with everything and threaten not to sign. I'm not just anyone; if they are too arrogant, I'll hand full power over to the court!'

My grandmother smacked her lips, and said to my father in a wounded tone: 'It's up to you, do what you want. Those two girls have both got husbands: one a clerk, one who trades in thousands. What can they do with an insignificant 200 that you give them like that? If you want them to sign and accept the money, you must talk properly to them, not scold and roar like that! I beg you, don't use your position as the eldest son to refer the matter to judges and lawyers. I can assure you that others will take advantage of the situation and split all the money up until the house is completely lost.'

Listening to my grandmother speak, my father's face turned increasingly pale.

'You have great strength and broad shoulders; you are well educated; you have sufficient capacity to perform all manner of tasks, to earn a living in order to support your wife and children; but me, I'm already over seventy. A few years ago I was still fit and strong, still able to do business, but from now on, what can I do to make money? How will I be able to afford food and drink, medicine, contributions for festivals, for the New Year celebrations? If God allows me to live a little longer and my funeral is put off for a year, two years, or five, or ten, if I can't rely on my son and daughters, I can only rely on the sale of the house and that's all. To lose 1 sou will make me suffer. To lose 1 piastre will cut my insides. But to lose tens and hundreds of piastres, it would be better if you took a knife and murdered me slowly.'

My grandmother cried, then held her face, and wailed: 'Don't make me suffer so much. Don't be too sure of yourself. All of a sudden, you've stopped working for the government; you've also brought an opium-lamp home and smoke day and night … then suddenly you pawn the plans of the house for 500 or 700 piastres on which you pay a monthly interest of 30 per cent so that you can go to Saigon, spend money all over town, thinking that this will get you a high position, and it turns out that you remain unemployed and addicted to opium!'

The sound of her crying became louder and louder, and, from two dark holes in her face, tears flooded over her cheekbones down two wrinkled hollows like a bursting dam. As she cried, my grandmother yelled the names of my grandfather and father and went on and on complaining about them.

The gloomy life of an ordinary Annamese woman had passed quickly, but painfully, as the prolonged, hoarse wailing of my grandmother testified: 'From the moment I left my mother's womb, I had to bear injustice being brought up among my brothers; as I grew up, I was confused by the training I received from so many members of the family: from my grandparents, father, uncles, and relatives until I was seventeen or eighteen, when I became a wizened girl, always afraid, shy, and withdrawn. Next, I went to my husband's house with feelings of resignation and abject submission that choked my personality as they became stronger each day.

'After about three or four years of being a daughter-in-law, I was elevated to the status of a mother, then, after that, a grandmother. Old age and the years of decline had arrived. But then there was a little security and happiness. Old age was a time of disengagement from the life of ill-treatment, ignorance, and darkness that would be suffered by the members of the next generation as they dragged out their lives to the last minute. And when that Annamese woman dies, she will die beside a high-quality coffin that was already made ten years ago, beside the pile of scented wedding clothes that have maintained their folds from the time she stepped into her husband's house ... dies in the doleful mourning of the daughters, daughter-in-law, and family acquaintances.'

My father stood up and went inside, leaving my grandmother raving. I climbed on to the bed, shook my grandmother's shoulders, and said in tears: 'Grandmother, Grandmother, stop crying! Father will sell this house and build another one.'

A sobbing voice answered: 'He'll buy a few more opium trays! Your father is killing me.'

I shook my grandmother's shoulder harder.

'When I grow up, I'll go to school, I'll go to work, and I'll build one. Grandmother, please stop crying.'

My grandmother looked up at me. She lifted her bony hands covered with skin like dry parchment and pushed her white hair back. Tears were running down the side of her face, down to the back of her neck.

A month later, the rent expired and we had to move to another place. It was the twenty-third or twenty-fourth of the twelfth month. It was a dry cold morning. Along the street, except for the betel-nut stalls and crowded pawnshops, all the houses had been thoroughly cleaned and the doors were shut with red parallel sentences hung out on display.

Formerly, in peaceful years, people celebrated the New Year very early!

* * *

Early one morning I woke up all of a sudden. I felt cold, and my feet and my hands felt lighter. I sat up and rubbed my eyes to see: the mosquito net had been rolled up and the blanket had been pushed into a rumpled pile at the corner of the bed. My father, who always allowed me to sleep with my head in the crook of his arm, was not lying there.

'Daddy! Daddy!'

I called out louder and louder. My grandmother and mother got out of bed and followed me into the garden. My younger sister came along too.

'What's the matter, Hong?'

I looked at my grandmother, crying: 'Where's my Daddy gone?'

My grandmother scolded me loudly: 'He must have gone to the toilet. Don't cry.'

I pushed the toilet door: 'Grandmother, where is he?'

My grandmother took my hand and dragged me inside: 'Stop crying. Perhaps your father has gone to buy opium.'

I ran into the room and couldn't see the opium tray which was usually put on top of the trunk at the back of the bed. I couldn't see it anywhere and started to cry: 'The opium tray has disappeared.'

Observing that my father's sleeping place had been tidied so early and that his good clothes were missing, my grandmother panicked and asked my mother: 'Do you know where his father has gone?'

My mother shook her head. My grandmother became more nervous and exclaimed: 'That's strange! That's strange!'

That day the food was dry and bitter to swallow. The meat soup was salty with my tears. Since I was crying so much, my grandmother tried to comfort me, but she did not succeed. She joined in.

'Madam Prison Warder,'—my grandmother called my mother by the title my father had when he worked at the jail—'the Prison Warder went into the house and took the 100 piastres that I put aside. When I asked him, he said he wanted the money to do business in Laos. What do you think?'

My mother remained silent. It was the silence of someone who had suffered so much and who was so discouraged that she had no more faith in anything. Sometime later, my mother replied slowly: 'Mother, I don't know what to say.'

My grandmother let out a 'huh', before changing her tone: 'You must be joking. Before his departure, he must have given you instructions.'

My mother looked into the dark, airless room where my father used to sit or lie, smoking or sleeping, never going out and hardly talking to his wife and children. She sighed. Then, with her eyes as tired and as dim as her voice, she said: 'No! He has left without telling me anything!'

Autumn was short, followed by a long, sad winter.

That winter was as sorrowful as a sick widow, lonely in her poverty: the rain continued to drizzle as though it would not stop in the icy wind. It was as though people had dried their lungs from coughing so much in the wet air of the low sky.

My family lived with a coffin maker in Hang Su. In the house, aside from the altar, you could see different kinds and cuts of timber piled up everywhere: sheets and blocks of wood, round pieces tapered at the ends, and various coffin boards. In every corner of the house, you could see sawdust and wood shavings. All year round, soft aromatic canary and cinnamon woods gave off a strong pleasant scent that filled the air.

On wet, windy days when there were no customers, the owner and the craftsmen had spare time. At midday, the craftsmen would slip into the empty spaces between the piles of boards and doze off fitfully.

On those quiet days, when I opened my books to study after I had come home from school and eaten, I felt my mind wandering, flying away, even though I had already been very lazy in class. In the reading session especially, I didn't pay attention for a minute.

With one arm coiled around the desk to hide what I was doing, I fiddled with two empty halves of an almond nutshell that my father had left behind. They were rubbed smooth, like two pieces of tortoiseshell from the heavenly turtle that waits day and night on the opium angel. My childish imagination conjured up some very strange images in the quietest hours of the afternoon class.

The smooth, shiny surface of the hardwood desk was an immense layer of bright clouds on which the two turtles, the 'almond shells', were swimming away. I put my middle and index fingers on the two angels, one boy, one girl. Although they had become angels, they were still attached to life, they still longed for their loved ones. They were riding turtle spirits, flying in the air; they had spent months and years searching for their beloved father who left them suddenly without telling them either where he lived or when he would come back. The further they flew and the longer they flew, the more they only saw fields of rice and rivers and mountains and the sea ahead.

But at times when I suddenly remembered my father at school, my sad longing was alleviated by the happiness of my friends, and it was on returning home that my mood was most sombre. I would sit on the same bed as I had always done. There was a yellow light in a transparent light shade, always square, a thin wisp of smoke giving off a sweet smell, and I felt as unsettled as on the days when I had watery soup.

Drops of cold water from the roof guttering dripped down to the bronze container, the cold seeping into my heart; the soft call of a lonely sparrow fluffing its feathers on the roof made me forget the little warmth I had left in my soul; clouds floating in the blue, green mossy roof-tops, and an old unpainted wall were tangled before my eyes in the thin, cold veil over my vision.

I was very sleepy! I couldn't study any more because when I finish reading one sentence, the words I wanted to recall disappeared from my mind before I could revise them. It was as though my brain was made of iron; it could not absorb or remember even short easy lessons.

Sitting with her legs crossed on the quilt in the middle of the bed next to the brazier, my grandmother would quietly raise her eyes and look at the bronze crucifix hanging between pots of white lilies and gilded candlesticks. If there had been no deathly whisper, if there had been no dry fingers moving over that rosary, my grandmother would have been a monument to old-fashioned prejudice, to the dark spirit of despotism that came out on her haggard face and the dark rings around her eyes.

'Lord, please forgive us!'

'Lord, please have mercy on us!'

The imploring words groaned on.

'Lord, please hear us!'

'Lord, please destroy evil, please give us peace!'

All the sparkle had gone from my grandmother's sad eyes. She would look at the crucifix of Jesus, exhausted, sad, blood coming out of his hands, and slowly bend to kiss the small round silver medal on the rosary. Her whispering would become increasingly tremulous.

'Lord, please forgive us! Christ, please have mercy upon us!'

'Lord, please destroy evil, please give us peace!'

Once more, my grandmother had repeated the imprecations she taught me and made me say so many times from the time I began to speak.

Decadence

Except for the hardwood tea closet that was not beautiful but solid, we didn't have anything that was worth any money. The wardrobe, the sofa with the mother-of-pearl inlay, the high writing table, the big armchair, and varnished sofa had been sold one by one. So had the bronze and the porcelain items such as the pot, tray, large vase, and large antique plates. Poverty had also robbed us of another precious thing: the pendulum clock.

I don't know how long my family had that clock before I was born. I only know that the wooden case had become shiny, the white paint had become yellow, and the several lines of lettering on it had faded away and become illegible. The pendulum also remained tarnished from the smoke no matter how many times we tried to polish it. My cousin had taken it away to repair many times, but, before long, the clock would run slow again and finally stop.

That clock could have been sold a long time ago. But each time somebody came to buy it, my grandmother smacked her lips and sighed. Seeing that, my father didn't sell it.

My grandmother's brown eyes looked dimly at the clock, that vestige of a stubborn husband and drunken fool, and her look showed that her old heart shrivelled as she thought of her former hardships. This saddened me too.

I didn't know how to smack my lips, I didn't know how to sigh, I didn't have tears in my eyes, but the haggard expression on my face was enough to prove that I had the same feeling as my grandmother. Each time was the same; when someone came to buy something and take it away, I sat there for a while, not knowing what to do, then looked around for something to fill that empty space. I was also unreasonably jealous when I saw those items well looked after by the people who bought them.

With my father's decline, my mother's business also declined.

There were no baskets full of bright red or fresh yellow Western apples on her round stands in the market, no baskets of Yunnan peaches shining canary yellow; no young green leaves from ornamental shrubs, no crates of juicy American oranges, no white cabbages and bunches of carrots, cauliflower, snow peas, celery, and delicious Chinese leeks were piled up waist-high.

Her ear-rings and golden rings; I'm not sure when my mother sold them. Now, the small basket, that was usually full of money after the market was over, was only dotted with a few sous. Many times waiting for my mother who had gone somewhere else, I sneaked in and gently lifted the basket cover, intending to steal some money. But I only saw that the basket was empty.

So many years have passed, but I am unable to forget one summer afternoon. It was after three and the market was still crowded, and my mother walked back alone, carrying a basket under her arm. On the sidewalk, beneath the clumps of lilac trees that twinkled with red flowers, she was quiet, with her head slightly lowered, and her eyes downcast.

As she passed groups of noisy bustling people, I saw my mother looking tired and very sad. At that time, I'm sure my mother's mind was completely numb with painful thoughts of the irreversible decline of the family, which resulted naturally from the forced marriage, the efforts to bear the situation, the resignation, and dark meaningless sacrifice.

A father and a mother with different personalities, without mutual understanding or love, who came close to despising each other but had to appear intimate in front of two playful children and an old mother who was only fond of her own offspring.

The long, cold nights of sleeplessness, worry, and useless deliberation were nights when one person was drugged in the opium smoke, the other with deep insomnia: the one was so discouraged that he'd lost interest in life; the other grieved and bitter, feeling that her life was cold and incomplete when devoted only to nurturing children. And both felt deeply that they were slowly dying, dying of sorrow and intolerable resentment.

* * *

Day after day, my father took money from my mother to buy opium. I knew very well that 20 or 30 sous was never enough for my father to smoke. Previously, when my father had been wealthy, it had only taken him five or six days to finish a *lang* of opium. From nine in the morning to midnight, my father only came out of his room twice to eat. Often, after finishing her rosary and reading hundreds of verses from the Bible, my grandmother, who was outside and could still hear the continuous 'ro ro' of my father smoking, would ask him in a sweet diplomatic voice: 'Is Hong's father still awake?'

'I'm nearly finished, Mother.'

'Nearly finished!'

My grandmother would repeat my father's words and sigh. The irritation and anger of my grandmother had become extreme, and so she had now dared to question him in this fashion since he had started to become sickly and cough up blood and my mother had to worry about taking care of everything in the house. In asking that question, my grandmother was also skilfully reminding my father: 'Your wife has no more respect for me! You should find a way to quit opium.'

No! My mother didn't dare to have such a thought. Her life was the short shadow of a thick wall. And, that gentle, sensitive woman, when would her heart be stained with marks of arrogance and hatred? Wasn't my mother resigned when she looked haggardly at my father to see him holding his chest and coughing non-stop? She would shake her head and sigh. How many times have I seen tears in her eyes?

One day, my mother took my little sister Que to Hanoi, saying she was going to visit a friend and also take the opportunity to borrow some money from her to pay a debt. Before she left, my mother measured out a few days' rice and left enough money for my father to smoke opium for a week. Neither did she forget to slip me 10 sous for lollies and cakes.

The morning before she carried her basket off to catch the train, my mother stood outside the door and asked my father's permission, and lowered her head silently waiting for my father to reply. But my father kept quiet for a long time before answering in the indifferent tone of a stranger.

For over a week, I didn't see my mother or little sister. I went down to the station to wait for them many times, but returned alone, disappointed and very annoyed! The money my mother gave me was finished the day after she left. It was the summer holidays, and I played around in the streets alone. Looking at the cake and fruit sellers going past me, I felt very miserable. I didn't know who to ask for money, I couldn't ask anyone at home except my mother. At times I intended to dip into my father's opium money. But when I thought of the rattan whip which made my backside bleed, I decided not to.

But, while I could go without eating cakes, I couldn't go for long without playing street games, especially hit-the-coin, a game in which one player throws a coin over a line and another one has to try and hit it with his. Without playing, I would become uneasy and unable to sit still. I was so unhappy I wanted to cry because the other children gathered in groups, disputing and cursing one another in front of my house.

One afternoon, my father gave me 18 sous to buy some opium. I didn't go straight to the shop; I joined the children in front of the house to play a few games.

The children in this group were street kids who sold lollies and newspapers. Some were thieves. They had plenty of time to practise this game and were very skilful at all the moves. Furthermore, they knew how to keep calm when they were down to their last sou, just before the game was over.

But I could match them. I used to go to school early for many months to play hit-the-coin, so I had become a very skilful player who was full of tricks.

Near the group of children, there was a group of coolies and barbers playing. They didn't play for half a sou, but for a copper sou and each one had to put in three. I left the children's game to join the adults: although their arms were long and they had a strong throw, they had to be accurate or they'd toss their money away.

After I'd played for a while, my 18 sous had become 40. I was then worried that if I continued to play, I might lose, so I decided to quit. I was smart enough to buy 5 sous of opium extra, and also thought up an explanation in case my father beat me for coming home late.

The following day, I got up early. Having washed my face, I went straight out into the street to play for money. I managed to get 5 sous. That small sum was quite a lot for the poor children with whom I played. One must be clever, hard-headed, and resourceful to get money (which they carried carefully fastened inside their trousers) out of them.

That afternoon I won again, and this time it was even better! It was double the amount of money I had won the previous day, and I won it very easily and quickly. Those who lost the money were kids from wealthy families who played in secret places hidden from their parents.

For a few days, when I had finished eating, I went out into the street, looking for those games.

I lost some and won some; I lost to the poor children and I won from the adults and children of wealthy families. The experience taught me that if I wanted to have money to buy cakes and go to the movies, I had to go to the street near the market, near the quay, near the bus-stop to find the kids from wealthy families or join the wild games of coolies and excited workers who got together in the afternoon after work.

From the day I knew I had that skill and recognized my advantages and disadvantages, I started to wander around the streets with a thick shiny coin for a taw and a little over 10 sous as capital. I also had the desire to get a lot of money to spend.

Every day I managed to get 20 or 30 sous. I was very happy and proud of myself. My happiness now overflowed; I was like a person who had experienced the glory of freedom through his own worthy profession.

* * *

One wet, windy afternoon, squatting on the bed with his knees up to his chest supporting his chin, my father called me gently and sweetly: 'Hong, come here, I've got something to ask you.'

My father rarely called my name as tenderly as that, and so not only was I not pleased, but I was also anxious and worried by this unusual occurrence. My face turned pale as I walked towards him very slowly. He smiled, and waved at me once more: 'No! Daddy's not going to beat you, he's only going to ask you a question.'

I went up beside my father with my heart beating fast, my legs trembling, and tears in the corners of my eyes. He remained calm as he placed one arm over my shoulder and slipped one hand into my pocket: 'You've got some money, haven't you?'

The silent lamp and clean opium tray that had been pulled right to the foot of the bed made me think immediately that it was after four, and I still hadn't gone to buy opium for my father's afternoon session. I also remembered immediately that the day before yesterday he hadn't smoked and, that yesterday, relying on my grandmother to sell something or other, he had 20 or 30 sous to buy a little opium. But this had only been just enough for last night and four or five pipes this morning.

My anxiety passed in a minute and was replaced by feelings of anger and indignation. I was so choked with tears that it was almost impossible for me to say a word. I knew well that, if he didn't have opium and he saw that I had money, my father would surely take it from me. But 4 or 5 sous wouldn't be enough! A string of over ten nickel coins, 5 sous, was hidden in my money belt—a rather large sum that I had brazenly hung around the streets and markets and gone all around town to make.

It was as if my resentment boiled over when I thought of this money being converted into spluttering opium that would be sucked quickly into a small pipe before the sunken, dim eyes of my father. I turned away my face, wet with tears, and plainly answered my father: 'I haven't got any!'

My father smiled again a smile which made his grey face darker, the purple bluish colour of a whetstone.

'Are you sure?'

After saying this, my father fingered the hem on my pants. I shrank from him and yelled at the top of my voice: 'Leave me alone! I beg you! I really haven't got any.'

My father scowled and scolded, 'Be quiet!', then pulled my body towards him.

I was on the point of freeing myself from my father's grasp, but seeing the whites of his eyes bulging as though they were about to pop out and feeling hot on my face a breath which came from a mouth he tried with difficulty to close, I gave up my struggle and stood there quietly.

My father groped behind my back, and poked his hand into my pants to find the hidden coins.

There was not a trace of love left in my heart at that moment.

My father felt around the front of my pants. My face turned more and more pale and my throat became more and more constricted.

Then I let out a scream when my father's hand touched the piece of string which fastened the money belt inside my pants.

Suddenly, the string snapped. Pain knotted my insides. I ground my teeth and stamped my feet on the floor. My father's face suddenly became menacing, and he jerked my chin up.

'Hong! Where have you been going after you've eaten these last few days?'

I cried and didn't dare to answer. But in my mind I had a very clear answer: 'I don't have any pocket money, so I had to go out and play hit-the-coin. Where else could I have gone?'

My father still glared at me: 'Hong! Who allowed you to go and play hit-the-coin? Who allowed you to play around with street urchins? Get down. Quick. Or I'll kill you. Hong!'

I withdrew to a corner of the room, my eyes filled with tears. I clasped my hands, imploring him: 'I beg you, Father, forgive me, I have been stupid.'

My father smiled: 'Yes, you've been stupid, stupid, so get down here.'

In a flash, he pulled the rattan whip down from the top of the mosquito net.

'I beg you, Father! Father, forgive me. I won't dare to do it again. If I do it again, you can kill me.'

My father's lips tightened, and his nostrils puffed out. All the flesh on my body trembled. I imagined pain stabbing through my body under the supple whip, leaving me with no regrets about having to give up the money. I cried to my father: 'I beg you, Father, please let me give you all the money I have. I beg you, Father, forgive me.'

As I finished those words, the whip was being held high above me: 'Go and lie down on the bed, quick! Be quick!'

Before he'd finished that sentence, my father's eyes had filled with tears, his grey forehead broke out in beads of sweat, and his face became darker. 'Quick!' He began to yell, but this time his voice was not clear and stopped short like the sound of a cork breaking in the neck of a bottle when someone has used all his strength to remove it.

My father did not beat me, and he didn't touch my money. Pleased and surprised, I couldn't understand it at all!

From that day, my father's attitude towards me changed. Whenever he spoke to me now, he consulted me and discussed matters with me gently and sweetly! And he always raised his tired dim eyes to look at me. From time to time, he also smiled at me, but his smile would fade quickly from his pale lips.

Although my father's way of speaking, his eyes, and his smiles were full of love, they often terrified me. This was especially so at times when my father sat with his knees up in that dark airless room; except for a small glass skylight in the ceiling to let in some light, the room had no windows.

In My Mother's Heart

I had already taken off my funeral turban; not because I had cut short my mourning for my father, but because I now had a white sun helmet with a black band.

It was almost the first anniversary of my father's death. My mother had still not returned from Thanh Hoa. I heard that she was selling lanterns and gold foil at the main markets there. I say 'I heard', because people spread the news that my mother made her living that way, and one day my aunt called me to her and asked me with a smile: 'Hong, do you want to go to Thanh Hoa to visit your mother?'

Thinking both of my mother's gentle face and the affectionate nurturing that I was missing made me cry, and I was going to say yes. But recognizing the cruel sarcasm in my aunt's smile and voice, I lowered my head without answering.

I knew very well that when talking about my mother, my aunt wanted to plant seeds of suspicion and scorn in my mind. She wanted me to forsake my mother, a widow, who, because of poverty and debts, could not stay in her home town to bring up her children, but left them to their grandmother and aunt while she went off to make some kind of living elsewhere.

But my love and my respect for my mother could never have been damaged by the evil intentions of my aunt, even though it had been nearly a year since my mother had sent me a letter or any news or pocket money!

I answered my aunt with a smile: 'No, I don't want to go there, my mother will be back at the end of the year.'

My aunt's voice halted momentarily, before she continued with her smooth tongue: 'Why don't you go? Your mother has become rich. It isn't like before.'

Her eyes sparkled as she stared at me, as if trying to stimulate my desire to go. I kept quiet and lowered my head to look at the floor; my insides became knotted; my eyes were burning. She tapped me on the shoulder and continued with a smile: 'You fool, go ahead, I'll give you the train fare. Go there and tell your mother to buy you clothes, and also visit your new baby sister. Why not?'

Tears ran down my face and chin and neck. The sound of the words 'baby sister', that my aunt uttered so sweetly and so deliberately, made my heart shrivel as she had wanted it to. But I didn't have that painful feeling because my mother had a child with another man even though my father had not been dead a year. I had it because I felt so much for my mother; I was angry because she had become separated from us because of her fear of old-fashioned prejudices; she had to go away to give birth secretly, and hide like a clumsy murderer with a blood-stained knife. I laughed in my tears and asked my aunt: 'How did you know that my mother had a baby?'

My aunt went on relating in a cheerful tone the news that a member of the family had been in Thanh Hoa to buy rice and, on passing a market, had seen my mother sitting breast-feeding a baby beside a bamboo basket full of lanterns. She was dressed in rags and her face was pale. Surprised and full of pity, that person intended to call my mother, but my mother turned her face away and covered it with her conical hat.

When my aunt had finished this story, I was so distressed that my crying was noiseless, and I went pale with anger. If those ancient customs which hurt my mother had been objects of rock, crystal, or wood, I would have taken them, put them in my mouth, and ground them to dust.

My aunt suddenly changed her tone, tapped me on the shoulder, and said: 'You should go and ask Aunty Thong, the relative who went to Thanh Hoa, where your mother lives, then send your mother a telegram telling her that, no matter what, she should return; that sooner or later she will have to face her shame and shouldn't leave this town forever because of it.'

As if to show love and respect for my father, my aunt continued hesitantly: 'You should remind her especially that the fifteenth day of the eighth month is the first anniversary of your father's death. If your mother doesn't come back, she will hurt his spirit, and the relatives will torture you by saying that your mother is a bad woman.'

When the anniversary came, my mother came back even though I didn't write a letter to her. She came home by herself bringing a lot of gifts for me and my sister, Que. That afternoon, walking home from school, I suddenly saw someone in a rickshaw who looked like my mother. I immediately ran behind her, calling out with excitement: 'Mother! Mother! Mother!'

If the person who turned around was somebody else, it would have been a big joke for my classmates who would have teased me by taking off their wooden shoes and clapping them together noisily. It would have caused me not only great embarrassment, but also self-pity. I would have been like a traveller who had collapsed in the desert before the mirage of a stream of fresh water, running through the shade of a hibiscus bush.

The rickshaw slowed down, and then my mother used her hat to wave to me. A few seconds later, I caught up with her. I was panting, my forehead was covered in sweat, and, when my mother affectionately touched my head and asked me how I had been, I started to sob as she cried with me.

'Don't cry any more. I've come back to be with you and your sister.'

My mother dried my eyes with the panel of her brown tunic and lifted me into the rickshaw. I could now see that she didn't look as ragged and poor as my aunt had recently described her to me. Her face was still bright, and her clear eyes and smooth skin still seemed to make the rosy hue of her cheeks stand out.

Or was it the sudden happiness of seeing a loved one in person that made my mother look as beautiful as when we were rich?

I sat on the cushion with my thigh against my mother's, my head resting on her chest. I felt the warmth I had been missing in my life flow through my body. The smell of my mother's clothes and the scented breath that came from her lovely mouth as she chewed betel were unusually fragrant to me.

Just think when you were young and in your mother's lap, how infinitely gentle a sensation it was to have your face against her milky breast, and her hand caressing your face and chin, and rubbing your back. From the time I met my mother in the rickshaw until we got home, I don't remember either what she asked me or what I replied. I cannot remember whether I thought in those excited moments of what my aunt had said to arouse feelings in me of rejection and disdain for my mother: 'You fool, you should go to Thanh Hoa, I'll give you the train fare. Go and tell your mother to feed and clothe you, and also to visit your little sister.'

Christmas Night

At the beginning of the ninth month, my mother went back to Thanh Hoa. When she left, my sister and I accepted her departure calmly and we were happy with her instructions:

'You two stay with your grandmother and aunt and let me go and make some money so that I can provide for you and buy you some new clothes for Tet.'

Cherishing the idea of having beautiful clothes and a lot of pocket money, I was quite happy to go to school and my younger sister stayed home to play.

Soon winter came.

Talking about winter, I had the funny feeling that the previous winters were wetter and colder and sadder than that one was and future ones would be.

Those strange long days of quiet drizzle and cold seemed never-ending.

The street I lived in was Hang Su. It was only busy from April or May to September or October. From November through to February, few people passed through it; the rasping sound of sawing and the clatter of carpentry could no longer be heard. Activity came to a complete stop.

I still remember the numb feeling I had at times when dark black clouds massed unevenly in the sky like the furrows in a freshly ploughed field or like the piles of pungent smoke that rotten vegetation gives off when it's burnt in the cold.

Once I had finished spending the money my mother had given me, I waited eagerly for the day of her return. The more I waited for the lunar New Year to arrive, the more slowly time passed, as if it was about to come to a standstill. But when Christmas came, still half a month before the end of the lunar New Year during which time my mother would still be at Thanh Hoa, I prayed that, from 23 to 25 December, the time would pass even more slowly. This was because I had the intuition that the earliest my mother would arrive home would be the twenty-ninth or thirtieth of the last month of the lunar calendar, and this meant I had no expectation of a joyous Christmas as in former years!

During the two days' break from school, I only appeared in the house once to eat and spent my time wandering around the streets looking for a game of hit-the-coin or odds and evens. When I saw half-sou coins tossed into the air and land on the ground, when the taws thrown at a pile of coins flew up and hit other coins which in turn turned up with their faces odds and evens, I became excited and wanted to satisfy my greed for money. Being with people who had money made me feel uncomfortable.

Why were they so happy? Their red faces, gleaming eyes, and noisy laughter showed that they were extremely pleased.

Hadn't I enjoyed the same pleasure two years ago on hot summer days? People said that I became a street kid who wandered around the street playing games to earn money to buy rice for the family and opium for my father and that no one bothered to look after the family tombs. Ignoring the criticism and contempt of these people, I calmly enjoyed a free life with the street children and workers, and a close relationship with my father.

At times, when I was with my father, I noticed the sparkle in his eyes, the affectionate smile on his pale lips: I now realized that they contained deep love which was mixed with the pain of parting from this world. My father knew he would soon leave us, two children whose lives he had surely damaged with his neglect, and a wife who died slowly in forced love.

The evening of 25 December had arrived! My young sister was carefree. She borrowed money from her old school friends to buy some grapefruit and star fruit to take to the gate of the nearby Convent the following morning. She was hoping to compete with the other street vendors. My aunt had gone to play cards; my grandmother was at home but did not bother to talk to me.

After 10 p.m. I went out quietly, wearing a loose black coat, but no hat or shoes.

The bell tower of the cathedral was illuminated by an arrangement of electric light bulbs which I saw turned on in the shape of a five-pointed star. Mist swirled in the glowing beams of electric light, rising thickly and dispersing far off in the night. The sky looked like a dark blue velvet curtain that was about to be raised. Then, suddenly, parallel lines of bulbs which hung down from the bell tower to the stone steps of the church were also illuminated, forming a tree of dazzling rays.

Christians from the outskirts of the city had gathered, sitting in groups of five or seven people that covered the wide, elevated stone courtyard of the cathedral. I don't know how many cake sellers had gathered around the sidewalks on either side of the cathedral.

Wearing only a set of thin cotton clothes and a dark loose coat that was torn at the shoulders, I felt the cold piercing my flesh and chilling it. Each time the east wind lashed my face, I felt as if my cheeks had been cut with a knife. I walked around the church over ten times, often trying to work my way into the crowd. My legs were giving way beneath me.

The bell suddenly pealed, and the sky reverberated with its ringing. The cathedral door was now wide open. A dazzling vault of candlelight interspersed with glowing beams of glass and crystal appeared glittering like gold before my eyes. French people moved in first. They chatted as they went slowly into the very wide isle and up to the front pews on which were covered cushions. Next Vietnamese officials, people with power and wealth, entered the cathedral with an important stately air.

When the church heated up with the shining colours of the congregation's clothes and the smell of make-up and strong perfume, when the choir broke into song as if to welcome the haughty wealth and serene calm of people whose class permitted them to enter first, the church wardens who had spread their arms to block the rest now dropped them. At once a wave of ragged unkempt people surged in, jostling and pushing each other, not at the main entrance, but at the two side doors which only now were opened. It was as though, in the wailing tumult of a poor hungry city that had been destroyed by flood and smitten with famine, people had to wrangle and rob each other for a place to stand in front of a charity house.

Quickly jumping up a few steps, I tried to slip through a part of the crowd so as to see the altar, but was not able to do so. As it happened, each time I put my head forward and tried to burrow through from the far end of that stinking throng, I was pushed back, and if I hadn't ducked, I would have felt the blow of someone's knuckles.

Gradually, I lost all interest in seeing the mass. I became more aware of the piercing cold. Gradually, I felt bitter at my abject loneliness, at my plight as a destitute orphan, while so many happy people were being carried away in the soft ambience of the service.

The sound of the organ pipes and the singing of the hymns rose joyously over the congregation. But I had only reached the top of the steps to the stone courtyard that was still covered with people who had come a long way from the country and arrived late. I turned around and walked off by myself down the steps in the opposite direction, then turned into Paul Bert Street.

I didn't go home.

* * *

The mist had spread out like a curtain drawn in the night. Indistinct and still, nature appeared in a light sea of fine vapour. The foliage on trees on either side of the road was darkening green, wet and heavy. It was cold. But each time a gust of wind blew across my face, I felt particles of water seep into my flesh.

Only being soaked in a storm could give such a sensation of the fierce chilling cold. That was how I felt walking that night in the wind, in the quiet, with my thoughts of a gentle mother, agitated, unsettled, and numb with pain.

The wind became stronger! The cold midnight air became more penetrating! Leaves stirred on the surface of the road, and it was as if their rustle had entered my soul.

That vague sound was like the whispering of birds. The glow of the electric lights that illuminated the silent landscape became dimmer and now sank into the deep mist that came whirling off the rim of the moon.

I felt as though the rustle of the leaves would never end. It was so cold! In my soul, the dead leaves were being crushed and churned, crushed and churned in a process of perpetual disintegration. I continued on my way, not conscious of anything but a funeral.

It was on the fifteenth day of the eighth lunar month, the time when every child is full of joy at the banquet held to look at the full moon, to watch the somersault dance with the lion's head, to listen to the loud beating of the drums and the crashing of the cymbals. My little sister, Que, and I were dressed untidily in a set of rumpled clothes with the hems let down as a sign of mourning, as we followed a small coffin on a wooden frame that over twenty people were carrying.

As the funeral procession proceeded slowly through the streets, everybody looked on with interest, because of the two little children who cried: 'Daddy! Daddy! Daddy!'

The cute sound of those endearing words, which came out with our sobs, made many women cover their smiles. My aunt had to take a step back and whisper in my ear: 'Don't cry "Daddy"; cry "Father".'

But we were only able to correct our cries for a few moments, before we remembered what came usually from our mouths and continued: 'Daddy! Daddy! Dear Daddy!'

For many years, the word 'Daddy' had been the one beginning so many phrases that were addressed to the most beloved person in our lives. How could we suddenly change it! To cry 'Daddy', it was as though we were showing that even though my father had now passed away, he was still remembered by his two children: remembered with almost maddening pain and sorrow in an intimate expression that everyone thought was so cute: 'Daddy! Dear Daddy!'

On Winter Nights

The back of the calendar was already covered with words! Each time I felt pain, resentment, or shame, I would write a couple of lines on the front of the calendar, summarizing the details of when, how, and why I had been insulted, despised, or made miserable.

12 November 19. . .

Aunt C . . . drained the stale water from the pot of chicken soup into a small bowl. She said to give it to me. Who would want to eat it, even if they were starving? She has more consideration for her servants than me.

14 November 19. . .

I will remember the slap and this curse which accompanied it until the day I die: 'Hey, Hong, your father has died, but you still have your mother to teach you. If your mother sells herself or chases men and leaves you to fool around, you could say you've still got us.'

Oh Mother! I'm so miserable, Mother! Why do you go away for so long? My aunt beats me, because I dared to take back the toys her children took from me. She also curses me and you too. You are away from me, do you know all this?

After hours of walking in the wind and rain, I wrote:

1 December 19. . .

Oh Daddy! You were kind in life, and now that you're dead, please answer my call. Do you know how I feel? Since I beg your supernatural assistance, I don't think you will refuse my request. Daddy, help me to gain 10 sous. I'm very hungry, dear Daddy! It is raining again and very cold! For a week, I haven't had a sou to buy snacks.

4 December 19. . .

Why didn't my aunt send her children out to do errands? I'm even sent to buy half a sou of salt and soy sauce. When I came home from school, I was so hungry that I couldn't see clearly. I was just about to get some rice to eat, but I had to put my bowl down and run an errand. It makes me cry to think about it.

Oh Mother! Why have you gone for so long? Why don't you ever come home?

I wrote a lot more. But I hope that the examples I have given you over a few days are enough for you to understand clearly the dark tortures that filled my childhood once my father died and my mother went away to earn her living. I have also given a quick summary of my diary in order to prepare you to come into the nights when I had vague dreams.

Those nights were the last nights of my thirteenth year.

* * *

We didn't live in Hang Su Street any longer. We moved to Ban Go Street to live with Aunt C.

Because we were dependent on Aunt C for shelter, my grandmother, Aunt G, my father's younger sister, Aunt G's daughter, and my younger sister and myself were squashed into the outhouse which served as Aunt C's kitchen!

To use the word 'squashed' is not an exaggeration, because we were extremely cramped.

The room was about 20 square metres; along its side there was a kitchen for three families, altogether sixteen people; along its width was the passage leading through the rear courtyard and up to the house; the remaining surface was just enough for a bed, a table, and a trunk jammed in without a centimetre between them.

The table was cluttered with a teapot and cups, a betel box, and my grandmother's things. Piled on the trunk were my clothes and three or four baskets of torn rags!

Of course, those rags belonged to my sister and me.

It was impossible for me to lie on the bed which was claimed by so many people and which could also collapse at any time on the cooking pots, baskets, plates, and firewood that were piled underneath it. I had to lie on a piece of wood on the edge of the passageway that was slightly bigger than the bench pushed up beside the bed.

It was on this piece of wood that I lay awake so many silent nights when it was drizzling, when the dew was so thick that it seemed to be woven into a grey cloth that covered the landscape, and when the whistling of the wind went deep into my soul.

I covered myself with the mattress that my father used to lie on when he smoked opium. It was short, narrow, and thin. I took it out to dry in the sun many times, but it still kept the burning smell of the peanut oil, the *lao* tobacco, and the sweat and dirt of the body that had lain on it so many times before. Since I could not cover my face, I wrapped it in a piece of brown cloth that my aunt had discarded. In order to cover myself completely, I also used a sleeping mat and curled myself up with my knees touching my chin and my head on my chest.

From nightfall to midnight, I could sleep a bit, but from cock crow to daylight I lay awake, changing my position from one side to another, face down and face up, holding my legs up against my chest. At that time, the cold caused me pain from the tips of my toes to the tops of my ears. Sometimes, I stretched myself out with my arms folded in front of my chest trying to sleep, but I could only stay still for a few minutes, because it felt as though there was a block of ice on my stomach. I continued to toss and turn.

Outside, the wind occasionally wailed, while a shower of rain beat down, then both stopped and were lost in the silence of the night. All those sounds made me think of clumps of wet vegetation pushing up chaotically through thick-matted grass that looks like freshly washed curly hair: clumps of cauliflower and ragged herbs struggling to rise in the wind and lift themselves out of narrow thorny gardens and gutters choked with mud.

Lying awake for many hours, I was so exhausted that I succumbed to sleep. The cold quickly carried my soul to faraway dreams.

There, so many sweet absorbing impressions and feelings vibrated and warmed my heart! My mind was no longer beset by anger and jealousy, and so my innate personality—that of a young child—was able to blossom fully in those bright familiar dreams.

I call those dreams familiar, because the landscape in them was not remote or complicated at all. Those landscapes had once appeared before me in daylight when I wasn't more than eight years old. . . .

One night, my younger sister, Que, and I leisurely climb a staircase to get to the attic of the house with few windows and no ceiling in Jules Ferry Street; the house that my father will sell for money to buy opium.

My sister carries a small basket of sweet potatoes, rice popcorn, and rice cakes. And I, I carry a basket of mussel shells, the empty opium tin, an empty condensed milk tin, a knife, a small chopping board, and a tiny pair of chopsticks.

Dear Readers, here before you are two children who are about to embark on an adventure in the middle of the jungle that is deep in the mountains of their childish imaginations!

The jungle is the area where my father's potted ornamental shrubs stand on the brick parapet. The island of wild beasts where no person has yet set foot is in the corner of the narrow attic. There is a cave in the heart of the high mountains that almost touches the blue clouds and covers hundreds of acres of fields, and this is in the space between the bed and the wall.

The food that Que and I arrange carefully in small baskets is hung on a piece of timber that we imagine is the branch of a tree. If we don't store our provisions carefully, we will be worried that the tigers and bears might come to destroy them, and then we will have neither anything to eat nor the strength to struggle against the terrible forces of nature and wild animals.

We eat very cautiously. Each month—a few minutes is a month—we kill a pig which is really a sweet potato which we stand on four toothpicks. The first lumpy slice we carve is the head, the second longer thinner piece is the neck, and the big fat slice behind the neck is the belly. Naturally, we have to throw away the legs! Chickens, ducks, birds, and fish are made from peanuts and discarded rice crisps that we boil and cook in butter tins and condensed milk tins, at the rate of a few a day. We take the food from the tins and put it into the mussel shells and dip it into crushed rice cakes or sugar.

I am bigger than Que so I should eat more, but being a man in the middle of the jungle, I have to make sacrifices for my female companion. Whenever my sister kindly offers me some extra sticky rice or peanuts, I have to tell her gently: 'You eat it. I have had plenty. I'm strong, I can eat less! You are weak, you need to eat a lot in order to have the strength to fight the wild animals with me.'

Outside, the rain pours down. The wind wails. Occasionally, lightning flashes in the black clouds.

I go downstairs to get some burning coals and put them in a biscuit tin so that I can take them upstairs to warm ourselves. We warm our hands over the coals, pretending that it is very cold. My younger sister talks affectionately to me using very cute words. In the end, she puts her head on my shoulder and pretends to sleep.

We had run out of food! Our father had finished smoking. We had to put our toys away and go downstairs so that my father could sleep.

That was part one of the adventurous life of the young wanderers! Immense and light, the dream of it was like the smoke of evening cooking fires that silently attracts the evening sunlight as it disperses. And it left in my heart its infinite softness for weeks to come.

It seems I have been reliving the innocent period of my life that everyone says is the rich source of feeling.

One night when I was harshly scolded by my grandmother, I was so indignant that I cried quietly for hours, before I fell asleep exhausted.

Then, having escaped in sleep the pain, the shame, and the self-pity that tormented me, my soul returned to a restful state and entered again a world of bright dreams. . . .

Beneath the far-reaching light of the moon, the appearance of a slender woman, stepping lightly in the shadow of a lilac tree, vibrates dimly along a glistening tarred road, and I hurry after her without calling. She turns around. I can see two sparkling eyes looking at me from a fair fresh face. Her hair blows in the wind like silk threads fluttering in the moonlight. I quickly take the supple hand that the young lady offers me.

I don't know how much time has passed since I and the young lady with warm skin and tender voice have put our heads on each other's shoulders and looked passionately at each other. I don't know what sweet feelings are caressing her, what profound impressions are blossoming in her. As for me, I am nervous, and it is as though my chest has gone cold.

I no longer worry about my persecution. At times, I want to say a few words in her ear, but when I see her faint face and eyes half-closed and her light hair fluttering in the air, I tremble and remain silent. Gradually, I fall asleep in the naïvely passionate eyes and fresh cool breath of that slender girl.

On the footpath where we sit, broken yellow leaves from the lilac tree fly up constantly and then scatter everywhere. But, at the same time, there are other broken leaves. They have been churned and crushed to dust that spreads in the shining light of the moon and settles like gossamer on our hair and in our souls.

Thu—this gentle girl, who has shared my life in the most gentle moments of that dream—was a classmate about my own age who usually walked home from school with me.

Thu's school was about 100 metres from mine. To avoid any trouble between the two groups of students at the girls' and the boys' schools, the principal of the girls' school always let her students leave a little while after the boys went home. But I always went back to meet Thu or waited under a veranda at the corner for her to come past.

At thirteen, how could I have the burning passion of an adult for this girl? I was waiting eagerly for her, as I remembered something that happened one particular morning.

That morning, under the drizzling rain, I put my arm around a person who I thought was a male classmate, while we watched the activities to celebrate Armistice Day. A little while later, a cold slippery feeling of hair rippled on my skin, startling me. I lowered my head to look at the face of the person around whom I had just put my arm.

Oh God! It wasn't that cross-eyed, dark-skinned boy; it was a girl who was a bit shorter than me, with ebony-coloured hair shining on her lissom back. She had bright brown eyes with soft black lashes and fresh bright lips.

From then on, this small girl was always on my mind. I could not forget the beautiful hand that had gently lifted my arm, and her innocent brown eyes that looked at me as a blush came quickly to her cheeks and faded.

For months when I was suffering from hard work and pain, whenever I started to cry, I thought of Thu, that pretty young schoolgirl!

The more tears I had in my eyes, the more clearly I could see the flap of her brown crêpe tunic and her shiny hazelnut hair.

The Taw

The first few days of the warm spring that year were as bright as the litter of exploded firecrackers fluttering on a gleaming white sidewalk.

After lunch on the afternoon of the second day of Tet, my mother ordered me to put four Xa Doai oranges, ten fresh areca nuts, and ten yellow betel-nut leaves into a small betel box.

Going out into the street, I was just about to call a rickshaw, when my mother told me not to. I complained in an endearing voice: 'It's a very long way from the house to Phu Long, I can't go on foot.'

'But there's no money for the fare!'

'Then you go alone.'

We had reached the street. A number of rickshaw coolies rushed towards us, and, on getting no business, dispersed and went elsewhere. I handed the betel box to my mother: 'Here, Mother, you take it. I'm going back.'

My mother looked quietly at me for a moment, then said slowly in an unruffled voice: 'Let's walk, I want to talk to you.'

Never had I seen my mother with as grave an expression on her face as she wore at that time. Although I knew she was very determined, she was still not strong enough to control me if I decided to become obstreperous. However, I didn't dare to ignore her. After so many months of shame and ill-treatment and of missing a mother's loving attention, I had promised myself that I would never offend her. Even if excessive love engendered by her absence had made her afraid of me and turned her into a willing slave who would happily spoil me as I pleased, I decided not to take advantage.

This pledge had another significance: to let my mother see that her child respected her and would be extremely sad and miserable when she abandoned him again.

Acting immediately, I helpfully took the betel box and said 'yes' in a sweet voice. But after going a long distance beside my mother, I suddenly became anxious and worried. Why had my mother told me to walk so that she could speak to me?

In the past, when had my mother talked to me as strangely as that? Is it good or bad news?

I was even more surprised when I saw my mother lower her head and look down at the road with a dark look on her face. She suddenly let out one word: 'Hong!'

I didn't reply, and just looked at her with wide eyes. She called my name once more, then said, trembling: 'I want to ask you something, answer me truthfully.'

The broken words of her question, spoken with sobs and pants, reverberated in my ear. In confusion, I quickly took my mother's hand and shook it: 'Mother, what is it? What is it?'

My mother quickly raised her eyes and looked at me and then looked back down at the road: 'Do you agree?'

Vexed, I said: 'Why would I not agree? But what is it? Tell me what it is.'

My mother was cautious: 'All right, I'll tell you, but don't....'

My mother, a mother of twenty-nine who still had a fresh face, asked, after hesitating for a few moments, the following question in a small voice that was quivering with anxiety and worry: 'Would you consent if I brought your baby sister back here?'

Good heavens! Such a humiliation! The ancient rites and customs of Vietnam force a mother to regard the bearing of children before the end of the mourning period for a deceased husband as more disgusting than the most evil, cruel, and wicked thing. And, following the slavish adherence to past prejudices which are still binding, a boy of less than fourteen is raised to a position of such importance that his mother has to submit herself to him and beg him.

I tapped my mother lightly on the shoulder: 'Mother, stop crying! Of course, bring the baby home! Why wouldn't I consent? You didn't have to ask me.'

But angry resentment suddenly came into my mind. Agitated, I said very quickly: 'Mother, don't be afraid of anyone! Bring her back openly.'

When she heard my unflinching words, I didn't know whether my mother could feel the indignation that had boiled up in me. And, after enduring so much ill-treatment, deprivation, and lack of love, I ground my teeth in order to crush the meanness of those who despised me because I was the son of a gentle widow who was forced by her suffering to become involved early in another relationship.

My mother didn't reply. She only raised her eyes and looked vaguely at me with a smile that seemed as though it would never disappear from her pretty lips.

Once she'd dried her tears, her cheeks became rosy, and her eyes sparkled. The red of her cheeks and the flash of her sparkling eyes were like fresh young bamboo shoots sprouting in the bright spring sun.

* * *

Soon January ended, then February. The happy time of love and affection was interrupted. But my life was not as tormented as before; this time my mother had asked my grandmother and my aunt to look after us.

But actually my grandmother and aunt did not provide for me, because I looked after myself with the money I earned.

Money for soap, school books, and tickets for the movies or a soccer game all came from me.

The day my mother went off with her basket under her arm, she emptied her pocket to give me her last 5 sous and said slowly to me: 'Hong, be a good boy and stay at home. I'm going to Hai Phong to borrow some money from Aunt T, so I can go to Thanh Hoa to get your baby sister and come back here to start a business and look after you all.'

Two weeks passed, then two months, and my mother had still not returned. Nor had I received a letter from her.

The days of heavy skies with black clouds and drizzling rain towards the end of January reflected my feelings. During the long nights, I lay awake, thinking of my mother's disappointment at not being able to borrow money, and of how this meant she had to stay in Thanh Hoa and experience the hardship of being a street vendor so that she could take care of the baby sister I hadn't seen.

My painful memories of my mother were more bitter when I turned the calendar over to read quietly bits and pieces of the diary I had been keeping on the back of it.

But from the beginning of March, I rarely felt pain and worry. Gradually, calm and good spirits returned to me. I began a new life that was free and full, because I had an extraordinary idea about a new way of playing hit-the-coin.

When my father was still alive about four years before this, I was the child who could do without food and proper clothes, but not without 'playing'. However, at first, I always lost the game, some days losing little, others losing up to 30 or 40 sous. My father then tied me up and beat me until my bottom bled, because I had dared to disobey his orders and gone out playing in the street.

By the year that my father was dying, I had become a very good player who could compete with other smart, cunning children without losing. Furthermore, I knew how to talk workers, coolies, and kids from wealthy families into playing so that I could beat them.

Two years after my father died, the way of playing changed. Although my old way had been very clever, it now became useless. I started losing again. Any sou I put down to play disappeared. Once my mother sent me 2 piastres from Thanh Hoa to buy school books, and I lost them in two days.

Playing this game for a whole year, I always lost. There were times when I was able to save 60 or 70 sous by not eating cakes, but lost them in a couple of games, and all I wanted to do was cry.

Having no money left, I still hung around to watch the game. I tried my best to imitate the playing style of the champions.

Then one afternoon, I knew I had learned the secret of the game. My trouser legs were heavy with mud, my hair was dripping wet, and I continued to play with success. Not only had I luckily found a good taw, but with it I had also worked out that, if I used less force, my throw was more accurate.

Soon, one pocket full of sous was so heavy that when I bent down to throw at the half-sou, my left hand had to hold the pocket so the coins wouldn't spill out and, also, lift it up so that it wouldn't be in the way. A little while later, the other pocket in which I didn't want to put the money for fear that it would be in the way was full too. I had to change those coins into 10- and 20-sous ones, and I had to give the street vendors an extra half-sou when they changed the money for me.

All the students who were early for school came to look at our game. Each time I raised my arm to throw at the target, the kids cheered and all eyes were on the half-sou coin which bounced a long way.

The youngsters who lost became angry, and many times they forced me to play again thinking that I used my finger to flick the half-sou coin quickly, or how could the taw always successfully knock the other coins over the line? My classmates objected strongly. They defended me by saying that the way I threw the taw, my hand never touched the target coin.

The school drum sounded once. The kids lost all their money. With both hands holding my full pockets, I ran to the fountain to wash my feet and clean the mud off my clothes. I was followed by a crowd of classmates asking for money. I couldn't refuse, because one of them pushed my arm up behind my back, and, calmly plucking the coins from my pocket, he distributed them to the others.

* * *

My lucky taw never slipped out of my hand. When the game was over, I pried the mud out of the letters which were stamped on the coin and washed and dried and polished it until it was really shiny. After that I put it into a delicate wax paper covering and hid it in my pocket. Once every few days, I even more carefully dipped it into some brass cleaner, then took a piece of thin felt, and polished it for hours.

When I held the coin up in the sunlight, it sparkled like 24-carat gold.

I was pleased and proud and had the impression that it was more valuable than gold. Because of it, I was able to make 60 or 70 sous a day. If I added up the money I made, it was worth more than a piece of gold the same weight.

When I went to sleep, I didn't dare put it in my pocket because I was afraid it would fall out on to the bed and that someone would take it and spend it. I always had to slip it into a piece of cloth, put a string around it, and hang it inside my trousers.

On one occasion, I had thrown it down too strongly during a game, and it flew off into a thorny bush, so that I had to miss a whole class to find it. I wasn't as afraid of getting the cane when I went to school on Thursday or even of being expelled than I was of losing that rare taw.

I valued it the way sexy women value the beauty of their attractive figures; the way tyrants value their hardened troops and treat them well because they bring them many brilliant victories.

Lying at the foot of a tree in the park, I never got bored with looking at my taw. Rubbing my hand over the sharp edge of the coin, I felt elated and sad. Four Chinese characters, some French words, and the image of the woman on the sou piece brought an unusual idea to my mind: cast a sou that had my image and name on it so that I could go around all the towns earning my living as a professional hit-the-coin player.

I never used my rare and precious taw for practice. I was afraid that I'd wear it down or chip it for nothing. And, what is more, I suddenly had the idea of placing it in a higher position than every other coin, to commemorate with great respect that afternoon when I suddenly hit upon that terrific way of throwing the coin.

I didn't need to throw it down hard, just aim it accurately at a half-sou piece and hit a thick sou coin with the sharp edge and hole in the middle. The edge of the taw could send a half-sou coin flying up and sometimes leave a deep cut in the earth.

A few months after I discovered this style of play, all the children in Nam Dinh Province knew how to play it. But I was the best. They couldn't be as good as me, because I was the first one to think of this way of playing and put it into practice. Wherever I played, I could always knock the half-sou piece over the upper line.

All my playmates gave me a nickname: 'Coin Eater', because they knew I could make enough to feed myself from playing hit-the-coin. I wasn't ashamed, but proud to have received that sarcastic title.

Delinquency

I didn't seem to have anything to do with my family any more.

I used to get up early. Sometimes, I didn't even wash my face or put on a long tunic. I tucked my shirt into my trousers and left for school. At lunch-time, I ate a little for the sake of it. After I washed my bowl, I took my school bag and left straight away. After school was over in the afternoon I hung around in the school-yard or in the street where people were playing hit-the-coin. At seven o'clock I would go home, and at eight I would be at the movies, watching a Chinese film. If no one opened the door for me when I came back late at night, I would sleep at someone else's place.

It went on like that for three months. There were times when my grandmother glared at me when I went past. That gesture showed that she was more disgusted with me than the phlegm she spat out of her mouth. When I lifted the food cover, I could see that she was glaring at me as though she was cursing me quietly: 'So you are living like the devil; the authorities will have to teach you a lesson!'

In the past when I was despised and rejected, I stood up and walked away from the meal to protest against the way I was so unjustly treated! But now I remained cool and nonchalantly ate each grain of rice, carefully picked up each piece of vegetable, and slowly sipped the soup to annoy my grandmother.

On the days when there wasn't enough food, I went out to buy some minced pork rolls, brought them back and cut them into small pieces, and ate them noisily like the men who enjoy food with wine.

My grandmother was furious; she cursed me, but I only smiled back. When I saw that she was about to resort to the whip, I ran away.

My aunt did not dare to scold me any more because once when she was going to use my mother's name to curse me, I pointed at her daughter and answered in a nasty way: 'Her mother hasn't been cursed by her father's family; why do you always curse my mother?'

I was pleased and proud that I had dealt with the cruelty of my grandmother and aunt with this contemptuous provocation. I felt that was the appropriate revenge for the ill-treatment and humiliation I had recently suffered.

Anyway, my grandmother and aunt had to provide me with more adequate food than before, because they were embarrassed that I had left the house many times and stayed away for a few days and remained healthy and happy as usual.

Thanks to that taw with its sharp edge and my great talent for playing hit-the-coin, I was able to live a relaxed, full life. I bought myself clothes, shoes, and hats; I could eat anything I wanted; when I went to the cinema or to a soccer game, I didn't have to sit in the cheapest seats any more.

I didn't need to think about whether the influence of the life I lived as a vagabond was good or bad. I only knew that I had to live like that, because I was left more miserable and hard up than a prisoner by the indifferent nurturing I received from an old grandmother who gave all her love to my aunt and who considered my mother to be a terrible object of shame for my father's soul and the whole family line.

In the park, at the market, the wharf, the bus-stop, the football field, I shared my life with lost children from the dregs of society. These children lived by petty occupations: selling papers, rice pudding, cakes, lollies, sundry toys, carrying babies for busy mothers, collecting tennis balls, begging, or pilfering fish and vegetables. They were always ragged, dirty, hungry, and cold. Whenever they were able to make some money, they would squander it. They'd eat anything without worrying about how much it cost, and gamble without regretting their losses. In their ill-treated lives, it was as though they had to have some passion to carry them away and lose themselves in debauchery as a consolation. But each mischievous, dishonest, or wicked personality was the result of a family's degradation; of a father who gambled, drank, and smoked opium until he was worn out, or of a mother who was ignorant and too vulgar or suffered a physical handicap at the end of a life of dark labour, oppression, and exploitation. Such personalities could also result from the tragic, slow death of a mother who is gradually strangled by a system of slavery, and is born only to a life of resignation, shame, and suffering.

I shared my life with that group of wayward, uneducated children. Mixing with those wily urchins, I used those games of hit-the-coin to plunder the naïve ones whose experience had not yet taught them really dirty tricks.

Once, I tapped the shoulder of a young friend who was lying sprawled out on a grassy field, puffing a cigarette: 'Come on, why don't you pay him for the tea? It's only a few sous.'

He ignored a little boy of nine or ten who was standing crestfallen and crying nearby. The boy was carrying a teapot with a hemp cover in one hand, and a few earthenware bowls in the other. My friend pursed his lips and replied: 'Damn him, he has to pay for his naïvety; that will open his eyes.'

On a previous occasion, he had kicked another small boy in the kidneys and left him fainting in a vacant piece of ground beside a house. Running away, he panted: 'Have you seen enough?'

I didn't answer, because as I ran away with him I didn't have the strength to reply. I was also choked with fear. Now and then, I looked back to see if anyone was chasing us. Then, for over a month, I didn't dare to go past the street in which that little boy lived. I was afraid his parents would mistakenly think that I was the vicious boy who had beaten their child to take revenge for not being able to come into the courtyard to look for a lost taw.

Under the bad influence of my little band of nondescript friends, my mind was gradually filled with daring risky ideas. I always bore a grudge or was jealous of someone, I wanted to spurn them or longed for revenge. The chaos in my heart and mind prevented me from sitting still in one spot. If I wasn't playing hit-the-coin at school, then I was kicking a football or playing some dangerous game. In class, I was always talkative and finding ways to pester my shy friends. After school, especially on holidays, I wasn't at home for five minutes. I had to be in a crowd playing hit-the-coin, odds and evens, or cards. Whether it was raining or sunny, I went bareheaded, spending hours looking for a game if the ones going on in my street were too small to interest me or there was nothing happening at all.

In the care of loving parents, a youngster of thirteen or fourteen like me would have given a happy yell to see his family buy him a bicycle, a toy car, or a toy gun, or rejoiced when he was taken out to visit unfamiliar places. But me, my pleasure was that of an explorer who suddenly discovered a mine of precious gems when he saw a dirty, ragged crowd of people jostling and cursing each other in the distance. Such a crowd immediately aroused in my imagination thoughts of half-sou coins scattered on the ground, of red playing cards being thrown down and discarded, of the metallic rustle of money in iron bowls.

A Short Step

'Hong, come up here!'

My teacher was red in the face and shaking his index finger at me. I had just reached the teacher's wooden platform, when he stood straight up. His chair made a very long screeching sound on the floor as it was pushed back hard into the wall. I folded my arms and waited, not knowing why I had been called out. Since school was almost over for the day, all the class had left to do was to sit and listen to the marks for the weekly assignment of each student.

My teacher jumped straight down on to the ground, jerked my chin up, and fixed a stare on me with his shining eyes.

'You stay still, or you'll be dead!'

Slap! Thump! Slap! Thump! I felt the back of his hand slap into my face with all the force of a wild animal. Then another slap ... and another ... then several more.

My teacher had lost the colour in his face. His eyes were like two marbles that flashed light from their green veins. His square chin was pushed out like a coal miner's shovel.

There was not a sound in the class. Each student held his breath.

I withdrew behind the blackboard and sat down on the floor.

Rac! The ruler that had landed on my head hit the ceiling. My teacher yelled. He pushed me in the back with the heel of his shoe. But I had already fallen on the ground with my body curled.

'Hong, come here!'

I stood up unsteadily, and, in a daze, I staggered in front of the platform.

'You are a villain!'

'I beg you, Sir, I don't know anything.'

'Shut up! Shut up! You're a thief! Shut up!'

The teacher went on in a very soft voice: 'You are a villain. Here, let me ask you, what did you say when I was about to read the marks?'

I stood motionless, thinking. No! I didn't say anything impolite to offend the teacher. And at that moment I wasn't even making trouble. I hadn't stuck my foot out to pull at the tunics of my friends or turned around asking anyone for anything.

The teacher still glared at me. In order to remember what had happened, I had to control myself before his threatening eyes in which the red veins were dilated. Suddenly an incident came to my mind. My friend sitting on the left had tapped me on the shoulder and said: 'Hong, look here.'

I didn't want to watch him playing some trick under the table, and I raised my chin to reply: 'Leave me out of that.'

'Leave me out of that.' Good heavens! This is the way I usually spoke, and the teacher heard it when he said to the class: 'Everyone sit quietly and listen to me read the marks.'

* * *

Whenever school was in, I had to kneel down. This went on for four days; behind the blackboard at the foot of the wall was the place I studied.

This study was not of a literary nature, but I realized in a way I would never forget that, although it was cruel, the great shame and pain of the punishment was intended to correct the attitude of a bad boy and to eliminate his mocking, wicked ways.

At times when I looked out, I saw clearly those uneasy intentions on the cold poker face of the teacher.

But he was mistaken! Contrary to what he thought, unusual punishments only further fired feelings of indignation and resentment. What did I have to repent?

* * *

I was increasingly indignant to see my classmates becoming more distant from me every day. This included the lazy loafers who used to quietly undermine the teacher, because they were often punished indiscriminately by him. They seemed to be proud of themselves when they saw someone who was despised and degraded to a lower position than them.

My heart shrivelled each time I heard my classmates laughing hilariously because of a funny answer from a student who was absent-minded or stupid. And in that gay atmosphere some of my classmates looked at me cunningly as if they wanted to say: 'Hong, come back to your place, and join us.'

But then one of my friends would ask me sarcastically during recess: 'Hong, didn't you feel like laughing then?'

Or they teased me with words of false consolation: 'You've been kneeling since Monday, haven't you? For four days, poor you!'

Fortunately, the one who said that didn't have an unlikeable appearance. But if he'd been cross-eyed, pock-marked, or had a harelip, I would have spontaneously hit him in the face.

* * *

It was not yet one o'clock on Saturday afternoon and I had arrived at school. Lying on the grass under both a hibiscus bush and a big tree with my hands folded behind my head and my eyes half closed, I looked up at the vastness of the crystal-blue sky.

Three years ago when I was in fourth grade, I used to come to school early like this. The cool shade of the same hibiscus bush was thinner then; also the branches of the tree had been low enough for me to reach up and pull down as I lay quietly to let my mind follow the fine white clouds dispersing gradually in one corner of the sky.

The wind whistled softly, and, in the sunlight, butterflies fluttered on flowers.

During that time, the birds stopped singing. Only the noisy rustling of the yellow reeds on the other side of the school-yard could be heard. It was as though the activity of a prosperous city had come to a stop.

That great silence blended very well into the thoughts of a pupil who was not yet ten and imagined himself to be a general at the head of a Chinese army as it faced the terrible strength of the enemy's attack.

I was that tiny general, tossing and turning, busy thinking of a way of trying to take the enemy citadel in a corner of the school-yard. I wanted to save his brave entourage and capture provisions and weapons.

A sandy battlefield appeared in the imagination of that little general. Resounding in his ears was the tumult of battle, as the shock troops of two armies, all drunk on the essence of excitement, clashed in the fierce sunlight and hot sand, stabbing and hacking at each other with hibiscus branches, lilac branches, and leaves of grass. Three years ago ... those days which were so full of exuberance are now over for ever! Although I had grown up a few years, I still liked to play around, and still criticized or judged according to my feelings.

My eyes filled with tears. I tilted my face a little so that they would run down my cheeks. Salty liquid dripped into my mouth. The bitterness of my grief and indignation became more and more intense. My eyes gradually became dim behind a thick wet curtain of tears. Gasps built up in my throat.

I turned over and placed my face on my right arm.

It had been five days since I had to kneel in class, and now I really felt the pain as all my hopes of being let off the punishment had disappeared. That morning I waited at the back door of the classroom for the teacher to arrive so that I could ask him to forgive me—I would accept I had been wrong—and be allowed to go back to my seat. But he turned his head away, waited for a while, raised his bottom jaw, and said: 'I won't change my mind! You can kneel in class or stay home; it's up to you.'

So saying, he walked quickly into the classroom.

No! I couldn't endure the humiliation any longer! Kneeling for five hours a day, I had thought that my knees would get used to the pain. I didn't suspect that on the fourth afternoon the pain would become unbearable. When I heard the drum sound for recess, I stood up and had to massage my knees for a while to prevent myself from staggering.

I resented and worried about the more than sixty days ahead in which I would have to kneel at the foot of the stinking wall behind the reversible blackboard; the blackboard whose black colour oppressed my mind hourly with heavy feelings of weariness and boredom like the coat of tar that grips the door of the prison.

The piercing sound of the cicadas reached a higher and higher pitch. In the bright atmosphere of a summer noon, the lively twittering of birds suddenly burst out intermittently as they flew from branch to branch in the big shade trees above where I lay.

Unexpectedly, a gust of wind blew a coil of dust in my direction. I quickly shut my eyes. My eyelids blinked closed as the tears spilled out. But when I opened my eyes wide, the veil of tears still clouded my eyes. I used my sleeve to wipe them away.

Immediately sunlight flooded from the sky. I had the sensation that I could see thousands of flowers and butterflies, fluttering in the golden dust and crystal light.

Another breeze. Then another breeze.

The rustling in the clump of bitter fruit-trees, in the canopies of the big trees, and in the reeds rose higher and higher.

The sky was brighter, deeper, and wider, wanting to draw people's attention to its infinite horizons.

Suddenly, the second drum. One roll of sound reverberated, then died away.

A chill ran down my spine. I felt as though a thin steel hand had caressed the back of my head and neck, then hooked its fingers in around my collar bone to drag me into the courtyard and the ranks of the school assembly. I rose quickly and ran helter-skelter into the street.